PRAISE FOR EDWARD RICHE AND *EASY TO LIKE*

"Witty and stylish…smartly written…The book lives up to its promise by offering a spry, light-hearted defence of cultivated taste and an artists' prerogative in the face of entertainment by committee." — *Globe and Mail*

"Hilarious…laugh-out-loud funny…" — *Maclean's*

"It's easy to like." — *National Post*

"A fast-paced, sure-footed read…sparkling [with] wit and spice." — *Telegram*

"[Edward Riche's] new satire wasn't just easy to like, it was finish-the-bottle-and-order-another delicious." — *Telegraph-Journal*

"Riche is a breezy writer who creates fast-paced satires… enjoy [his] acid wit [and] have a good laugh." — *Here NB*

"Riche's prose is astute and bitingly comic…the real pleasure comes from his richness of characters, ridiculous situations, and surprisingly believable comedic timing." — *The Coast*

EASY TO LIKE

EDWARD RICHE

ANANSI

Hardcover edition first published in 2011 by House of Anansi Press Inc.

This edition published in 2012 by
House of Anansi Press Inc.
110 Spadina Avenue, Suite 801
Toronto, ON, M5V 2K4
Tel. 416-3363-4343   Fax 416-363-1017
www.houseofanansi.com

Distributed in Canada by
HarperCollins Canada Ltd.
1995 Markham Road
Scarborough, ON M1B 5M8
Toll free tel. 1-800-387-0117

All of the events and characters in this book are fictitious, and any resemblance to
actual persons, living or dead, is purely coincidental.

House of Anansi Press is committed to protecting our natural environment.
As part of our efforts, the interior of book is printed on paper that contains 100%
post-consumer recycled fibres, is acid-free, and is processed chlorine-free.

16 15 14 13 12   1 2 3 4 5

LIBRARY AND ARCHIVES CANADA CATALOGUING IN PUBLICATION

Riche, Edward
Easy to like / Edward Riche.

Also issued in electronic format.
ISBN 978-1-77089-105-0

I. Title.

PS8585.I198E38 2012   C813'.54   C2012-901185-1

Cover design: Brian Morgan
Text design and typesetting: Alysia Shewchuk

We acknowledge for their financial support of our publishing program
the Canada Council for the Arts, the Ontario Arts Council, and the Government of Canada
through the Canada Book Fund.

Printed and bound in Canada

for Frances

PART ONE

"This Champagne didn't come from France."

— Orson Welles

ONE

"IN THE MOUTH," Elliot said. "Feel it. Its weight, its heat."

"When are we going to drink some American wine?" Robin asked.

Elliot had first heard Robin described, by Veronica, as "my extremist gal pal." Doubtful that one of the many Islamists reported crowding the shadows would attend a wine tasting in Bel Air, Elliot assumed Robin to be a former dabbler in, or groupie-come-concubine of, the Weather Underground or the Panthers or the Symbionese Liberation Army or the like. (You met those people in Los Angeles, hostages and their takers together again on the same talk show.) On further learning that Robin "just one hundred and ten percent had to come to the tasting," Elliot gathered that Veronica meant that Robin was her "*extreme-est* gal pal."

The friends were eerily similar in appearance, like fraternal twins, though they probably shared a trainer or a surgeon rather than a womb. They were both a hay blond, with thrust pneumatic boobs. Their eyes were differing blues, Veronica's

1

Aegean, Robin's a colder, deeper sea, each equally improbable. Repeated injections of botulism made their faces taut but leathery and shiny, like the hide on a well-played drum. They were such stalwart defenders of a certain cliché of Southern Californian womanhood that they surpassed it, attained something higher, were masters of their practice, priestesses. These were not the post-age-of-irony spending-for-democracy porn-positive Barbies one saw nowadays; they were purer, and, like their hometown, of irony they simply knew not.

"If we did this again I could take you through some better examples of what California's self-styled 'Rhone Rangers' have on offer," Elliot answered.

"Good," said Robin. "Cabernet Sauvignon, I like that." She was proud of this knowledge, however erroneous.

"Well, actually, no," said Elliot, "they don't use any Cab, that's more of a Napa and Sonoma thing, these vintners —"

"Fred Hanover has the most beautiful ranchy thing in Napa Valley, not far from St. Helena," Robin cut in.

"He has this barbecue," said Veronica, "every year. There are always a lot of celebrities there, A-list people too. I hate it when it's B-list. I get depressed by 'B.' And 'C,' Jerry keeps telling me, is for 'cancelled.' Fred's is fun. It's for a charity . . . can't remember which one. Is it a childhood cancer?"

"I think it's for animals. Animals in Africa, I think. Can animals be displaced by a conflict? Something was displaced, anyway," said Robin. "Janice Everston was there last year and . . . who is that guy on *Murder Squad*?"

"Kevin Stewart," said Veronica.

"Do you know about Fred's barbecue?" Robin asked, remembering that Elliot was sitting across from her.

"I was there last year."

"You WERE?" Veronica warmed to Elliot for the first time that afternoon.

"Yes."

"Did you see Janice Everston?" asked Robin.

"No. Though I wrote something she was in, years ago, for television." It was a pilot for a *Mannix* remake that never went. This was before Janice Everston was on any list, "A" or otherwise.

"So, you know her?" asked Veronica.

"We've never met. Now, this Chianti —"

"Who else was there?" asked Robin. "That we would know."

When Elliot agreed to direct this tasting, as a favour for Jerry Borstein, he never imagined it would prove such a trial. Veronica was Jerry's trophy wife, one of such high shine as to require constant polishing. She was, Jerry told Elliot, trying to improve her skills as a hostess and learning all she could, which was very little, about food and wine. There was a new (and to be short-lived, Elliot prayed) fashion in Hollywood for seriously themed dinner parties in honour of an invited guest, a thinker or humanitarian, who could expound on his or her area of expertise over a (typically catered) gourmet meal. Jerry had hosted one such soiree for Yuri Smeltlotov, a Russian scholar who was to speak about the crisis in the Caucasus, real estate from which Jerry's ancestors were long ago chased. Elliot supplied the wines, starting with a freakish sparkler from Georgia and finishing with an intensely sweet Tocay Yuzhnoberezhny from the Massandra Collection in the Crimea. It was a wine, made for a czar, that survived the Nazi occupation of Yalta by being shipped to Tbilisi, a singular and treasured wine that seemed to impress nobody but Elliot himself.

That fete exposed Veronica's need for tutelage. Near the end of the evening, with regard to the situation in Georgia, she'd given the Yellow Jackets even odds for the Gator Bowl.

She posed another question. "That's a winery, right, Fred's place in Napa? I think he served his own wine at the barbecue."

"Yes. He produces a Cabernet Sauvignon–based wine there. It's a large, extracted wine, excellent with, or as, barbecue sauce."

"Lot of fruit?" Veronica parroted something she'd once heard said about wines.

"Very much so. 'Fruit bombs' they used to call them. They're easy to enjoy."

"I thought so," said Veronica. "I remember loving the label."

"Yes," said Elliot, "Fred produces one of the better labels in California. Features a horse, if I'm not mistaken?"

"I think it does, you're right. It was *very* western."

Elliot had not been able to refuse Jerry Borstein this favour. Jerry regularly hired Elliot to rewrite or "beat" scripts and to give his more nebulous ideas some semblance of order on the page in the form of an outline or a treatment. An outline penned by Elliot, for *Goldie's Piece*, was part of insider Hollywood lore for being only five words in length: "Guy with the biggest gun." A treatment credited to Jerry but of Elliot's hand went on to become *The Nevada Girl*, another success, and Elliot knew for a fact that his *The Invader* was the source for *Total Conquest* — on which Jerry'd made more than a few shekels. As a rule, Elliot never brought up his part in these authorships. He knew that Jerry knew that he knew, and that some adjustments would be made. Let Jerry have the glory. (Sure enough, in the end, Jerry gave him one of six producer credits on *Conquest* — a nice gesture, as it came with fees.)

Most critically, Jerry was a silent (*mute* was a better word) partner in Elliot's vineyard and winery. Though she obviously didn't know it, Veronica's extreme-est friend Robin also had a piece of the action. Her husband, Lucas "Lucky" Silverman, with whom Elliot had spoken on the phone but had never met in person, was also, on Jerry's recommendation, a major investor. Silverman was big-going-on-huge in the business, producing hit after swollen mega-hit, never stumbling. If Elliot could write just one of those sorts of pictures, he could easily pocket enough dough to sort out the mounting problems in the vineyard. Elliot's plan was to meet Silverman by bringing him a couple of cases of his wine — their wine — but the early vintages weren't showing yet, and Elliot thought it prudent to wait until he could deliver something delicious.

"He's using 'easy' as a pejorative." This was the first thing Eva said. She was the third invitee. A new neighbour of Jerry and Veronica's, she looked nothing like the other two women. Her hair was a sick-making cobalt, more Goth girl than the middle-aged woman she was. Broad in the hips, shrink-wrapped in lustrous black, she resembled an eggplant. Eva had followed her husband, some big cheese in digital animation, from New York to Los Angeles. Elliot gathered she'd been asked along out of a sense of obligation on Veronica's part, a one-time-only gesture, but with Elliot and Robin sharing in the awkward socials.

Eva was sitting with her arms crossed, gathering up the too-long arms of her black sweater into her fists. The garment was unnecessary — the vast solarium in which they were gathered was warm, and the air-conditioned interior only slightly less so. It was August in Los Angeles, for heaven's sake. At least being overdressed seemed — thus far — to induce a lethargy in Eva that diminished her will to complain.

"Not entirely," said Elliot. "Nothing wrong with a wine that makes a lot of people happy." He did not believe this. "Back to these two wines. Chianti Rufina is just outside Florence. Galletti is a modest producer. The wines are made in a traditional manner on the estate. You don't have the degree of technological intervention we see in some larger operations. As a result we are getting a much less mediated experience, we taste the soil and the weather in the grapes. On the left is the 2002 Ascella . . . Please, a sniff and then a taste, remember what we said about it in your mouth."

Was Robin making eyes at him over her wineglass? Elliot never knew whether women were being flirtatious or fidgety. The last woman he thought was coming on to him had only been itchy. Like Eva, who sniffled and scratched as though generally allergic. She nosed her glass wetly.

"It was not a good year in Tuscany," said Elliot, "and the wines are rather thin and dried out."

"Dried out?" wondered Veronica.

"Let's say instead they aren't generous . . . 'generous'?"

"For sure."

"Sangiovese, the principal grape being used here, has a restrained and enigmatic aroma at the best of times, it —"

"'Enigmatic'?" said Eva.

"We smell some dried cherry or cranberries, violets, and leather in the best examples, but it is hard to nail it down." It was a maddening aspect of wine tasting, this search for taste and smell equivalencies. There wasn't a risk of sounding pretentious; there was a certainty. And the reporting of various fruits seemed to have induced some winemakers to chase the taste of raspberries or plums. If you wanted strawberries, thought Elliot, go to the Santa Monica Farmers' Market and buy a basket.

"Could say it smells like Sangiovese grapes," Eva pressed.

"Indeed, but then very few people would know what we meant. Besides, when a wine tastes of the grape variety from which it's made, it's failed. It's too . . . literal."

No one seemed to grasp this. Elliot elaborated.

"Good winemaking uses the grapes to express a place at a certain time. The best winemaking is none at all."

Still no help.

"We don't want to taste the hand of the maker, we want the wine in the bottle to be an expression of the plant growing up through those stones in that field in that year. The wine is made in the vineyard, not the cellar."

Blank stares.

"The point is that the 2002 is not expressive, it lacks *fruit*." Elliot said the word anyway, the sooner to get it over with. "This enables us to better appreciate the mineral profile of the wine." Elliot sniffed his glass. "There are some old-world spices there too — clove and cinnamon, but muted."

He sniffed again. For a fleeting moment he detected the note that he most relished in wine, that of forest floor — *sous bois*, said the French — wild herbs and fungal growth amidst the fallen needles of a conifer and, atop all that, more faintly, the musk and scat of passing animals. It was a scent he rarely detected in wines. Once, having passed out face down on a mat of leaves in the woods near the Tuscan hill village of Trequanda, and waking in the dawn to the sight of a boar scenting a cypress stump, Elliot had experienced it, unmediated and in situ.

"You like this wine?" Robin asked.

"*Like* isn't a word I ever use. To make my point, now try the 2003. Look at it first."

"It's darker," said Veronica.

"Good."

"Yeah, it is definitely much darker," said Eva, seeming, to Elliot's surprise, interested. "You say this is the same wine?"

"Same wine. I don't know if you remember, but 2003 was the year of that incredible heatwave in Europe."

"Remember?" said Veronica. "I'll never forget it. We had this fantastic trip planned. Jerry had rented a yacht and we and Linda and Kent and Linda and Bernard were going to sail from Antibes to Capri . . . well, it was too hot. We spent like a day aboard this boat and then we said, like, totally forget this. We rented this castle in Scotland instead, which was nice except the boys played golf a lot cuz, like, this castle had its own nine-hole course."

"Right. This wine was made during that heatwave. I think if you smell and taste, you will get that. This wine is baked."

"I like it much better than the 2002," said Robin.

"For sure," said Veronica.

"It's a bit much," said Eva.

"My view exactly. I find it's too alcoholic — hot, it's high in sugars, low in acid. It's big but flabby. There's a raisiny character that I find offputting. Will it come around with bottle age, or will it crash? It's puffed up, but there is no structural support for the Medicean architecture."

Elliot measured two beats of silence.

"I like the sweetness," said Veronica. "Californian wines are sweeter than Italian wines."

"The Italians, to their great credit" — Elliot thought how much he would like to be, at that moment, in Italy — "appreciate bitterness in food and wine."

"It's also a question of patriotism," said Robin. "I mean, especially since 9/11, should we be drinking Italian wine?"

"Italians didn't crash those planes into the buildings, Saudis did," said Eva.

"All the same, when we have perfectly good wine grown right here in California," said Veronica.

"Rather too much of it," said Elliot. "And as for 'perfectly' . . ."

"What about your wine?" asked Veronica. She turned to Eva and Robin. "Elliot has his own vineyard. Is it in Napa?"

"Paso Robles region, place called Enredo," said Elliot.

"Will we taste your wine?" asked Eva. "If only for America."

"I hadn't planned on it. Most of our vines are only eleven years old, our fifth vintage in the bottle, none of it is really drinking."

"It's not ready?" asked Robin.

"No. It's made to age, a *vin de garde*. Now if we can return to Fattoria Galletti, do you . . . ?"

"Which of the two is your favourite?" asked Robin.

"Both are utter failures. While I find the 2002 the more interesting, it is impossible to drink."

"Why are we drinking wines that are failures?" Robin was confused.

"Let's drink some successes," Veronica said, clapping her hands. She was rocking slightly as if trying to hold her pee.

"The point here is to . . . There comes a time, if you're being analytical, when failures are more intriguing than successes."

"But," Eva cut him off, "I thought wine was all about pleasure. I'm sure you said that."

"And getting a buzz," added Veronica. What wine she'd consumed had lowered her already limited inhibitions, for with these words she, without a care, manually hoisted one of her boobs into a more comfortable position. Surgically altered or not, thought Elliot, they were great tits.

"People draw pleasure from different things. I, for one, don't like a wine that gives too much of itself, I —"

"So there is no Cab in the wine you make," Robin concluded.

"Correct," said Elliot, to make life easier.

"Is it like a Chardonnay?"

"No. It's a red table wine. It's made from many different grapes, nine different varieties, none of them Chardonnay or Cabernet Sauvignon."

"What do you call it?" Veronica said, and laughed inexplicably.

"It's called 303 Locura Canyon Road."

"Why?" wondered Eva.

"Because that's where it comes from and what it should taste like."

"Why so many grapes?" asked Robin.

"It's . . . I don't like to say 'emulate' but — well, it's *in the tradition of* a Châteauneuf-du-Pape."

"I think I've heard of that," said Veronica.

"The most intriguing wine I ever tasted was a Châteauneuf," said Elliot. "We don't want to mimic it, it would be impossible, but Châteauneuf is our inspiration." Elliot saw that he was losing Robin and Veronica. "Châteauneuf-du-Pape is a wine they make in the hot part of France from a bunch of different grapes, some of which we also grow here in California." Yeah, he was only talking to Eva now. "We also use a bit of the old-vine black mix, mostly Zin and Carignan and Cinsault, that was on the estate when we bought it." (This presence of the Zinfandel in his wine was bothering Elliot of late. Tiny portion though it was — probably less than one percent — he felt it might be imparting a note that he could identify only as "aluminum syrup.") "People mistakenly think, because it's a blend of grapes, that it's some sort of *concoction*, but you grow different grapes on different sites to best represent the land and the conditions. It's a meadow, not a lawn."

"That was absolutely THE BEST wine you ever tasted?" said Robin, who Elliot now saw was drunk.

"Well, no . . . what's 'best'? The best wines anyone ever tastes are Burgundy Grand Cru, Musigny, or Les Clos. You don't compare every play to *Hamlet* . . . that's not the . . ." Finally Elliot thought he had it. "The most beautiful lover you ever had isn't necessarily the one you think about all the time."

This appeared to give Robin pause. Either that or she was becoming dizzy.

"What did you say it was called again, Château something something?" Veronica's pen was poised above a notepad on which she had yet to write a word.

"Châteauneuf-du-Pape. It was an old bottle — a 1961 Isabelle d'Orange. It should have been long finished when I drank it, too old, but no."

"Orange County?" wondered Veronica.

"Why didn't you bring some of that 'intriguing' wine along, instead of two wines you say are failures?" asked Eva.

"The one I drank was the only bottle I have ever seen. Nineteen sixty-one was the last year the vineyard existed. They never made much. And the family was always at odds with the syndicate. I've tried tracking any down that might have been lying around but . . . to no avail." Elliot heard himself starting to sound precious.

"Why was it such a memorable lover?" Veronica asked.

Good question.

"Oh, I'm not sure." Elliot had worried for a time that it wasn't the wine at all but the context, the confidence and contentment he'd felt drinking it with Lucy on that perfect day in the South of France. Then, hearing one day, about a not very good movie, that "everything is context," he realized that everything wasn't. Some part of anything was context, some other part was substance. "It was a spectacular vintage for the entire appellation, and the blend of grapes at that particular vineyard was not typical; there was more of this and less of that than was usual. Isabelle d'Orange actually used fourteen different grape varieties, the extra grape being an obscure one, the Matou de Gethsemane. That's one of the reasons they were having trouble with . . . Regardless, it's not germane to this discussion."

"But you will bring some good wines the next time?" asked Veronica.

"I promise."

❧

OUTSIDE, THE GLARE punched. The stone of Jerry's vast sloping drive was the texture and colour of Rolaids. In the sun it was infernal. Elliot felt his pockets for sunglasses. The daytime highs in Southern California were approaching record levels; it was Al Gorey. Elliot dreaded calling Walt and getting a report out of the vineyard — no doubt another day over a hundred degrees and the newly formed grapes would be beginning to show signs of heat stress. The oldest Zinfandel vines seemed even to like it and the Mourvèdre could handle it, but every other grape variety he grew would be shutting down, the fruit cooking before it could mature phenolically.

He looked back at the house. It was a rectilinear thing, planes of tooth enamel and shimmering glass — Richard Meier school. There was a smog warning, and the sky, white as the centre of a spark in every direction, seemed to suspend something dusty and grey as cigarette ash. The palms in the rear garden that rose beyond the structure looked to Elliot as if they were about to ignite, like that tree line at the beginning of *Apocalypse Now*. "This is the end."

Worse, it was the middle.

Eva emerged from the house, her blue hair and bituminous sweater on the white stone in the midday sun some kind of experiment in the limits of ultraviolet tolerance in New Yorkers.

"That was interesting," Eva said, not bothering to sound convincing. "It's weird terrain, aesthetically. I mean, are there greater rewards for the viewer or listener or drinker if the work is more difficult?"

Elliot made like he wasn't sure whether it was he to whom Eva was talking, as though she was mistaking him for someone else standing nearby who might understand, or care, what she was saying. "'Aesthetically?' I'm a *screenwriter*, you know . . . *here*," he jabbed his finger down toward the scorching concrete drive, "in Los Angeles."

"You're being flip, right? It's hard to tell in California," said Eva.

"Sorry. I don't hear many interesting questions. If you'd asked me if the lead could be younger and more sympathetic or if the ending could be more uplifting, I might have better understood how to dodge the question."

Eva smiled for the first since they'd met. And she was right, it was weird and interesting stuff. He was being a prick. Elliot was about to say so, but Robin was upon them.

She came out the house like a shot and staggered, tipping forward on account of her heels, gravity sending her careering toward the street. By the time she reached Eva she had to put a hand out to arrest her momentum.

"Elliot," she said, "you live in Beverly Hills . . . didn't you say?"

"No. I didn't. I'm in the Los Feliz Hills, by Griffith Park. Beverly Hills," he sighed, "can be on the way."

"Awesome. You can drive me home, it's not far, 1085 Summit."

Given what little they had consumed — and that over a couple of hours — it seemed incredible that Robin could be impaired, but as she came unmoored from Eva her course to Elliot was as irregular as a torn kite. Elliot looked back to Eva as Robin dragged him forward. "Aesthetically," imagine.

On the drive to the Silvermans' house Robin explained how it was that she had become so intoxicated: Thursdays were "not-eating" days for her. On Mondays and Thursdays she would take no solid food, though she allowed herself fluids — that they might be alcoholic was no matter. Elliot didn't bother offering that booze, in any variety, was not particularly slimming.

So little did Robin care about getting smashed during her fasts that she invited Elliot in for a drink.

"I would love to," he said, on the off chance that Lucky Silverman was at home and that Elliot might finally shake his hand, give Lucky a face to remember. Everything went through six or seven page-one rewrites, minimum, these days; having your name rattling around the consciousness of a producer as busy as Silverman increased your chances of joining the queue of eligible hacks. Elliot had been on a conference call with Silverman once but knew that Lucky would never remember it. Even he couldn't recall what that one had been about. That Lucky would've known that the scribbler on the phone also had something to do with a winery of which he owned a piece was unlikely. Lucky Silverman had bigger fish to fry. Men in such a hurry only learned the dimensions of their holdings when the courts were seizing them.

Elliot pulled up to an iron gate at the bottom of a long, steep drive. Robin stuck her head out the window, waving to an invisible camera, and the security barrier opened. Parking was under a twelve-car pergola.

The interior of Casa Silverman was decorated in an Asian tropical theme. There was a preponderance of coffee-coloured wooden furnishings, the grain and heft of which said endangered and illegally logged. Indosamnesian? Javanu-atan?

Once onto the rattan matting of the living area, Robin gave a kick of each leg, launching her high heels toward the far end of the room, a punt for the help to return.

"Do you only drink wine?" she asked, making for a credenza the length of a Cadillac.

"No. I'll —"

"How about a vodka?"

"Sure," Elliot said, though he didn't really care for vodka. "You know, I've been meaning to come by. I guess you know that Mr. Silverman is one of a number of investors in my —"

"Lucky's overseas. Toronto, I think." She turned around with an offering of four ounces of clear spirit on ice for her guest.

"That's a shame." Out of habit Elliot swirled the liquid in the glass and sniffed its contents. Next to nothing. Maybe vague grassiness.

"Shame. Shame on me? Sorry? Nooo . . . I'm sooo high. I should sit. Sit with me." Robin took a place on a couch, one of three distributed seemingly willy-nilly throughout the place. She patted a space next to her as if beckoning a puppy. Elliot sat. He gave the place another once-over to avoid eye contact. It looked not like a home but like a furniture showroom. Over a concert Steinway hung a Warhol of his hostess. Elliot did the math. The painting, if genuine, would have to have been executed in the early '80s at the latest, when, judging from appearances, Robin would have been only in her teens. Unless she was mainlining formaldehyde . . .

"Nice Warhol," he said, fishing.

"Yeah, looks like me, hey?"

"Very much."

"It's Lucky's second wife, Melinda. It was in storage. I thought, she looks just like me, what the hell. It's a Warhol, right? And where, like, Warhol's dead, this is the closest I'm going to come to getting him to do me."

Thinking she was correct in her assessment of the situation, "It's a great place you have here" was all Elliot could think to say.

"Used to belong to some old Hollywood director. You know, the communist. Pissed everybody off."

"There have been a few."

"I heard the story so many times that I've forgotten," Robin said. She was grasping her vodka in one hand and, with the other, absent-mindedly brushing a nipple already hardened by wintry gusts of conditioned air. Perhaps she had been making a pass back at Jerry's place after all.

"It's a storied town," he said.

"What does that mean?"

"It . . . it has a lot of stories . . . in it. You know, a history." Elliot hadn't been laid in many months, and the last few exchanges, fraught with the tension of a terminal relationship, had not been rewarding. Robin was presenting. The prospect here was of sudden and meaningless gratification. There was a vascular manifestation.

"I thought, when I came out here, years ago, from Wisconsin, that it would be much more exciting."

"I'm from Canada originally. When I came down I thought the same thing."

"Hardly anybody drinks anymore . . . everyone goes to bed early. Lucky and I go to parties, everybody leaves around ten o'clock."

"Their bankers' hours are in New York, so . . ."

"There's nothing they can do until the overnights come in." The comment betrayed Robin's age. "Why not relax, enjoy yourself? Lying in bed at home worrying is not going to make people watch your stupid TV show or go to your stupid movie."

There was definitely something going on, for now Robin was working the nipple, pinching and rolling it between her fingers. Her long, pale coral nails were, if real, flawlessly manicured.

"There has always been a puritan streak . . ."

"Elliot." She put her hand up to stop him speaking. A thought seemed to have come to her, something she had to say before its sense was lost. "Can I . . . Well, listen, how would you like to fuck?" She placed her tumbler on the coffee table and turned around to face him, coming so close that he could feel her boozy fever. "I would love to fuck."

How many people had made such a request of Elliot? Few. None so directly. Maybe good-looking lifeguards or firemen heard it occasionally. Movie stars, even the B's, heard it. You got it on the other side of the Hollywood Hills, in "Silicone Valley" ("Let's take it again, from 'Fuck me, fuck me'"), but that was lazy writing.

Elliot was faced with one of the most intractable of choices: that between fucking and eating, between screwing some thriving producer's wife and the faint hope of working for the man. Elliot thought of a starving, horny rat sent into a maze, the path to one side leading to a mate, the other to a ration of feed. Today, facing, as he did, escalating debts and a diminishing professional reputation, he first considered the pellets of meal.

"I always like to fuck, but . . ."

"I had some work done down there" — she looked into her lap — "cosmetic, and this is the first day I'm allowed to test drive it."

"Unfortunately —"

"And like you said, even if you weren't the most beautiful lover I ever had, I might think about you from time to time."

"I'd love to be in your thoughts, Robin . . . and elsewhere, but —"

"Sex is tremendous for my self-esteem."

"Mine too, but I have an appointment, with my agent, that I cannot break." This was almost true. He did have an appointment with Mike Vargas, his agent, though, given what Mike usually had for him these days, breaking it probably wouldn't matter.

Robin snatched her vodka back off the table. "See! This town is a total bore!"

"I really appreciate the thought, Robin. Thanks for the drink."

TWO

VARIOUS CUTS OF what might have happened with Robin screened in Elliot's head all the way to Mike Vargas's office in Century City. No matter how gratifying or, as now, frustrating the experience, Elliot was left wanting more. He was closing in on fifty and desperately awaiting some diminution in his drive. The infrequent act wasn't such a problem, but the social theatre surrounding it wasted so much time — to say nothing of the thousands of hours spent thinking about it. Elliot was a creator, a man who made his living making things up; now valuable imaginative resources would be blown on the what-might-have-beens with Robin.

He was dealt a red at the intersection of South Beverly Glen and Wilshire. A long, tall white guy, a stork in a Speedo and a muscle shirt, crossed the street, glassy eyes glowering at Elliot through the windshield as he passed in front of the car. He mouthed something carefully, and with deliberate menace. Was it "chaff"? Elliot saw, as the man stepped up onto the curb on the other side, that he was wearing, for shoes, hollowed-out loaves of bread. Dude was one of those . . . what did they call themselves? "Farinists." Elliot knew of them. They were holed up in a compound in the hills west of Paso, near the site of the old Enredo Mission, not far from his vines. They were rumoured to be armed to the teeth. The latest in a line of apocalypse-hankering wackos, waving the Bible or the Constitution, neither ever read, under your nose.

"Hi, my name is Stereo Mike," Elliot sang to himself. The Bran Van number. "Hell Hey! L.A.! Hell Hell A! L.A.!" Indeed, the city was visiting more mockery and humiliation on Elliot daily.

How degrading to be so hard up for work that you wouldn't put it in some producer's wife. This was a low point. He needed a break, needed to get the fuck out of the industry town for a time, get his head together. Maybe France, among like minds.

As he pulled into the parking lot he saw Priscilla Smith emerging shoulder to shoulder with the director Dutch Waggoner. Waggoner was nodding enthusiastically at something Smith was saying. Waggoner was hot, Smith was hot, Mike represented both talented youths, something was probably happening. Bastards.

Elliot resolved to ask why it was that he was never part of some package deal.

"Feelin' kinda groovy, working on a movie! . . . Yeah, right."

⤖ ❦ ⤕

"BECAUSE NO ONE ever asks to work with you," said Mike. "There is no one to 'package' you with."

"Really?"

"You have to communicate your ideas to producers and directors if you want them to become interested in your script."

"Directors," said Elliot with disgust. He looked around. Mike's agency had recently expanded into the adjoining set of offices. Where formerly was a wall, shared with a dental surgeon (vibe retained), there was now floor-to-ceiling glass, through which one could observe Mike's ever-expanding staff of go-getters making their daily flatteries into headsets. "You fixed up Dutch Waggoner with Priscilla Smith."

"See them in the parking lot?"

"I've still got a few teeth in my head and a few friends downtown."

"Is that from *Citizen Kane*?"

"John Huston in *Chinatown*, but I don't think I got it exactly right. Yeah, saw them in the parking lot. "

"Dutch and Priscilla, they came to me with the idea. They took the initiative."

"They're young, they don't know any better."

Mike, while the same vintage as Elliot, didn't look it. He was as spry as his buff new clients. Perhaps he was drinking their blood to stave off aging.

"And it's not a film or show that would interest you anyway."

"What is it?"

"It's not storytelling, okay, Elliot? It's high concept."

Elliot started to speak but Mike cut him off.

"Yeah, yeah, high concepts are for the lower orders, you've said it a million times. Basically, Priscilla's thing, it's competitive rehab for celebrities. But it's interactive. The audience can vote and reward competitors with like a therapy session or methadone, or put hazards in their way, like booze in the kitchen cupboards or a kite of blow on a night table. It's interacploitation."

"So . . . what? They're filmed in their homes?"

"They live in a compound with surveillance cameras everywhere. Same old same old. What is entertainment these days, Elliot? Degradation and celebrity adoration. This has got both, in spades. It's a market-savvy pitch."

"How do you get away with . . .?"

"It's shot offshore, on a tropical island . . . what's the place called? Primitive, corrupt government . . . no American jurisdiction, no unions, and a tax credit to die for."

Washed-up celebrities battling it out, their cringe-inducing meltdowns, the audience transference and *schadenfreude* . . . it had a chance. Elliot recalled the delight the press took in reporting his son Mark's arrest on drug charges. A former child actor brought low, what sport that was.

"People are afraid of fiction these days," continued Mike. "I mean, if it works, they identify with the character, they say 'Hey, that could be me' — and that scares them. The thing that makes reality programming so much more comfortable to watch is the fact that you know that it's somebody *else's* reality you're watching. Reality is for people who can't handle fiction — and that is mostly everybody."

"I would have thought television had all the reality it could handle by now."

"It's not for television, Elliot. It's a new platform. This is a hand-held show."

"Hand-held?"

"Not as in hand-held camera; as in hand-held devices.

It's for smart phones and various micro and mini . . . portable . . . thingies. I saw a test on my watch."

"How was it?"

"I'm not sure."

"Picture quality an issue?"

"Quality is overrated."

"'Quality' *means* rated."

"These are lo-fi times, Elliot. The most important part of any program is that it is on somewhere. With hand-held the shows are not only on, they are literally *on* the audience. Increases the odds they'll watch." Mike looked out the window, his visage turning grave. "People have to scramble, client-o'-mine. The Internet is destroying this town."

"You sent the one-pager for *Nailed* to Fred over at Litehouse . . . right?" Elliot wanted to change the subject.

"I did."

"And?"

"They passed."

"Not even going to take a meeting?"

"No, they are not."

"Did they give a reason?"

"They don't think *Brokeback* meets *Passion of the Christ* has an audience. They don't buy the whole gay Jesus thing."

"Come off it, it is so obvious. In the new draft Judas betrays him because he's insanely jealous of this thing Jesus has with Mary Magdalene —"

"You've told me already."

This was impossible, as Elliot had only then made it up. There was no new draft.

"They think," Mike continued, "and they have a point,

that it doesn't bring the Christian or gay audiences to the picture, it manages to alienate both. And there was a question whether you were the guy to write it."

"Why?"

Mike wheeled his chair too far forward, pressing his torso, about where the diaphragm sat, against the desk. He was hurting himself. "You're not Christian, Elliot. You're not gay."

"I can be gay for a studio green light. I mean, what does it take?"

"There's also the issue of your age."

"My age? I'm forty-nine."

"Shhhhh," Mike waved his hands urgently. "Increasingly difficult to pitch a twentieth-century writer."

"What do I have to do to earn my twenty-first-century cred, Mike?" Elliot was fucking around, but Mike looked to be giving the question serious consideration.

"Become younger and more attractive? Move to Laurel Canyon? Bring your dog to work?"

"Hilarious."

"There comes a time after which plastic surgery makes things worse."

"Fuck Litehouse. Let's take the thing to some hot young indie outfit."

"Specifically . . . which hot young indie outfit?"

"What about Benny and Tara?"

"They're not indie. They sold out years ago. Indie is just a step to . . . what's the opposite of indie?"

"Dependent?"

"Then Tara is very dependent. She's an executive in charge of production at Paramount now."

"How many executives in charge of production do you think there are in Los Angeles?"

"How many will take your call is a better question. If there were ten thousand execs-in-charge, how many would take your call, Elliot? You're becoming disconnected from the trade. You've got to get out there more. People forget you fast in this town. Have you considered joining . . ." Mike hesitated. "You know what is popular now?"

"Surely the bloom is off Dianetecs."

"Have you heard of Farinism?"

"The bread people? Tell me that's a joke, Mike."

"You're not networking enough, Elliot. Not schmoozing. A lot of people are getting into this Farinist thing, you know. Faranist writers are being attached to projects with Faranist stars and Faranist directors. Priscilla was just in here with a bracelet that looked an awful lot like a bagel to me. I'm just saying. They're into wheat, how scary can it be?"

Elliot thought back to the loaf-soled freak from the way over. Chaff? Elliot was "chaff"? That sounded anything but harmless to him. Los Angeles would always have its Manson Families, its Jim Joneses. Elliot needed a breather.

"The winery has taken all my time," Elliot said.

"Well, it can't take any more of mine."

"What's that supposed to mean?"

"It means that I represent screenwriters, not winemakers. It means, unless something happens soon, I don't think there is any point in us continuing. I don't represent hobbyists."

"The winemaking isn't a hobby."

"I was talking about your screenwriting."

"You're kidding, right? What does it cost you to represent

me? Nothing. It's all take, no give."

"There are office costs."

"Paper clips and photocopying?"

"My take of your give doesn't cover those."

Though he wished to tell Mike to go fuck himself, he said instead, "Give me a couple of weeks."

"I'm beginning to think you prefer not working."

Elliot looked at his watch. He had another appointment to keep, at home.

☙ ❖ ❧

ELLIOT HAD ACQUIRED the matrimonial house, on Amesbury Road, fifteen years earlier. (Most of his scribe-tribe fellows lived in Sherman Oaks, the other side of the hills. Elliot was thankful, every day, that none of his neighbours were in show business.) He'd bought the place outright with his fee from *A New Arrangement*, a picture for which there had been great hopes. There was enough money left over for the patch of old Zinfandel up in Enredo (only five grand an acre back then), where he would plant his vines. It seemed then that things could or would only get better. Contrary to common wisdom, no one appreciated, from the top of the mountain, the height they had scaled. You only got it later, looking back from among the bones in the stillness and heat of the valley floor. Hadn't Nixon said something like that when he resigned?

Paying cash for the house was wise. As its value continued to madly increase, it became a critical asset in Elliot's continual refinancing of the winery. Now it was mortgaged to its rafters — with the Los Angeles market tanking, for more than it was worth. The last thing the bank wanted to do was call it. Elliot was too bad to fail.

There was living and working room enough for Elliot and, for a brief, happy time, Lucy (to whom he had promised a cheque) and their son, Mark, and then, for a shorter time, Lisa, followed by fickle Meryl and then, for a mere six months, Connie. It was a grand spot to entertain, though Elliot couldn't think of the last time anyone was over for dinner. The door to Mark's room was closed, and inside was as he had left it.

Elliot had furnished the place in the same way he'd purchased it, with cash on the barrelhead. The dining room was airy, with a view over a tangled garden (horticulture becoming a diversion for Elliot as he learned his viticulture), and so a good setting for his treasured Charles Rennie Mackintosh chairs and tables. It was the liquidation of these which he was now negotiating.

The asthmatic lug the dealer sent could barely squeeze through the front door. Perspiration caused his glasses to slip down his nose. To better survey the furniture he pushed the specs back up with a fat finger, whereupon they would steam up and again begin to slide.

"To provenance," he wheezed.

"Right out of Glasgow, same period as the Willow Tea Rooms."

"I can see that! I mean before you. Where did you acquire them?"

"Oh. From another writer, a countryman of mine, Lloyd Purcell. Writer's writer, classic storyteller . . . so naturally he sort of . . . ran out of luck down here. Also there was a criminal matter, vice related. No one much harmed but he lost his green card and had to sell everything quickly. Now that I think about it, Lloyd came to acquire the set in much the same way . . . another writer fallen on hard times."

"Like yourself?"

"Me? No. I'm doing well, professionally. It's my winery . . . The wine we make is proving a touch tougher than we expected, needs more bottle age than anticipated. Besides, the furniture has some bad associations for me."

"No one died on it or anything?"

"No. Relationships. Failed ones."

"Oh," he said with unmasked disgust, as if Elliot had spilled seed on them. He circled the table, reaching out to finger the oak of the high-backed chairs. "There is obvious wear."

"They're going on a hundred years of age."

"I mean, recent."

"I believe furniture is meant to be used. It wasn't purchased as an investment."

"Feel the same way about wine?" The intruder now lifted one of the chairs and studied the underside of the seat.

"Yes. Meant to be drunk," said Elliot. This caused his bulky guest to laugh, derisively, as though Elliot had that wrong too.

"Our house auctioned the contents of Barry Hart's cellar. There were bottles once owned by Bing Crosby, Vincent Price, Peter Lorre. Let me tell you, there's money in keeping it."

"Barry in financial difficulties?"

"No. Converting his cellar into a panic room."

"A room hardly seems enough; I would have thought an actor of Barry's standing would want a full-blown panic suite."

"I shouldn't have said anything. The table would be an exceptional piece" — he laid the chair down and pointed with his chin — "if it hadn't been repaired."

"That was done before I got it."

"Regardless," he said, taking a showy breath. "What were you imagining it might fetch?"

"I thought a few hundred thousand dollars."

"Heavens, no!"

"I've kept up with prices on the Web," said Elliot.

"This set is not . . . pristine, nor, I suspect, complete."

Elliot was worried this might arise.

"Perhaps not. Though no one knew of any more than the four chairs."

"Had six originally."

"Definitely?"

"Absolutely certain," He looked past Elliot and proceeded, unbidden, into the adjoining living room. "What about these?" he asked.

He was hovering over one of a pair of snooker-room chairs, also Mackintosh, also from the Purcell sale. They had low, curved backs, the line and ornament of which seemed to anticipate the modern. The wood was unblemished. They were still upholstered in their original white calico.

"I wasn't going to sell those."

"They are much the more interesting pieces."

"At auction?"

"Look, I've seen dining sets fail to meet the reserve. These . . . Are they snooker chairs?"

"Yes," answered Elliot.

"These will sell."

"Take them and the dining-room set as a package then. I won't break up the lot."

The assayer was still looking at the chairs covetously. He pulled a cellphone out of his pocket and held it up between them. "Will I call for a truck to pick it up?"

"What's your offer?"

"With these included, two hundred and twenty thousand, tops. I'll be honest with you, if you want to wait, get the word out to the collecting community in the U.K., then more, but right now . . ."

"No. I haven't the time to wait," Elliot said, even though it wasn't nearly enough. "Let's have on with it."

The fat man placed the call.

⌐ ❥ ⌐

ELLIOT MEANT WHAT he'd said: wine was to be drunk. It should be kept until maturity but never "collected," never thought of as an asset to appreciate. Nor should it be accompanied by too much palaver — he was beginning to doubt that tastings, such as the fiasco he'd led earlier in Bel Air, did much to increase most people's enjoyment. It was great fun for the fanatics and geeks but a bore to everyone else. Attaching too much importance or ceremony to wine's service killed its magical agency to spur conviviality. And above all, wine was culinary, to be taken with food. He loathed the practice, common in his professional community, of serving heavy red or white table wines at receptions or post-screening parties. He might allow for a more frivolous Champagne — better, the lightest Mosel Kabinett — but never anything built to wash down roasted joints of meat or game birds. Feeling so strongly about the matter of food's symbiotic relationship with wine was now the only thing that made Elliot eat at all. He had lost his appetite. (If he did not consciously force himself to take sustenance, he would waste. Lucy worried that he was looking thin.)

And so, if he was to have wine, he would have food. This night he sat at the cedar table in his yard with a plate on which were some thick shavings of a hard pecorino cheese, a few slices of beef tongue and salami, a small piece of bread, and some olives. To drink he opened a tart Barbera d'Alba. He would drink it all, tonight. He would fight and maybe lose to the desire to open a second. To drink by oneself was to be contemplative. Or depressed, depending how you saw it. Or lonely — definitely lonely.

A consequence of Elliot's rudimentary learning in viticulture was some knowledge of "dry" farming. (He was among those who held that drip irrigation made for lazy vines, while thirsty plants produced more intense fruit, fruit with an urgent need to preserve its threatened DNA.) Elliot had put this wisdom to use when he planted the rear of his yard with natives and other desert plants. A chaparral with yucca and laurel sumac, prickly pear and white sage. It was once a retreat, a place where Elliot got his best thinking done. Now he worried there.

Until Mike stated it so starkly, Elliot had been able to avoid confronting the fact that he hadn't worked as a screenwriter for many months. Even then his most recent paying gigs had been "polishes," passes at dreadful scripts in a last-ditch attempt to save them — unsuccessfully, it turned out. His heart wasn't in it. The screenplays were too poor to inspire interest or hope, and Elliot's changes were forced and arbitrary, changes made for their own sake, nothing that bettered the original.

The strictures of the pictures, the heroic leads, the love interests, the reliance on gun violence to up the dramatic stakes, the damned "inciting incidents," the three or four or nine (depending on the current operating theory) prescribed acts, their value as star vehicles, beginningmiddleend — none of it had anything to do, as far as Elliot was concerned, with telling stories with moving pictures. The cinema was to have freed the story, abandoned linearity, cut loose the nineteenth-century novel.

He put his final disillusionment down to being asked of his screenplay *The Feinting Spell* (blue-balled teen pretends to be vampire to get girls), twice, at different pitches on the same day: "This is a comedy, right?" But then, what did Elliot's feelings on the condition of the contemporary film narrative have to do with anything? His job was to provide a service, and he did not. He'd seen this problem coming but assumed that by now he would have left Los Angeles and the entertainment industry for his idyll. There, looking out over his rolling rows of vines, combed over the contour of his land, he supposed he would continue to write. Never again screenplays or scripts for television. Prose, he supposed, maybe something for the theatre. But maybe, just maybe, nothing at all.

The sun drowned in the Pacific. The sky was Fleurie. The bottle of Barbera was empty. Elliot went to fetch another.

THREE

IT WAS IMPOSSIBLE to beat the traffic. Ever. Traffic had won a decisive victory and held Los Angeles pinned in a triumphant chokehold. The 1, with its views north along the coast, was less congested than Highway 5 but added an extra hour to Paso Robles. Those times he'd gone farther, up to the prison in Soledad in a futile attempt to visit Mark (who continued to refuse to see him), he'd taken Highway 5 up and, to try to soothe but finally only numb his broken heart, the coastal highway back.

Elliot found that keeping a fleet pace on the road, particularly with stirring music played at an injudicious volume, cleared the head. A sluggish advance had quite the opposite agency and induced black rumination. He saw the line of cars ahead slowing and gathering.

Mark's trial was the end of Elliot and Lucy. The excruciating bureaucracy of the proceeding, the dull, grinding inevitability of the thing, gave them time to consider nothing so much as the space between them, to notice that even after all these years neither could be fully and freely themselves with the other. Neither Lucy nor Elliot could let themselves howl in despair at what was happening to their son and expect complete and utter forgiveness from the other. They loved one another. But not enough for that.

There wasn't any courtroom drama. Everybody knew the ending. It was the slow agony of dying not by a knife but by a cudgel. When it was said and done, the shocking sentence passed, Mark was led away and Elliot called to him, "I'll come and see you as soon as I can." And Mark turned and said, "Don't bother."

It was the most horrible thing he could recall. The memory was so unendurably painful that Elliot felt no shame in running and hiding from it.

The traffic inched up the coast. One started seeing the occasional vineyard from the highway a few miles south of Montecito.

They'd been at it in California from the time of the Spanish missions, planting vines so they could make wine. Perhaps it was because of that term, "wine*making*," that people imagined the enterprise was by man's hand, that the drink was created from a recipe. But at its best wine was an expression of the place, not the ingredients. One wanted to taste the oyster shells in which the Chardonnay of Chablis grew, the lime in Alsatian Riesling. There was sometimes tinkering, in Bordeaux — softening a Cabernet-based wine with chocolatey Merlot, seasoning it with small admixtures of Petit Verdot or Malbec, co-fermenting Syrah with a dash of floral Viognier in Côte-Rôtie — but it was essentially, when done right, farming, not cooking. Châteauneuf-du-Pape was unique among serious wines in being made from so many grapes, but even so, its alchemy was as much in the agriculture as in the mix.

The primary (and occasionally the only) grape in the majority of wines from Châteauneuf-du-Pape was Grenache, a black, hot-climate grape of Spanish or perhaps Sardinian origin (no one seemed willing to admit it did best in Sardinia) that produced a potent though pale juice. Easily boozy, most of the Grenache grown in the world became plonk. It did so well. It was unpretentious; it made a carafe wine, a wine for the people. But low-yielding old vines could also produce something much more.

Châteauneuf-du-Pape began with Grenache — to which could be added Syrah, for a shiny pepper pelt and the durability of reinforced concrete; Mourvèdre, for the funk of blood; and Cinsault, for volatility and polish. Counoise gave a fermented essence that Elliot called "raspberry kimchi," and it brought to the wine what Mick Taylor had to the Stones. Vaccarèse was a spice: a pinch did the trick. Terret Noir added crisp acidity. Muscardin's role was an utter and essential mystery.

White grapes, in tiny proportions, were part of the blend too. Roussanne gave beeswax and honey to the palate and white flowers to the nose. Clairette, while soft, added alcoholic heat for the tongue. Bourboulenc kippered; Picpoul puckered against Picardin's sugar.

Beyond the official truth there were more grapes than these. There were, in fact, several varieties of Grenache, from black to white; there were spontaneous hybrids; there were mischievous oddities from faraway corners of the vineyards of the southern Rhône Valley. But nowhere, it seemed, was there any longer cultivated Matou de Gethsemane — the grape in the admixture that contributed the critical element that Elliot sought in the wine.

The Matou de Gethsemane (*Vitis vinifera* subsp. *Golgotha rutilus difficilis*) was alleged to originate in the Middle East — from the garden on the Mount of Olives where Jesus suffered his agony, if one took the name at face value. It was said to have been carted back from the Holy Land to the south of France by Crusaders, in the belief it had made the wine that filled the Grail, the very wine that became blood. But given the vine's traits, this made little sense. Unlike the other hot-climate grapes in the Châteauneuf mix, Matou de Gethsemane could not bear heat and sun.

They said you could see this in the pallor of its fruit. Botanical accounts from the nineteenth century, including a few poor drawings, described a faintly blue skin with amber freckles on any exposed shoulders. Because the vines did so poorly in the light, they were planted in the shadiest areas and trained to have heavy leaf canopies. Only in this relative gloom could the grapes mature in such a way as to produce juice useful for wine. Those few who, long ago, planted any of it, often did so in the shade of a stone wall between properties, on the edges of their *clos*. Exposed to the midday sun, the grape, like Jesus on the cross above, was finished.

The top of the name, *matou* — "tomcat" — tipped one off to its nose, reminiscent of the spray of just such an animal. In colour it was not at all purple, but copper. The palate, wrote one monk who grew it, was enigmatic, having a distinct flavour, something earthy or of metal, that wasn't quite there.

He ascribed to it a taste that compelled one to continue to smack the lips and roll the tongue, searching. But monks tended to exaggerate the few pleasures they took.

Among reasons speculated for the decline of cultivation of Matou was that, vinified on its own, it was thought to be nearly undrinkable. In concentrations of up to an absolute maximum of 10 percent and in concert with Grenache and Cinsault, there were reports of its producing rosé wines of simultaneous lightness and gravity. These, the stories went, "refreshed" like no others. As a component of a beefy southern Rhône red, it would provide relief against a tendency to be boozy and sweet. It made wine of only 9 or 10 degrees alcohol with no residual sugar and it was, in all accounts and with complete conviction, said to add critical "tension." When Elliot pressed the oldest vignerons of the southern Rhône, in his Canadian high school French, for a further explanation, for an expansion, there was a Gallic shrug and that shaking of the half-opened hand, like the turning of an invisible dial, that said, "If you cannot understand what I mean by 'tension,' then you cannot understand what I mean."

Lastly, every account, every bit of geezer-imparted lore, held it a bitch to grow. More than the fussy canopy management required, the Matou was prone to every disease known to grape — fungal, viral, and bacterial. It was particularly susceptible to mildew-like growths that thrived in the same leafy vines necessary to protect the grapes from too much sun. Its yields were poor, except in those years when the berries spontaneously shattered. It was impossible to harvest mechanically. Its vines had to reach fifteen years of age before the fruit showed its characteristic modesty. It was in need of constant and individual attention, possibly why it held a reputation for being "jealous" of other varieties.

By the early 1960s only one or two growers were known to bother with it. The Thibodeau family at Isabelle d'Orange vinified it with success, as did a secretive group of monks who'd long ago made wine for the Avignon popes. The monastic order, whose allegiances were suspect after the Church returned to Rome, was extinguished by papal bull in 1964.

Cultivation gradually ceased. The Matou was by no means unique in this. Grapes like the Penouille, the Troyen, the Camaralet, and the Arbane Rouge were almost extinct too. Gone the way of the Snouthouse apple and the Ribston Pippin: casualties of a globalized marketplace that could not find a niche for an apple known as "Perfect."

Elliot drove into Cambria, on the coast, to get a sandwich for lunch and a cup of coffee. Fog made the place as damp and chilly as faraway St. John's, Newfoundland, the town in which he was born. Given the right conditions, these Pacific mists could creep inland to the most westerly vineyards of Paso Robles, cooling and slaking them. (Vigneron wisdom in the South of France held that the Mourvèdre grape didn't grow properly where one could not smell the sea.) But the tendrils of relief that snaked their way through the Templeton Gap in the Santa Lucias too rarely made it as far east as his thirsting vines. Standing beside his car, looking out at the surf, he shivered. In a short twenty minutes, he would be in an inferno.

THEY WERE ERECTING another building on the grounds of the neighbouring property, Haldeman Estates. (Elliot called the place, owned and operated by a retired cavalry general — an Apache helicopter his last mount — "Haldeman Laboratories.")

Haldeman were, in philosophy and practice, in direct opposition to Elliot's operation. They believed their product was *made* in the cellar. Where Haldeman deployed forward osmosis and microminioxygenation to create their Frankenwine, Elliot endeavoured to be as non-intrusive as possible. Haldeman raised their wines in spanking new barrels, specially coopered extra-small so as to impart the maximum characteristic of American oak. Elliot used *foudres* and concrete tanks to minimize the influence of wood. Haldeman harvested fruit that was verging on deliquescence to make blowsy, sugary wine. Elliot harvested early to ensure acidity, austerity, and minerality. Haldeman called Elliot's wine a "Châteauhuit de Dope." Elliot likened Haldeman's wine to a rootbeer float.

The starkest difference between Elliot's operation and his neighbour's was that Haldeman's was successful.

A crane was in there at Haldeman's, lifting some machine off the back of a flatbed. Probably an Israeli centrifuge.

There was no sign marking the entrance to Elliot's winery.

Elliot made his way to the vineyard offices. His operation was not plush but practical, built into the hill to facilitate gravity feeding as opposed to rough pumping. Visitors were discouraged. Winery tours were right out. He thought he could feel the heat of the gravel coming through the soles of his shoes.

Day-to-day business operations had fallen to Bonnie Sherow, whom Elliot had hired, originally, as his secretary. She was greatly overqualified and only took the job because it was close to home. She and her husband, early back-to-the-landers from the '60s themselves, ran a biodynamic farm nearby. She hadn't been on the job a month before Elliot named her manager. He never did hire another secretary — there wasn't call for one — and so was always uncomfortable asking Bonnie to perform functions below her station. But the situation was approaching an emergency. Bonnie was worrying over a litter of invoices.

"Elliot," she said, "we have —"

"I know, I know."

"We need thirty-eight hundred bottles. I have to get them on credit."

"Cash flow, I understand."

"That's only part of it. Sales are . . . The wine cannot market itself."

"Sure it can. We've been through this, it's cult." Elliot hated the term. "Advertising works completely against the image. Does Rayas advertise?"

"Marketing means more than advertising. You can't have it both ways, you can't be this cool thing with integrity, that only those in the know know, and be, like . . . popular. And the wine you are making . . . forgive me, Elliot . . . it's no Rayas."

"Rayas was a bad example. Beaucastel." Like Elliot, Beaucastel grew and made wine from many grapes.

"Beaucastel advertise. And you know what? Locura Canyon is even less like Beaucastel than Rayas. Beaucastel is a terrific business."

"I know you're right, Bonnie, but . . . I think vineyard problems are our priority, I know what's got to be done. I haven't got much time."

"You sure don't."

"How long?"

Bonnie looked down at her desk, pretending to consult some papers when Elliot could see she just couldn't say it to his face.

"Without refinancing, we've got two more vintages. Maybe. With the drop in land values around here, the asset side makes talking to the banks impossible, even if they were lending. Probably best to keep our heads down."

"Then I've got to get on this immediately. Can you book me through to Paris or Marseilles? First flights available."

"Is this a new partner?" asked Bonnie.

"What?"

"Are you drumming up some investment? In France? A partner? Because if you are, I think it's great idea."

"Yes," Elliot lied, "that's part of it, it's an ancillary objective of the trip."

"Ancillary?" Bonnie took a moment. "What's the primary objective?"

"Matou de Gethsemane. I'm going to make one last effort to find some."

Bonnie caught and held her breath, ultimately failing to suppress the urge to say something.

"Do you really think . . . It's not my place to question you but . . . Really, Elliot, do you think that's going to make any kind of difference to the situation here?"

"I think, if I can find some, it will make the wine great." Elliot straightened, lifted his chin.

"I understand that. I've understood that for some time. But our problems, your problems, are financial and they are immediate."

"If the wine is great, then . . . It came up yesterday during this tasting I was leading and I thought again how that was really what got me into the business, and —"

Bonnie held up a hand to stop him and turned to her computer screen. "I think you have more pressing concerns, that's all. Besides the money situation, Walt tells me he's gotten phone calls. ATF and the Department of Agriculture are worried that you have root stock out there that didn't go through quarantine." She continued without looking at him. "If that's true, you have recklessly put the entire California industry at risk." She let the accusation settle in silence. "Any particular carrier?"

"Just the quickest way to the South of France."

So Bonnie thought that his search for the grape was an excuse. Indeed, in the South of France, worries could seem very far away. The perfume there, the *garrigue*, the lavender and tobacco smoke on the air, put one's head right. But Elliot was being forthright: whether or not he had a chance of locating the vine, he knew he was getting near his last chance — in many regards. If all that came of the journey was a release from confusion, from nascent panic, if there was only a moment of subsequent clarity, it would be worth it. "I have to go, Bonnie."

"Sure, boss."

"I'll talk to Walt about these ATF jokers. Where is he?"

"He's up in the third block of Counoise with a rifle."

"A rifle?"

"A zebra has been eating the grapes."

"A zebra?"

❧

BY THE TIME he reached the older block of Counoise, the sun was weakening him. He should have driven. It was the other side of hot, beyond the barrier at which one could distinguish any change. He would return in Walt's truck.

Walt Stuckel was meant to hold a rifle. He was a tall and lean native Californian. If his ancestors hadn't been actual pioneers, then they had at least been in Westerns.

Seeing Elliot, Walt put the rifle on his shoulder and walked to meet him.

"A zebra?" asked Elliot.

"A fucking zebra, if you can believe it."

"Well, no, I can't."

"Something was eating fruit, I assumed it was deer. I saw some tracks but . . . what do I know."

"Back up. A zebra?"

"I came down in the dark before dawn, two days ago, and I saw the goddamn thing. I wasn't even sure if I could shoot a deer or even a coyote, Elliot. I've never shot anything. But then, I see, you know, a zebra in here eating the grapes . . . I didn't know what to do but shoo it away. It didn't budge. Showed its teeth. I thought it was going to attack me."

"I don't know how to put this . . . I'm not being flip . . . but this zebra . . . it's not in your mind, is it?"

"No!" said Walt. He looked at the gun. He seemed to be judging its weight. "I think I can do it now. I think I can shoot it. If I see it again."

"Zebra."

"From San Simeon. Hearst had a private zoo and kept them."

Elliot now remembered hearing this before. He nodded.

"They're still there, the descendants," Walt continued, "left to range on the estate. This one must have found its way over. It's sixty miles through the hills."

"Did you call anyone over at Hearst Castle?"

"Yeah, they said they'd come over but they didn't hold out much hope of catching the thing. They wouldn't have done anything if I hadn't said I was planning on gunning the thing down. Zebras aren't endangered, are they?"

"The gun suits you."

Walt seemed insulted.

"I'm glad I got one, with those Faranistas over there." Walt pointed eastward with his chin (yeah, he was definitely descended from actors in Westerns) and raised the rifle, as if he was going to put the butt against his shoulder in readiness to fire.

"Faranists. Not Faranistas."

"They're crazy, Elliot. I've seen them in Paso and SLO, freaking bread on their heads."

"I didn't know they put it on their heads. I've seen them with loaves on their feet."

"It's all bad signs lately. I'm getting spooked."

"Signs?"

"There was a tremor the other day, 5.5, and then these folks from the Department of Agriculture calling."

"What did they want?"

"They want to see the paperwork on the vines, especially the Counoise, proof you got them from UC Davis."

"What did you tell them?" said Elliot, looking down at

the vines. At this tender age the trunks were as insubstantial as a young girl's arm. At maturity they would be as thick as a man's leg, their bark cracked and frayed and the plant no higher than it was now, pruned back to a vulgar bonsai.

"I told them that was your department, that I didn't know where you got them, that they were here when I came. And that's no lie," Walt said. "They know they're suitcase clones, Elliot, they aren't stupid. They asked about coming down to take cuttings, check the DNA."

"You told them they needed some sort of warrant."

"No, I didn't. This is my career, Elliot, it's not a hobby for me. I can't afford to piss those guys off."

"It's not a hobby for me, Walt. Never has been. Where do think I'd rather be, here or in Los Angeles?"

"This is it for me. I have my future to consider."

"You have a future here, surely."

"This is serious, Elliot."

"If they go after me I'll start talking about all the suitcase clones up in Napa. Nobody's gonna want that." It was an open secret that much of the source rootstock of Napa's top wineries had been purloined from the best vineyards of the Médoc and imported without any controls.

Walt didn't respond.

"Did the zebra have any sort of palate? Why was it eating the Counoise? Is it doing okay?" The leaves were wilting, drooping over bunches of grapes of uneven shape and size.

"It's hurting in the heat and drought, and it was in bad shape to begin with, what with the powdery mildew. Keeping the canopy so thick, we should have sprayed Rubigan, and earlier."

"Bad call. My mistake. How about the other varieties?"

"They all are in bad shape, 'cept the old-vine Zin. I swear it likes these conditions."

"I've actually been thinking we should sell all the Zin."

"It's the best fruit you've got."

"It's giving the wine this metallic thing, and I'm thinking that by the time the rest of the blend is coming around the Zin will be crashing."

"'By the time'?"

"It's not appropriate anyway. It's not authentic."

"Authentic? Christ sakes, Elliot, how can anything be authentic in a Rhône blend made in California?"

"Can we not go through this again."

"This isn't the South of France, Elliot." Walt paused and drew a breath. "I was going suggest we make a Zin."

"Under the label?"

"However you want to do it. A Zin is about as authentic as you can get here."

"I don't think so. Anyway, I am more convinced than ever that the solution is adding Matou to the blend."

Walt spun on his heels, his heavy boots kicking up dust. He could not look at Elliot.

"That's crazy talk, Elliot. It's wishful thinking. You've got all your hopes wrapped up in a grape people stopped growing fifty years ago. After a certain point you gotta get realistic about this."

"We have to strive, Walter, and if you're going to say that, there also comes a point when you accept that this is the best you can do . . . We're not there yet." Elliot reached down and picked a grape that looked to be ripe from the bunch.

"I'm saying that there comes a point when you learn that what you were chasing was never there in the first place. Imagine if you actually found some Matou stock. Your false hope could end your best excuse."

Elliot forgot what Walter said as soon as he bit into the grape. "Fuck sake!" It tasted like Sweet'N Low.

"It's been so goddamn hot that some of the grapes already have all the sugar we need, and some others, because of the uneven véraison, are weeks from being ripe. We'll have to pick before they've developed and there will never be enough acidity." Walter paused. "We could make a nice sweet Zinfandel, butterscotched up with American oak, zebra on the label, that lots of people could enjoy. 'Zebra Zin.'"

Elliot looked past his vines, over rolling country, land that begged to be covered on horseback, out to the other wineries that had sprouted in the area. Most of them, heeding the desires of the consumer, were going from strength to strength. Elliot, making decisions impulsively, half aping his French heroes, ignoring California viticultural orthodoxy and the public taste, was going from bad to worse.

But Elliot couldn't shake his conviction that giving consumers what they "wanted" was to fail to respect them. To his mind it was limiting their possibilities, diminishing their capacity to grow and change, and so holding them in contempt. There would come a time, he supposed, when all the other winemakers would realize they'd made a terrible mistake. But, like Haldeman Labs with their uniform green rows, their drip irrigation, their approved clones, and their marketing, they hadn't yet come around.

As for Elliot, he would sooner have his winery go down in flames than produce one fucking bottle of "Zebra Zin." Feeling the heat of just such a blaze, Elliot's reflex was to run.

FOUR

PACKING FOR FRANCE back in Los Angeles, Elliot didn't even fill his carry-on. He thought this was a sign either of his essential freedom or of something sad that he could not understand because it was about himself. He had one stop before the air-port. Lucy's place in West Adams was out of his way, but the cheque was late. The books said he didn't owe her anything. She was doing better than him. He was just too proud to admit it.

Lucy's was now the only Arts and Crafts house on Victoria Park Drive that hadn't been restored. She didn't seem to care.

"I'm moving anyway."

"Where?"

"Ascencion and I are going to get a place in Pico-Union. It's close and it's like half the price."

"The Peoples Temple — why not?"

"It's not far from there, actually."

When they were by for drinks last Christmas, Connie read the situation perfectly, but Elliot would not be convinced that his ex-wife was having an affair with her Salvadoran house-cleaner. When he saw it was true, Elliot assumed Lucy was, with her acute liberal guilt, confusing pussy and politics. But moving in with Ascencion made it more than a dalliance.

Hefty, hirsute Ascencion was glowering at Elliot now from an exquisite chair he'd given Lucy years ago. He'd found it in a small antique shop in Marseille. It was at a time when he was actively trying to rekindle the romance. He thought giving her a beautiful thing from France would make Lucy recall their time together there. But Lucy had only ever seen it as a chair, a gift from Elliot that was actually for himself.

Elliot believed, because of its measured use of Art Nouveau ornament, that the piece might be by Édouard Colonna. He couldn't see it in a place in Pico. Lucy didn't know its worth. Would it be inappropriate to ask for it back? Put it along the lines of relieving her of the burden of moving it.

"I have a cheque for you." Elliot held up an envelope. Seeing no one coming for it, he laid it on the coffee table.

"Gig?" asked Lucy.

"No. Wine sales, actually."

Ascencion scoffed at Elliot's lie. What did she know about wine or his business?

"Wow," said Lucy. "I never would have thought . . ."

"You? Any work?" Elliot punished Lucy for her lover's presumptuousness. Of course there was no work: Lucy was selling the house. She was grey-listed in town. Her last two features were modestly budgeted, justifiably lauded by the critics, and still lost money. And she was deducted points for being a woman and over forty. Lucy said she was abandoning "entertainment" and focusing on a couple of documentary projects. Elliot knew they would pose surprising questions, be filmically inventive, and connect, in a profound way, with a tiny audience. She was as whip-smart and original as when he'd first met her, when they made that film together, discovered France, sought their fortune. He still loved her.

"You don't really want to know about me, Elliot. So I will tell you that, yes, I saw Mark last week, and there's been a positive development."

"Really?"

"They've determined, the corrections people, that he is functionally illiterate."

"What the fuck?"

"Yes. And if you think about it, that explains a lot."

"No. He had a full-time tutor on *Family Planning*, what was his name? Kenneth."

"Did you ever know Mark to read?"

"I . . . thought so. He played a lot of video games, so . . ."

"And it was Kenneth, I believe, who introduced Mark to narcotics."

"I thought it was Harvey, the best boy."

"In any event, he's taking a literacy program they offer there. The Muslims are encouraging him."

"Muslims?"

"He's converted to Islam."

"Be serious."

"I am."

"I don't think that's good."

"They've got him reading."

"What? The Quran? In Arabic?"

"I don't know."

"You can't convert if you're not anything to begin with. We raised him with no beliefs."

"*Nunca queria salir en television,*" said Ascencion. "*Nunca queria que todo el mundo le miraba!*"

What was she saying? Elliot's Spanish was hopeless. Mark never wanted to be on television? Sure he did.

"I want to do a doc," said Lucy, "about the social cost of draconian drug laws in America."

"Not been done?"

"Name one."

Elliot couldn't.

"Not a polemic, use Mark's story as a thread."

"Mark won't talk to me because I got him a job on a television show and now you want to make a movie about him. Didn't you just hear your girlfriend say —"

"I think he will see a difference between network television and an independent documentary. And he was a boy then, you don't 'get a job' for a little boy. He's a man now."

"Maybe. Listen, Lucy, when you're speaking to him, please put in a good word. I'd like to talk."

"I tell him every time I visit."

"Thank you. That cheque is dated for next week. Some stuff has to clear."

❦

THE QUICKEST ROUTE to the South of France was swift indeed and via, of all places, Toronto, Canada. Everything direct out of LAX or San Francisco or via Atlanta or New York was booked for the next several days. Elliot thought this was impossible, believing it a lie that was part of some sort of price-fixing conspiracy, the mechanics of which he couldn't yet comprehend. He explained to Bonnie that many of the seats offered online were mere phantoms, posted to give consumers an illusion of choice. You could search and click and call until your head fell off, but you would never get that cheap fare. Besides, on a long flight, anything over three hours, Elliot clung to a demand, stated in a rider in the nether regions of his contracts, that he travel in the front of the bus.

He was on Air Canada to Toronto with a change to another Air Canada flight on to Paris and then a quick regional flyer to Nîmes. One way. It was a rush to make it, but at least it was with a top-drawer airline. It had been years since Elliot had flown his native country's national carrier, but he remembered it as having excellent service.

At the gate at LAX an Air Canada representative informed Elliot that there had been some mistake, that although he had purchased a business-class ticket, he was seated in row 23.

"Is business class oversold?" Elliot asked.

But the ticket agent looked past Elliot as though he were no longer there. Elliot asked again.

"Sir, please, there are other customers in line." The agent was a woman in her late forties, early fifties, mannish. Her hair was up in a bun, drawn masochistically tight.

"I don't care," said Elliot. "You haven't finished serving me."

"Yes, I have." She was almost a baritone.

"But I've booked and paid for a business-class ticket. I want to know why I am being assigned another seat."

"Then I recommend you call 1-888-247-2262."

"What? Now?"

"Whenever you like. If you try now, though, you will miss your flight. You have to turn off the cellphone once you board."

"Why should I call an 888 number when you are standing right in front of me? There's a computer terminal right there. You're perfectly situated to sort this out."

"You're not a terrorist, by any chance, are you, sir? I'm not going to have to call security, am I?"

The whole point of taking this flight was how soon it was leaving Los Angeles. Vowing he would write a letter, to which no one would pay any heed, Elliot stomped off to the plane.

BUSINESS CLASS WAS almost empty. There were a couple of sleepy-looking Air Canada pilots in one row and a nattily dressed black man of at least seven feet in another — that was it.

The plane was old. The shape of the cabin, the particular curve of the tubular enclosure, was familiar, but in distant memory. Seat 23B was threadbare and stained — with coffee, Elliot hoped. When he sat, his knees were against the seat in front of him. He would shortly explain the mix-up to a flight attendant and move forward to where he belonged. He searched the seatback pocket for one of the illustrated escape manuals to determine in what model of — jet? surely it was a jet — he was to be riding. The pouch hadn't been cleaned since the inbound flight and contained several plastic wrappers, a couple of sections of the previous day's *Toronto Post and Leader* — a paper Elliot remembered as a vaguely right-wing daily business rag — and crumbs. The edges of the three-way emergency escape foldout were getting furry, and there were ridges and blisters in the lamination. Elliot read that he was on a 737-300. He saw the problem: the aircraft scheduled for the flight must have been unavailable for some reason. That explained the trouble with his seat assignment and the antique flying machine. As long as it got him to his Toronto connection.

A flight attendant now passed, looking with disgust into Elliot's lap and counting under her breath. Judging from her age and disposition, this woman evidently came with the plane. An occasional visit to the barber, hot towels and the fixings, might cheer her up, thought Elliot. He thought he would wait for another stewardess with whom he might bring up his problem.

The other woman patrolling the aisles in Elliot's section of the plane looked grumpier than the first. She sighed loudly and closed the overhead storage bins with projected violence. Elliot was too frightened of her to even ask for a glass of water.

Only after they were airborne and the seatbelt sign had been switched off did Elliot go looking for the attendant responsible for the business-class compartment. He found a man in his forties with baby blue contacts and a carotene complexion.

Elliot explained his situation. The man looked at Elliot's ticket, nodding as though he were agreeing, and then shrugged.

"What a company, hey?" the steward offered. "Piece of shit outfit."

"They told me —"

"— to call an 888 number. Yes, I know. Don't bother, you'll be on hold to Mumbai longer than the charge in your cellphone."

"I don't want to make a fuss about it. I would like my seat in business class."

"You can try in Toronto."

"But then I will have already flown."

"I would really like to help you," he said, "but I think that's what they want me to do. They are trying, you know, to make us take on the responsibility of the ticketing agents. Once they do that, they'll start laying them off. I was supposed to groom the aircraft today because the service in LAX didn't show — they haven't been paid in over a hundred and twenty days. I'm sure you can see my point."

Elliot shuffled back to 23B.

If the blood-pooling confines of his seat weren't bad enough, an hour into the flight miniature screens dropped from the ceiling and the in-flight entertainment commenced. The 737-300 did not provide a choice for viewers: you got a package of Canadian news and a movie.

Some bald guy hosted the newscast. (You would never see that in the States.) Life in Canada didn't seem to have changed all that much. The RCMP were reported to be turning into a bunch of bumbling crooks. Quebec separatism was back, having briefly waned, so the federal government was announcing more spending in La Belle Province. The disgruntled premier of Newfoundland and Labrador, wielding evidence of yet further Canadian colonial malfeasance, was either righteous or insane. A woman in British Columbia had fended off an attacking grizzly with her guitar. The hockey playoffs, featuring two teams Elliot had never heard of, were, inexplicably, still going, even though it was nearly fall — there was a danger they would overlap with the beginning of the next season. That was Canada this day. There followed some short travel features, an episode of *Happy Days*, which Elliot couldn't remember as having been this terrible, and then, one hour into his five of mile-high confinement, the feature.

Though he had never before seen a frame of the finished film, the first few seconds of image sent a chill of recognition down his spine. A poison began to transit from his optic nerves to his sphincter. Here was young megastar Barry Hart, his face flattered by applied hypoallergenic stage filth, eyes gleaming against the half minstrel, making his way, solo, through the overgrown hills of Laos, somewhere in Mexico (near Oaxaca, Elliot remembered). Elliot's Vietnam script was — he'd thought — a transparent satire about the blood-soaked debacle in Iraq. But Marv Hinks over at Warner read the whole third draft, enthusiastically, straight. He saw it immediately as an action vehicle for Barry. So did Barry's agent, Herb Devine. Elliot was only looking out for Marv's and Herb's feelings by not correcting this misinterpretation. Why insult the guys? And hadn't Mike strongly advised him against writing it in the first place, quoting, *for like the hundredth time*, the George S. Kaufman chestnut "Satire is what closes on Saturday night"? Elliot would, it was understood, reshape the piece into the drama Marv thought it to be on the next pass. But Marv did not like Elliot's next draft, in fact thought it "a step backward," thought it had lost most of what he enjoyed about the previous draft.

In Hollywood, a producer's waning enthusiasm meant a new writer. After Elliot was shown from the project, seven more screenwriters were put on the case. Elliot ran into the last of these scribblers not long after shooting commenced on the picture, and felt it safe to reveal that the original premise had been misunderstood. This was a lapse in judgement, for when the movie was eventually eviscerated by the critics and tanked at the box, the credited writers, among whom Elliot was not, knew whom to blame. (Unjustly, thought Elliot now: the first couple of lines to emerge, haltingly, from Barry's exquisite lips bore no resemblance to anything Elliot had ever typed.) Jesus, was it bad! Elliot pulled off his headset and turned from the screen.

How long to Toronto? In his haste to get on the flight, Elliot had neglected to bring his book or to score some Bromazepam with which to knock himself out. He fished around again in the seat pocket. There was the in-flight magazine, dedicated, as fate would have it, to the Napa Valley. Elliot flipped through the pictures. Napa looked better than it drank. It was a vile example of how the rich got richer, how dabblers, in concert with some mercenaries out of UC Davis, managed to charge suckers over a hundred dollars a bottle for their syrup. Three parts water to one each of vodka and Ribena: voilà Napa Cab. The only thing worse was those bubblegum Pinots out of Santa Barbara — Elliot could taste nothing but banana in those. In the year after the movie *Sideways* came out, that was all anybody served. Elliot despised obvious wines.

Coming to a feature article on Fred Hanover and his Cab ranch, Elliot put the magazine back in its place and pulled out instead the rumpled newspaper.

Elliot deduced he was looking at a Central Canadian edition, for there seemed few stories from Canada's fringes. The economy was fucked, but less so than in the USA. This was cause for several columns of smug self-congratulation.

There was a wine piece, actually having the temerity to recommend Canadian plonk. (Though maybe, with global warming, Elliot reasoned, it was becoming possible to grow grapes to ripeness in the north. It was certainly getting too hot in California.) There had not been any serious Canadian wine when Elliot was growing up. There were concoctions that were *made* in Canada — pinkish products full of bubbles, called things like Baby Duck — though whether of grapes, it could not be said. These drinks were considered a step below even the brand wines from Europe, the Black Towers and Mateuses, though, in truth, they were probably not that much worse.

All the new Canadian wines discussed in the article were still named, like the Ducks, after animals of the boreal forest: foxes and owls and wolves. Elliot's own label featured no tasteful line drawings, no watercolours of the rows of vines on the estate, no portraits, no critters, no elaborate wordmark, none of the branding that he had been told was essential to success in today's marketplace. Elliot even insisted on employing a bland sans serif typeface. Someone once wondered aloud whether the bottle contained medicine. No matter, thought Elliot: his bottles wouldn't require "packaging" because the content would speak for itself. And it did, but in a plaintive voice. Or, as in the case of vintages 1997 and 1998, in the banshee scream of a crack whore fighting off the police. Even 2002's early whisper had become an agonized moan once the wine was in the bottle. The admixture wasn't right. A touch, a seasoning, two rows' worth of Matou de Gethsemane in the blend, for tension on the palate: that was the answer. *Then* Elliot's wine would sing.

He turned the newspaper's wrinkled page. "Leadership Vacuum at Pubcaster," said a headline above many column inches of print and a small, mysterious photograph of a densely treed gorge. It looked good as a sleeping pill.

"On Tuesday, CBC chairman Jean Bousquet cut short a trip to France, where he had been attending the Cannes Film Festival, to address the widening crisis affecting the public broadcaster's English-language television service."

Cannes ended months ago, thought Elliot: must have been the TV market, MIPCOM. He continued to read.

"In a hastily called news conference, Bousquet announced that he had, yesterday, accepted the resignation of Executive Vice President of English Television Stanford Heydrich. 'Stanford Heydrich came to the CBC with a vision of renewal,' said Bousquet. 'I accept his resignation with great regret.'" Heydrich, apparently, had become embroiled in a scandal stemming from the creation and scheduling of a new daytime chat program on CBC television, *Afternoons with Mac*, slated to be hosted by CBC employee Jill MacDonald — to whom Heydrich was romantically linked. Ms. MacDonald was described as a sometime on-air personality who occasionally provided weekend national weather forecasts for CBC NewsWorld.

"Mr. Heydrich," read Elliot, "has stated that he plans to return to the private sector. According to Mr. Bousquet, an executive search for a replacement has already commenced. No interim VP will be appointed."

Heydrich's resignation had come at a crucial time for the CBC, just as the fall season was set to begin. Moreover, a gleeful sidebar explained, it was not the first such woe to befall the CBC that year. In March, the highly touted, and reputedly costly, late-night talk effort *The Benny Malka Show* was cancelled due to abysmal ratings. The eponymous host of the program disappeared soon after the announcement. "Toronto Police investigated numerous sightings of Malka in area parks and green spaces," explained the caption below the photograph, "but were unable to conclude whether he was even still in the GTA." Reports that Malka was living as a sort of wild man in the ravines near the Don Valley were dismissed as urban mythology.

Elliot had grown up watching the CBC, simply because it was one of only two stations available in his hometown. It had never been much to get excited about but did possess a certain charm in its inability to be slick. The CBC could do adequate, vaguely liberal but cautious news and information, but its frequent forays into entertainment were cringe-making. The CBC, maybe Canada in general, was too self-conscious. The grown-ups couldn't pretend in a way that was second nature to Americans. With his years in the screen trade, Elliot now believed that the best film actors did nothing other than be utterly convinced by their own lies. The best performances came from actors who merely thought they were, at the moment, the character they were playing. They were dissociative psychopaths. They weren't method actors; rather, they were method humans.

The CBC programs Elliot best remembered, and then only fuzzily, were about nature; typically, documentaries about the people and fauna of the north. Most memorable were the "Hinterland Who's Who" public service announcements, produced by the National Film Board of Canada for the Canadian Wildlife Service and dropped into plentiful unsold advertising slots. Elliot could hum the forlorn flute part that signalled the beginning of each one, and still knew that the muskox formed a circle to defend against wolves (a strategy that a proved a failure against the rifle), that the beaver's teeth were yellow and never stopped growing, and that the moose was the largest member of the deer family.

It was quaint, really, that a vice president of the CBC could be forced to resign for having fucked the weathergirl and then given her a show as a reward. In the Darwinian world of television in the States, it wouldn't have mattered until the ratings came in.

There were other stories in the newspaper about sundry goings-on in Canada, stories of too small or too regional an interest to have attracted attention outside the country. At least the disgraced former VP of English Television had some excitement in his life. It was a shame the CBC turfed him; he was the kind of leader Canada needed.

The paper had done the work of a couple of Lectopa. Elliot dozed off.

FIVE

"**BIENVENUE À TORONTO**" said the voice over speakers the moment the plane's wheels finished bouncing on the runway at Pearson. But it was only after waiting another hour and a half on the tarmac, waiting to be assigned a gate, that Elliot set foot on his native soil, or at least its flooring, for the first time in more than a decade.

His scheduled connection was tight. He jogged to his departure gate. Studying the ticket for the next leg, to Paris, he saw that he was again assigned to the back of the bus. This time he took it up with the ticketing agent at the gate.

"There was even room in business class," he complained of the last flight.

"Can I see your ticket, sir, and your passport."

She was the youngest Air Canada employee Elliot had met that day, but she looked tired. She picked up the phone and said something Elliot could not make out. This was Canada. Elliot felt himself relax, his shoulders dropping. Action was finally being taken. Business class. To France.

"So you've managed to sort it out? I'd prefer an aisle seat."

"I'm afraid not, sir," she said.

"But it's —"

"The issue is not with your ticket, sir. It's your passport."

"What about it?"

"It expires in six days."

Elliot snatched the document back from her hands. It was true. In the photo, taken but five years earlier, Elliot looked a decade to the good, less drawn, eyes reflective. Those were happier days; the first bottlings of Locura Canyon were nearing early maturity and would, Elliot mistakenly believed, soon to be ready to show. Lucky Silverman's EA was telling him that the coverage on one of his scripts — none other than *The Feinting Spell* — was positive. Lloyd Purcell had a thing that was sure to go with HBO and had guaranteed Elliot a couple of episodes. Patricia Franchini from Warner was asking whether he had time to take on an adaptation of a hot chicklit property. None of it would ever happen.

"I've called Border Services," said the ticketing agent. "Someone will be here in a moment. If you wish to re-book the flight, please call 1-888-247-2262."

His Border Services escorts fancied themselves cops but were, in the main, too fat for a beat. Elliot dared not make a crack; he could tell from the way they carried themselves, and from the number of African and South Asian women sitting around the office weeping, that they were drunk with power. For an interrogator Elliot drew a blockhead — once of Newfoundland, judging from his accent. The fellow typed some details from Elliot's dated papers into a computer. The profile the machine produced must have been particularly dull, for the bulky official yawned, an effort that pulled his lips above his gums and aired his tonsils. He made no effort to cover his mouth.

"Why would you change your name from Johnston to Jonson?" he opened.

"Lot of Johnstons out there, my name is my business. I'm my own brand."

"And you go by your second given name, Elliot?"

"That's correct."

"Pierre Elliott Trudeau?"

"He wasn't yet a public figure in English Canada when I was born, he was still just another anonymous Jesuit Franco-ist, catholic in his sexuality."

"What?"

"Or perhaps by then he was a socialist playboy. I went to university in Montreal, and my Québécois friends, they kept changing the story."

Mr. Border Services took a moment to simply stare at Elliot and scowl before returning his gaze to the computer screen.

"What's a bayman like yourself doing down there in Tinseltown?"

"I'm sorry?" Elliot said, though he well understood the question.

"What's wrong with Canada? You have a problem with Canada?" He was leaning back in his chair and pushing his gut toward the roof. Was he displaying the great mound in an attempt to somehow intimidate Elliot? Maybe he was doing some sort of exercise to try to reduce the thing. He remembered his agent pushing his belly into his desk.

Maybe it was a new exercise craze.

"No, not at all. Why would you even suggest such a thing?" Elliot said.

"You've been living down there for years. Is there some reason you left Canada?"

"Yes, there is. I'm in the film and television business. There wasn't a whole lot going on here. I got a green card in the lottery, went from there."

"I know someone who works in the Canadian television business."

"Lucky them," said Elliot.

"You know a program called *The Littlest Hobo*?"

"I have a vague recollection."

"My cousin . . ." He thought for a second. "My second cousin, actually, he moved up here from Leading Tickles in Notre Dame Bay. Up to Guelph it was. His daughter is — was — married . . . they divorced . . . was married to the fellow who owned the dogs that starred in that show."

"Dogs?"

"They had two or three that looked alike, pack of Hobos."

"I remember now. Alsatians, right?"

"German shepherds. Good show."

A dog barked. Elliot convulsed. The border guard tensed and congealed. In a moment he relaxed and grinned. He slapped his wooden desk with an open palm.

"Fuck me," the guard said. "Talking about dogs!"

The dog barked again. The sound came from a room beyond, might have passed a couple of walls, but travelled easily on account of its deep pitch. Sourced from a bigger breed of cur, Elliot reasoned. The heavy official came forward, leaning over his desk. "That's bad news for someone trying to bring a souvenir back from down south. You should see 'em, the expression on their face when there is this dog barking at their bag. And then they realize they're caught. I've seen fellas shit themselves."

"I can see how they might," said Elliot.

The agent moved back and straightened in his chair. Perhaps he had completed his full set of gut thrusts.

"By comparison, your problems are small," he said. "You have to get a new passport."

"Can you issue me something temporary?"

The man laughed. "It's not a hall pass."

"But I have a ticket to Paris," said Elliot. The man now stood and turned around to a stack of filing cabinets; on the top of these was a levered press into which he slid Elliot's passport. He grabbed the lever and pulled it down with swift force. The passport was Swiss-cheesed. He put the punctured booklet in a small plastic bag and then into his desk drawer.

"The French would turn you back."

"But —"

"Where will you be staying?"

Staying? Jesus, this could not be happening.

"I'll wait at the airport."

"Mr. Jonson, this is going to take days, if not weeks."

"No."

"Yes. This is your fault. All you had to do was read the expiry date."

"I've gotten a new passport from the consulate in Los Angeles. It didn't take more than a week, and that was in another country."

"You've obviously been away a while."

Elliot put his head in his hands. The tile floor was speckled with something that Elliot's shuffling feet had streaked.

"If it's going to take that long I might as well go back to Los Angeles."

"Mr. Jonson, you're not grasping what's happening. You aren't going anywhere."

Elliot sat up.

"No?"

"You can travel within Canada. That's it. You could go back to the Rock for a visit. Back to Newfie?"

Elliot grasped it now.

"Fuck that. I'll stay here. I'll stay here in . . ." Elliot had to think for a moment. ". . . Toronto."

"Have you been in Toronto before?"

"Of course. Years ago."

"So. Where do you think you will be staying?"

"In a hotel. Downtown, I guess."

"Okay. There's a passport office on Victoria Street. You won't make it today."

Elliot looked at his watch. It was true.

❧

A SIKH CHAUFFEUR took him from Pearson Airport to his hotel, the Four Seasons in Yorkville, via the Gardiner Expressway, a downtown feeder. Everywhere repairs were being undertaken. The asphalt was like a rope binding the city and coming unbraided under strain. This eight-lane strip was as clogged with smoking vehicles as anything in Los Angeles. It conveyed Elliot alongside the shore of an Ovaltine lake and presented, from its elevation, a vista of the city's downtown. The place had surely doubled in size since Elliot last saw it: the spire of the CN Tower now seemed to rise out of an actual metropolis and its exhalations, rather than look down upon a little city north of Cleveland. When the landmark came into view, his driver sighed loudly. When Elliot said nothing, he did it again, more theatrically.

"What is it?" Elliot asked.

"The Tower is no longer the tallest free-standing structure in the world."

"I didn't know."

"Now what do we have? Ontario was capable of greatness, sir. But with the manufacturing jobs going to China, we have become a have-not province. Imagine our shame at this. We are like Newfies now. How many are needed to pick peaches? I will end up back in the Punjab."

To signal his disinterest Elliot opened his window. He sniffed. He was possessed of a natural gift for smell that he had refined in the cellars of Locura Canyon: making wine required, more than anything, olfactory acuity. When he travelled he could place himself with his nose. He guessed he could identify blindfolded Aix's telltale lavender and Gauloises or Firenze's distinctive diesel and cooked fungi. The town of his birth, St. John's, was easily known by the brackish and fecal hum of its harbour. Eucalyptus and ominous woodsmoke told him Los Angeles's ground-level ozone was about to be cut by the Red Winds.

Could he, similarly, recognize Toronto by its tang? The atmosphere outside the airport terminal had been indistinct, the fumes and hurried breath of transit everywhere. He'd hoped that, once en route, he'd be able to sense something familiar from the open limousine window. But the noxious billows of the road were in such concentration as to mask anything natural. The air quality was as bad as in Los Angeles. Toronto had come a long way, and, from the stink of it, it had come by car.

HAVING CHECKED IN and dumped his bags, Elliot hit the street. He was in need of a glass of wine. He headed for College Street, which he remembered as being the spine of a Little Italy. When he was last in Toronto, the strip had housed a few serviceable restaurants, and he hoped he could find a place that might offer the modest plate of antipasti he desired.

The neighbourhood, while still ostensibly Italian, had been buffed and deodorized by colonizing scene-seekers. Where once were boisterous families of Calabrese and the occasional artist or student, there were now throngs of poseurs. There was preening and posturing and, most hopelessly, searching sideways glances to see whether anyone noticed. Everyone was awaiting someone else's arrival, only they didn't know who that person might be.

To be fair, you could see the temptation. The scale and situation of the street were perfect for staging urban adventure. The Los Angeles hipsters searching for parking on the wider avenues of Silver Lake would covet such a prospect.

The couple of workingmen's bars seemed more Portuguese than Italian now, but finally Elliot came upon a joint with a promising menu and aroma and, owing to the stark lighting of the interior, an absence of wannabe boulevardier.

The coffee-with-cream beauty who took his order explained that while there were no antipasti on the menu she was sure something could be put together. The wine list was not as accommodating, so Elliot settled on a tolerable, if internationally styled, bottle of Tuscan table wine.

Out the window, Toronto appeared to be internationally styled as well, a condition its inhabitants undoubtedly mistook for being cosmopolitan. Still, things had visibly improved since the '70s and '80s. The diversity of the population, and the ease with which these hues and shapes and manners mixed on the street, was something of a marvel. In Los Angeles, people had drawn back behind their respective mud walls. Toronto, this segment at least, wore its prosperity well, seeming not to have unconditionally surrendered to the consumerism of New York or L.A. Livable, if unexciting. But with excitement came trouble — and Elliot had quite enough of that.

Elliot knew he wasn't being as generous as he might, that he held every émigré's conflicted contempt and nostalgia for the home country. One had to adopt a sort of chauvinism to justify or rationalize the decision to have moved on and, one hoped, up. Truthfully, the food now before him was as good as any back in Los Angeles. The two salamis on his plate were of the highest order, tasted to have been made by hand and dried in the air in the authentic fashion disallowed by North American health inspectors. The preserved red pepper, blistered sweet, was obviously homemade. The olives were surely sourced from North Africa, a better choice in a pinch than some mass-produced shite from Italy. The bread was excellent, a touch of salt improving on its Tuscan model, and the cloudy oil was the kind of fruit juice you found on the ground in Umbria. It was pleasant enough, the food even giving the ordinary wine a lift. Elliot was content until, after twenty minutes or so, he got the definite sense that the Norse thug tending the bar and the register was squinting at him, sizing him up. It was making Elliot uncomfortable enough that he called for his bill with a few glasses remaining in the bottle.

The barkeep was soon standing before him, Elliot's AMEX card in his hand.

"Elliot Jonson?" he said.

"Yes," said Elliot. The man's voice was familiar, as was the size of him, and the thick, nearly white hair —

"Didn't have the temerity to go with 'Shakespeare'?"

Elliot looked again. "Gunnar Olafsson?"

"Yeah, Wes, right? Wes Johnston?" He pulled out a chair and sat.

"Well . . . as you can see . . . I'm going by my middle name now."

They had been in film school together, in Montreal, back in the late '70s. They hadn't been in the same class or shared the same interests, Gunnar being a dedicated proto-experimentalist, making, if Elliot remembered correctly, long ("duration as an aesthetic") films with a delirium tremens camera. He did recall, clearly, that the films, which meant absolutely nothing to Elliot, were highly lauded by the faculty. Gunnar won a student prize. Elliot passed his courses and was little noticed.

"Right. And what's with 'Jonson'? Like Ben Jonson, yeah?"

"Lot of Johnstons around. It was a business decision, to

distinguish myself from everyone else. So you landed in Toronto after film school?"

"I was back in Winnipeg for a while, at the Film Co-op. I ended up taking a job with the CBC to make enough money to continue making my own films and then one thing led to another, I moved up in the organization, ended up coming here."

"Great."

"Well . . . no. I mean, obviously." Gunnar gestured to the room.

"Have a glass of wine?" asked Elliot.

"My shift is done in fifteen minutes."

NOW, AS IN university days, the Icelander became easily drunk. His head became too heavy for his neck. Elliot could remember seeing the same movement, the same swinging of the noggin, in the Greek dive Aidoneus, on Park Avenue. Gunnar could be nasty at school, never hesitating to make a crack about his peers' early and naive efforts in the cinema, but in the bar afterward, after a couple of *gros Molson* and a few spliffs, he became the sentimental fool.

Gunnar sat at Elliot's table with his supper, a carelessly scorched T-bone and a pint of beer. Halfway through the tile of beef (and his third lager), Gunnar abandoned trying to saw off another double mouthful and pushed the plate away. Betraying his roots, he took rye whisky for dessert. Gunnar wanted to talk about the good old days.

"And remember Bernadette, what a babe . . . Oh man, I actually went up to the Laurentians with her one time . . . Her parents had a place . . ."

"So you were in management at CBC?"

"At CBC . . . Oh yeah, I was a Creative Head."

This could mean many things.

"Which is . . . that you . . .?"

"Movies and Miniseries," answered Gunnar.

"In charge of production?"

"Yeah but . . . not really 'Production' production. Commissioning them, or taking an investment position. I'm proooud —" He burped. "Proud of the films that we helped make happen."

"Like?"

"Well . . . there was *Down a Mine*, and the Olive Diefenbaker biopic, which I think surprised a lot of people, and *Silly Goose*, that bird movie, and . . . anyway, a lot of . . . oh yeah, and, of course, *Cabane à Sucre*."

"Wow, that's impressive," said Elliot, despite never having heard of any of these films.

"And Louise, remember her, she was in animation? She broke my heart. Fucking hot. You know what she used to do?"

"With a track record like that — what happened?" Elliot asked, as if he'd not heard Gunnar's digression. Gunnar was probably soused enough to wonder whether he'd said the thing about Louise or only thought it.

"Okay, okay . . . audiences were in decline, but you've got to remember that, given the demo . . . demo . . . demographics, we were going to lose a significant number anyway."

"To the competition?"

"No, to death. The CBC audience skews kinda oldish. So I thought maybe more films about dying and disease, that sort of thing, I mean, Bergman did that all the time."

"Death was even a lead in one of his films, if I remember," observed Elliot.

"Right . . . anyway, some projects weren't as 'light-hearted' as some VPs might have liked. And a few were 'challenging.'"

"Challenging as in the art-movie-that-people-don't-watch way?"

Gunnar's head bobbed in vigorous affirmation.

"And you have no idea what a low opinion those guys have of their audience. They take them all for boobs and cretins. They were worried about their official mandate, so they had code words for it, stuff like 'more broadly accessible' or 'audience accommodation.' I mean, hey, sure, this is television, chicks in bikinis eating spiders for money, but this is *public* television, surely there has to be . . ." The thought filling Gunnar's head must have been giving it buoyancy, for when he lost its thread, his chin went to his chest. Was he snoring? No, it was a waking snort.

"People used to watch, Gunnar. I mean growing up, I'm sure we had the CBC on all the time."

"That was before there was a choice. How many channels did you get in . . . where was it you come from, Wes, out east, wasn't it?"

"'Elliot,' and we only had the two channels."

"You know, there is a gaggle of comfy liberals out there, a tiny educated elite, isolated in gilded downtown enclaves, in their bubbles, who like to imagine that this is a sophisticated, postmodern, secular humanist society. They have that smug, superior attitude toward the States, like they're all hicks and we up here are opera-going, art galleries on Sunday . . ." Gunnar burped once more. "But you go out there, my friend, out into the suburbs, get out into area codes where the people live. And . . . that whole funding system that was designed to bring all that art and culture to the masses, to subsidize it so that any Canadian could have . . . well, Wes, ol' buddy" — Elliot flinched at this — "they didn't want it. Even for free."

"Maybe it has to cost them something before they know its value."

"Nah. It's a Tim Hortons nation. Who should expect a population whose favourite food is Kraft Dinner to go in for documentaries about Stockhausen?"

"You have a point."

"Hmmm? I . . ." Gunnar was having trouble with his next thought. He looked at his glass with regret. He clenched his jaw in a last push to get out what he meant to say. "Regardless of the reasons, one day I got called before the bosses and told that I either resigned or took the position of Director of Radio for Nunavut. I told them where to go. I left my experimental film practice in Winnipeg for these people. I was happy to be out of there, clear of that institutionalized mediocrity. Besides, over the years I figured I had made a few friends in the independent production sector. There were people out there who had done well by my stew . . . stewardship of tax dollars and would return the favour by giving me a job." Gunnar's expression further soured. "The excuses I heard, Wes . . ."

Elliot was about to again correct Gunnar on the Wes front but thought better of it.

"'Production is way down this year,' they said, and 'There is this huge inventory of Movies of the Week,' and 'Reality is killing everybody.' Ungrateful bastards. I thought I had something at the OFDC, but I did a lousy interview and they really needed to hire a woman of colour. I was going lose my house . . . so I said fuck it, I'm going to do it myself, just some porn, low budget, quick turnaround, make some cash . . ."

"And?"

"I got it into my head to . . . when I was writing the script . . ."

"The *script*?"

"I started getting interested in the formal possibilities and the prospect of making a critique, more a metapornographic film than . . ."

"Oh dear."

"Yeah, well, it was a great film, only not sexy in the conventional sense . . . Anyway, I ended up workin' the bar here." Gunnar surveyed his domain and again let gravity have its way with his skull. Again it bounced back up.

"Hey! Do you remember Lucy Szilard from film school? She was really talented. Whatever happened to her?"

"She ended up in Hollywood."

"Wow. What about you, Wes?"

Elliot looked at his watch.

· "Oh, I ended up in the States too, in the beverage industry. Good seeing you, Gunnar, but I gotta go."

SIX

WITHOUT THINKING, ELLIOT, Angeleno though he was, walked
— walked! — back to the Four Seasons. There'd been a rain
shower; the city had shined its avenues and dabbed petrichor
behind its ear in preparation for a glittering evening. Toronto
wasn't such a bad little town. A couple of days here wouldn't
kill him.

In his room he turned on the television and, in mind of his
company that evening, found the CBC.

The program on offer looked to be one commissioned
by Gunnar himself. It was self-consciously arty, shot in high-
contrast black and white and with mannered performances.
At first Elliot thought that something was wrong with the signal or the set, for he could get no sound. He was considering
calling the concierge when the appearance of a title card on
the screen told him the silence was deliberate. They were taking great pains to emulate the films of the early montage-mad
Soviets — Eisenstein, Pudovkin, and cadre. They'd made the
new film look like something pulled from a dusty archive in

Leningrad, distressing the negative and chopping out a few random frames as if the print were ancient and much abused. The effect was visually compelling for all of thirty seconds, and ruined entirely when Mike recognized an actress he'd seen in a television commercial for Red Lobster.

At least the film's lack of soundtrack made it possible to watch while checking his voice mail at the same time. (There might be some future in silent pictures, thought Elliot.) The first message was from Mike, who sounded uncommonly keen. "Elliot, call me as soon as possible. It's urgent, like for real."

"Urgent" could mean only one of two things. Someone was taking a meeting — perhaps Litehouse had realized the potential of *Nailed* and reconsidered. Or, more likely, it was an offer of a quick polish job, perhaps trying to beat a few jokes into another lame comedy. Hopeful, and with nothing better to do, Elliot called Mike.

"Elliot! This is your cell number, right?"

"Yeah."

"Is there a pay phone anywhere near there? Are you at the vineyard?"

"I'm in Toronto."

"Toronto? Like . . . Canada, Toronto? Is there a shoot or something?"

"No, I'm here for a couple of days en route to France. There was some trouble with my passport."

"Trouble?" Mike swallowed the word, worried. Odd for Mike.

"Nothing serious. It was out of date."

"Oh . . . good. Listen, are you at a hotel?"

"Yeah, the Four Seasons."

"That's perfect. Gimme ten minutes. I'll call you back."

The moment the call ended, a blat of distorted sound leapt from the television set. Elliot dove across the king-size bed for the remote and muted the volume. The black-and-white piece had ended. Now there was too much colour and too much light. Onscreen were young people with forced smiles in an improbably spacious apartment. Their movements were halting but exaggerated; they were reacting to what was being said with the grandiloquent eyes and lips of desperation mugging. Elliot thought he might just be able to detect flop sweat blooming beneath the pancake on one particularly cherubic funny-maker. All too familiar, like at least half a dozen sitcom pilots in which he'd had a hand. Those had, thankfully, never seen the light of day. Perhaps this was a comedy *about* a failing sitcom. He'd mention that idea to Mike. He went back to his voice mail.

"Mr. Jonson, my name is Jasper Crabb, I'm a senior special investigator with the United States Department of Agriculture. I want to talk to you about some of your vine stock, issues concerning provenance. This is a serious matter and I'd appreciate it if you would call me as soon as possible at —" Elliot closed his phone. The jig was up. The USDA had determined that Elliot was cultivating grapes from unauthorized stock and was going to throw the book at him.

The first grape he'd smuggled into the U.S., back in 1992, was Counoise. The crowd at Tablas Creek had already acquired some from Beaucastel and had been responsible enough to put it through three years of quarantine up at UC Davis. It would be several more years before the nursery could make it available commercially, and Elliot, in his early enthusiasm for his venture, decided he couldn't wait that long. He needed mature Counoise and Mourvèdre and Syrah, five years of age minimum, to make a worthy wine. Elliot smuggled in the cuttings to be on an even playing field with the growers who had pioneered the region.

Yet for all that risk, the Counoise failed to contribute the missing element to the wine. There was definitely some desirable red berry pickle but . . . In for a penny, Elliot soon after got his source in Avignon to score him some shoots of Muscardin. Those planted on flat ground did well and, when introduced to the concoction five years later, gave the wine, while still undrinkable, a more floral bouquet.

He looked back at the TV, thinking again that he'd better pay closer attention; a homecoming to Canada might soon be his only option. They were now on to some sort of drama: it was set in an open-concept office, possibly a newspaper. The lead character was a twitchy old guy, probably playing the editor, who, in a way one would never see on American television, squinted all the time. To its credit, the CBC seemed determined to reflect the nation back to itself, for the performers were all plain-looking, cast, it seemed, to resemble regular folk. There was an aversion to extremes up here. While the stars might lack glamour, the people on the street were not the great waddling obese, the new land-giants you saw in the States. Americans were content to let celebrities be attractive and happy for them. In Canada, Elliot knew, they thought that no countryman was worthy of celebrity and were suspicious of anyone who might be too good-looking or pleased with themselves. Americans were determined to believe in better tomorrows. Canadians wouldn't take risks in case they should make things any worse. Americans couldn't perceive irony; Canadians chose to look away from it. Elliot was about to turn the volume back up when the phone on the night table rang.

"Mike! Sitcom about a failing sitcom?"

"Too *Inside Baseball*." Mike, like all agents, could respond to a question without having given it any consideration, as though he'd spent the night in study and rumination. "I guess this line is clean, hey? I mean, a foreign hotel, they couldn't very well . . ."

"Where are you calling from?"

"I'm in a gas station on Wilshire. I'm calling from a pay phone."

"A pay phone?"

"They're impossible to find these days. I've been driving around for half an hour. Elliot, do you remember that conference call with Larry Werner, about two years ago?"

"Vaguely . . . remind me."

"Remember you were joking after the call that he took a pass on *Pass It On*?"

"Right, the pandemic comedy. That was a funny idea."

"No, it wasn't. Anyway. It turns out that the conversation was tapped."

"So?"

"From an illegal wiretap."

"Why would anyone tap my phone?"

"Not *your* phone, Elliot, Larry's. Why would anyone tap your phone?"

"Who was tapping Larry's phone?"

"A private investigator working for Lucky Silverman."

"But Larry and Lucky are partners. I even think Lucky was on the call for a bit."

"They *are* partners, and Lucky was on the call. The details aren't important, what's important is that you not cooperate when the FBI come calling."

"The *FBI*?"

"There's an investigation."

"Back up."

"Everybody was tapping everybody else: producers tapping agents tapping actors tapping producers. It's a victimless crime."

"I don't feel in the least victimized."

"That's the spirit. The DA will prosecute the easier cases, and Lucky needs the waters muddied. They don't have any tape, only the bill from the private detective who did the deed. Unless a person who was on that call gives evidence, they won't be able to proceed."

"Okay . . . I guess."

"Great. And there is nothing the FBI could squeeze you on, to compel you to testify?"

"Like?"

"Narcotics, like that business that got Lloyd Purcell deported."

Elliot thought about the call from the USDA. Mike had made it plain that he was tired of hearing about the woes of Elliot's winery, and why worry the guy? "Nope," he said.

"Excellent. I know that if you let this go, if you don't cooperate, have a lapse of memory, you can't remember any call, your mind has been destroyed by alcohol from all that wine, etcetera, then . . ." Mike was panting. "I'm advised to inform you that you could be looking at a producer credit on *The Centuri Protocol*."

The Centuri Protocol was based on a comic, something to do with serial-killing aliens who took the form of sexually insatiable, cannibalistic interns at the White House. Early reports said the film was fantastic to look at, utterly moronic, and testing through the roof. It was a hit-in-waiting, and Lucky Silverman and Larry Werner were its producers.

For Mike to even have bothered calling Elliot said that the matter of the wiretaps was a grave one. There wasn't time, but Elliot knew he should get legal advice before taking a payoff on the advice of his agent. That was what the situation in Hollywood had come to: one needed lawyers to talk to one's agents, and agents to talk to one's lawyers. Even the agents needed agents.

"What sort of fee?"

"Well obviously something . . . not in line with Larry and Lucky. You weren't even the one they were listening to, you were collateral damage."

"Collateral casualties are the ones who get the compensation, Mike. That's the American way. I have to get the same fee as those guys or no one will believe it. They make it known that it's a real credit, not a courtesy credit, and I will endeavour to stay out of reach."

The line was quiet for a moment. Mike was either considering the offer or had been dragged away by the feds.

"I think that can be done," he finally answered.

"One worry, though."

"Yes?"

"I've said, many times, that I would never adapt a comic book and never do serial killers."

"Sure, but who heard you? And since you may soon be attached to the project, it's 'graphic novel,' not 'comic book.' You would never be in the running for a top comic book adaptation. Though one major upside to this is that being considered a possible co-conspirator with that company really ups your stakes in this town. It puts you in another league altogether."

"And all this time I've been trying to get ahead with writing."

"Don't call me about this, okay? I'm sure they're tapping the office phones."

"Who? The FBI or Larry . . . or Lucky?"

"Any or all of the above."

"Can more than one person be tapping your phone at a time? Can you tap a tap? That would be a good twist in a picture, eh?"

"That's far too complicated for today's audience."

"It is rather 'meta.'"

"It's 'meh-ta,' Elliot. If I don't call you back then you can assume it's done and you're a producer on *Centuri Protocol*. If asked, you say it was an honour to work with . . . blah blah blah."

"Have you talked to Jerry about this?"

"Jerry?"

"Jerry Borstein was on the call too. Are you gonna talk to him?"

"No! And don't you either. Someone else must be dealing with Jerry."

"Right. You know what is weird, Mike? I was at Silverman's house the other day."

"I know. What were you thinking, not fucking his wife?"

"Jesus, I thought —"

" You could have done yourself a big favour there, buddy."

"I so misread that."

"How do you think it makes him look, some hack won't fuck his wife? And now he's got to keep fucking her on top of Janice Everston. You insulted one of the biggest players in this town."

"Janice Everston?"

"Everybody knows this, my friend."

"Imagine, though . . . fucking her on top of Janice Everston, I mean literally, her in the middle while you —"

"Stop, please."

"This bullshit credit, Mike. It's the first work you've got me in over a year."

"Not true, didn't I get you . . ." Realizing Elliot was correct, Mike refocused. "What I would really like to know is, what was said in that phone conference that's got everybody's pee so hot?"

"I have to be candid, Mike . . . I probably wasn't paying close attention."

"You don't surprise me much, Elliot."

"I say 'yeah, that's great' and 'good idea' and doodle. I could check my doodles when I get back to Los Angeles."

"Sure, Elliot, check your doodles.

⌒❦⌒

ELLIOT'S CIRCADIAN CLOCK had not adjusted, a condition aggravated by all the television he was watching. When he should have been going to bed, it was dinnertime in Los Angeles, and with nothing over the course of the weekend to change his rhythms, Elliot had been keeping west-coast hours. He did not wake until ten a.m., seven in the morning in California. So much for his plan to arrive at the passport office first thing Monday.

There was not a spare chair in which to wait. The standing crowd spilled into the hallway outside. There was a narrow, elbow-riddled passage through the mob that provided access to a dispenser of numbered tickets indicating one's place in line. Elliot drew 68.

Was there a mass exodus underway? Had there been some dreadful news that was motivating Canadians in great numbers to flee the county? They were serving number 29. He checked his ticket again: 68. He looked around. The faces here were mostly brown, so maybe people were going back to a home that wasn't Canada.

After ten minutes, they served number 30. From the spot to which he'd retreated in the hallway, Elliot craned his neck to better scrutinize the system. There were six wickets, only two of which were manned. Something wasn't right. Had not staunch conservative leadership of the nation put years of deficit financing and accumulating debt behind it? Since the banishment of the profligate tax-and-spenders, were not the newer governments in the black? This level of public service was positively third world. Trouble was said to be pending for Ontario; he remembered his Sikh chauffeur observing that the manufacturing sector was going down the toilet, but this was a federal service — shouldn't it have been handsomely financed and adequately staffed, considering the cash on hand in Ottawa?

In the interior room a hefty West Indian lady collapsed. People went to her assistance. One less person in line, thought Elliot.

Thirty-four, and one of the clerks was closing her wicket. A few sighs was the most protest the crowd could muster. Canadians took it. In France there would have been a riot — to no avail, of course, but it least it would show evidence of a pulse.

Paramedics arrived before the number could change to 35. If their level of disinterest was any indication, all was fine with the large woman.

Standing next to him, leaning against the wall, was an attractive young woman — features and skin one found in the French Caribbean. Her hair was in a funky, unravelling afro. She wore a revealing T-shirt, loose silk pants, and flip-flops.

A full year without sex was a worrisome milestone. Was there any possibility, however remote, that the delightful young thing standing there might, under some, at this moment unforeseeable, circumstance, take him to bed? No, there was none. Absolutely none. She'd have to be mad to fuck a sunburned old bucket of issues like Elliot. He was so seriously unfuckable right now that he would selflessly counsel any deluded comers, "Spare yourself the ignominy!"

Two new clerks arrived at wickets. Evidently their station was as complex as the cockpit of the space shuttle, so long did they take arranging their pens and staplers and stamps.

His bitterness about his breakup with Connie was far enough in recess now that he could look back with some fondness on his time with her. They had split over what she perceived as Elliot's inability to see things for what they really were. Despite its being none of her business (though Elliot continually burdened Connie with his complaints), she'd questioned the viability of the vineyard. She took it upon herself to download an article from the Net about creeping sprawl in San Luis Obispo County and asked if he'd considered selling his land to a developer. The nerve. Eventually she brought that stuff to bed and that was that.

Connie missed a critical factor in her analysis of his problem. Sure, Elliot wasn't being truthful with himself; sure, he wasn't facing the facts. But he was also self-aware. His was self-conscious self-deception. It was how one coped.

Now the line was moving more efficiently: they were at number 60, the number of the beautiful girl next to him. He watched her hard and high ass go and fancied what it might be like governed, in furious up-and-down pumping, by his grip. He was as stirred as he'd been by Robin Silverman. If it really was a year since he'd had sex, then maybe his old reptile brain was taking charge, shouldering reason and doubt aside to take the wheel, or, more properly, the stick. Fuck something, fast! it was saying. He should not be listening.

Someone was screaming at one of the clerks in his native Eastern European tongue. The audience of his tirade was waving in a security guard. The uniform was already en route, obviously having been summoned by some hidden button. Back to the shtetl, sucker. One less person in line.

What if things went badly with the Department of Agriculture back at the vineyard? If there was some criminal proceeding, there could be problems with Elliot's treasured green card. Poor old Lloyd Purcell's crime hadn't been egregious, nothing Fatty Arbuckle, an indiscretion, really, and the heartless monsters at Naturalization had snatched his documents. Jesus, Elliot realized, he hadn't heard anything of Lloyd, nothing at all, since his old colleague had been forced back to Canada. Poor sod might just as well be dead.

Sixty-five. He'd be up any moment. And might not an American criminal record, especially one involving the prohibited export/import of French root stock, cause him future difficulties crossing the pond? Without the occasional trip to France or Italy, to lands dedicated to living, he would wither and die.

His number, 68, flashed on the display. He stepped up to the wicket at exactly the same moment as a stern-looking Vietnamese chap.

"I 68," said the Vietnamese.

"Sorry, Ho." Elliot showed his tab.

"You go back, Blue Boy, you full of shit, you blue 68."

"What?"

The clerk piped up. "We are doing red numbers now, sir."

"What?"

"You have a blue 68. We have to get through the reds first and then the greens."

"But I . . ." Elliot checked the paper in his hands: indeed, the 68 was in blue ink.

"We might get to you by this afternoon; otherwise, we'll be taking today's blues tomorrow."

"You have to be early bird," said the Vietnamese man, holding up his tab close to Elliot's face, as Elliot had to him. The ink was red.

⌐ ❦ ⌐

THE CONCIERGE AT the Four Seasons had recommended a place on Wellington — Bymark. Elliot found it alongside and partially under a lawn between commercial towers. Iron sculptures of lazing bulls, perhaps eight of them, were placed throughout the parkette. They were no doubt totems to beckon or celebrate positive movement in the financial markets. After civilization collapsed (soon), Elliot reckoned the alien anthropologists who found the statuary would reason that the doomed earth people venerated the bovine creatures from within the steel-and-concrete towers surrounding them.

The restaurant turned out to be a smart joint. The menu was simple but wisely chosen. Without a reservation, Elliot was seated at the bar. There was an adequate selection of wines by the glass, though Elliot could easily drink a bottle himself. He was not particularly hungry so ordered only a roasted wild mushroom salad, having with it, instead of the suggested Viognier, a glass of Rosso di Montalcino. Mushrooms were good friends to wine.

Elliot resolved to have lunch, find a bookstore, return to the hotel, and start the passport process anew the next morning.

He watched two women in business attire, jackets and rather short skirts, negotiate with the maitre d' and then be escorted to low chairs at his back. They were waiting for a table but seemed more interested in the martinis with which they were quickly fitted than in grub. You didn't see as much of the heavy cocktails at lunch these days. Elliot did not intend to eavesdrop but, with nothing to read, he made no effort not to.

"What's replacing *Jeopardy* and *Wheel*?"

"Not game shows."

"No?"

"They piloted one with George hosting, but the prizes were so lame that it wasn't going to work."

"How lame?"

"Year's supply of Vachon cakes and a family pass to Canada's Wonderland."

"How did George take it?"

"Badly."

"Tears?"

"Wailing. Weeping. Keening."

"He went into this with his eyes open. It's the Darwinism of showtainment. Besides, he's starting to look his age."

"Yeeeeew."

They sounded to be lower-tier television executives. It explained the early boozing. Elliot was intrigued.

"What are they going to schedule?"

"They want something 'Oprah-esque' — their word."

"Self-help nostrums, latest diet, getting over your mother?"

"You go, girl."

"Keeps down the revolution, anyway."

"How do you mean?"

"Makes the need for change personal and not political."

"You can't have tax players subsidizing a revolution."

"You said 'tax players.'"

"Did I? That's good."

"What sort of Vachon cakes?"

"Jos. Louis, Mae West . . . you want some?

"If they aren't picking up the show. Wouldn't want to see

them wasted. I'll bring them up to Belmont House. Mom and the other girls at the home love their sweets."

From whence had come showbiz folks' elevated sense of importance, Elliot wondered. Giving notes on a moronic sitcom was more important than family; the parking of trucks for a C movie was more important than all other commerce. And how willingly people accepted it. *"I'm afraid you can't go home tonight, ma'am, your street is a closed set. The production's Child Containment Unit have your son and daughter under sedation. You will receive a DVD in the mail."* What were the gals saying now?

"Have you heard anything about the VP job?"

"They're panicking, totally . . . It's rudderless and — Oh, I did hear they've hired an executive headhunter out of New York, Barnaby Vesco?"

"What is it with these people? They're obsessed with the U.S."

"Why did I ever leave CTV?"

"Will Vic the Dick be in on the interviews?"

"Rainblatt? He can barely stand up. And it comes with nausea, his condition. You don't want the president of the CBC blowing chunks on potential candidates."

"What is it he's got, exactly?"

"It's called labyrinthitis. It's a virus, apparently."

"Poor bastard. How long do the symptoms last?"

"That's the worst part, could be a week, could be a year . . . longer."

"Is it contagious? I mean, if it's a virus?"

"No idea. Gawd, why did I ever leave CTV?"

"Why don't you get out of television altogether?"

"And do what?"

Elliot finished his salad and his wine. He placed his credit card on the bar and stood, as if stretching his back, to better get a look at the two women to whom he was listening. They, too, were now standing, their table ready. They were in their forties, Elliot supposed. Too thin, too old for their outfits, with too much makeup needed to mask their fatigue.

Elliot, for the first time in a while, had a winning pitch for Mike.

AFTER A SINGLE ring Elliot got Mike's EA, Blair.

"I don't care who he's in a meeting with. I need to speak with him, pronto."

"I have strict instructions. Strict."

"What has that got to do with me? Put Mike on the phone or —"

"Oh, HUSH!" said Blair. Elliot was put on hold.

Blair was back on the line with surprising haste.

"I don't know what you've done to upset Mike so. He was very flustered when I told him you were calling. He said he would call you back after he goes to pick up some groceries on Santa Monica Boulevard. I have no idea what he's talking abou — Oh my! Oh my!" Blair was speaking with tremendous excitement. "There he goes. There goes Mr. Vargas. He just left!"

"Thank you, Blair."

It was not long before the phone in the room rang.

"I told you about the phones in the office." Mike was breathless. "It's not safe."

"How else am I going to contact you? Leave a newspaper at a dead drop?"

"What?"

"Never mind," said Elliot. "There's been a new development."

"First," said Mike, "let me tell you my news."

"Good?"

"Fantastic. The lawyers say that without you the federal attorney doesn't have a case, and if you're a Canadian citizen not resident here, there is nothing they can do to compel you to testify."

"Why is that good news for me?"

"For you?"

"If I'm going to stay in Toronto I'll need a gig."

"I'll talk to Lucky about getting you an MOW or some D2V thing. They're always shooting those up there. I'm sure they can fire a Canadian writer. Who would notice?"

"No. I'm talking about something substantial. Something with a golden parachute. That's why I called."

"You've lost me. You've got to speak up," said Mike. "I have to hold this phone away from my face, there's something gross on the handset."

"The CBC is looking for a new vice president of English programming."

On the line Elliot could hear the drone of traffic on Santa Monica. "What's the CBC?" asked Mike, after a moment.

"The Canadian Broadcasting Corporation. Like PBS, only with commercials."

"And do they have a Spanish service or something?"

"No, why?"

"Well, you said English programming."

"They have a French service."

Mike laughed.

"No, really," said Elliot.

"Oh, so . . . they really speak French up there? I always thought that was . . . like a joke or something, you know like Black Jack Shelack."

"Jacques. Black *Jacques ShelLAC*. Listen to me. I want the job."

"English programming at the CBC? How the hell am I supposed to help you with that?"

"Not you — talk to Lucky Silverman, tell him that would be the best way to keep me here for a year or so."

"What can Lucky do?"

"All I need is for the headhunting agency to come looking for me. It's Barnaby Vesco out of New York."

"I've heard of them."

"Exactly. Someone like Lucky will have a connection."

"That's it? That's all you want? To stay in Toronto, a job at . . .?"

"The CBC."

". . . yeah, okay. The CBC. In Toronto. I don't know what Lucky can do, but it doesn't seem like a lot to ask."

"See, I'm being reasonable."

"You sure about this? Canada?"

"I'm from Canada, or one of its colonies anyway. I'm used to it."

"I'll get on this. I've got . . ." He paused, no doubt to check his Blackberry. ". . . the opening of *Fire Blades* tonight. I'll talk to Lucky there. Don't call me." He hung up without a goodbye.

⟳ ❧ ↶

From: wstuckel@locura canyon.com
To: matou@aol.com
Cc: bonorg@locuracanyon.com
Subject: Ferment
Frementation probs. Syrh. 118 stuck, tried heat, advise
add yeast. Clock ticking. 122 and 126 peculiar aromas.

From: matou@aol.com
To: wstuckel@locuracanyon.com; bonorg@locura-
canyon.com
Subject: Re. Ferment
No to yeast. Label says native only remember. What
sort of aromas?

From: wstuckel@locuracanyon.com
To: matou@aol.com; bonorg@locuracanyon.com
Subject: Re. Re. Ferment
Veg. Sauerkraut.

From: matou@aol.com
To: wstuckel@locuracanyon.com; bonorg@locura-
canyon.com
Subject: Re. Re. Re. Ferment
Shit.

⟳ ❧ ↶

THE RINGING OF the phone woke Elliot from a horrendous nightmare of grapes. It was one of those non-narrative spookers, a Gunnaresque formal experiment of the subconscious. In it grapes appeared, simultaneously, in bursting clusters, tumorous and testicular, weighing down their vines, shaking and bouncing on a triage table, burbling sickeningly in vats — and they were nowhere but around him, hemming him in, an exhausting, claustrophobic, eternal purpleness, violets and mauves, sanguine juice, regal robes, bruises.

"Yes?"

"You okay, Elliot?" It was Mike. "You sound terrible."

"Just waking up . . . Shit, what time is it in Los Angeles?"

"It's five thirty."

"What are you doing up?"

"My yoga is at six and I have a breakfast meeting."

"You drove out to a pay phone?"

"No, I picked up a bag of cellphones last night. Lucky Silverman told me about it. I spent hours with this guy, valuable hours."

Elliot could not but imagine a sack, like a pillowcase, stuffed with cellphones, and recall his dream.

"A bag of cellphones?"

"It's what you have to do these days. A line can get compromised so easily. You have a sensitive call to make, you use the phone once and then discard it."

Now Elliot pictured power lunchers at Providence and The Grill, all of them with Louis Vuitton overnight bags of cellphones on purse stools beside their chairs.

"The landfills will be giant mountains of used-once cellphones. Imagine great ringing and vibrating mounds —"

"That's someone else's issue, Elliot," Mike snapped. "It's a business reality. You should be nice to me, I've got your arrangements made."

"Regarding?"

"Lucky is on the board of General Electric, as is Jack Barnaby."

"Who?"

"Of Barnaby Vesco."

"Right."

"It wasn't such a big deal, he went through six phones and it was done. In a week or two someone is going to discover you are in Toronto, you are going to be asked to apply, you will be at the top of the list of candidates. "

"Wow."

"Like I said, Lucky very much appreciates your not being around to speak to the investigators."

"You hadn't said, but I take your meaning."

"You can't change your mind now. People went out of their way."

"Why would I change my mind?"

"For one thing, the money is the shits."

From: bonorg@locuracanyon.com
To: matou@aol.com
Subject: Re. Re. Re. Ferment

The printers still have not been paid for last year's labels. Miguel says the bottling line requires mainten-ance. Another letter from Diehl at bank.

PART TWO

Clarence
Where art thou, keeper? Give me a cup of wine.

Second Murderer
You shall have wine enough, my lord, anon.

— William Shakespeare, *King Richard the Third*

ONE

ELLIOT DID NOT have time to get anything made but found a decent clothier where he was outfitted in a darkest navy Brioni suit, a Façonnable shirt with vaguely nautical blue and red stripes, and a bold, shimmering scarlet Talbott tie. Remembering how Lucy used to caution that his thick mane tended to mad scientist, he got a cut. But meeting his interviewers in a boardroom at the Barnaby Vesco offices in the Gooderham Building on Front Street, he worried that even these simple preparations might have been overdoing it and was glad not to have shown up in bespoke. Though the young woman from Barnaby Vesco was smartly put together, in a tapered black jacket with rounded shoulders (surprising in a woman's garment), a blouse of Mediterranean blue, and a straight silk skirt, the two interrogators from the CBC looked, from the dun-coloured sacks on their backs, to work in Ottawa.

They were introduced. One was a vice president of human resources, the other a senior bureaucrat from something called, ominously, the Heritage Ministry. Elliot promptly forgot their names. The VP HR attempted to look at ease, removing his jacket, loosening his tie, and rolling up his sleeves, evidently doing so with an eye to his reflection in the window, so scrupulous and regular were the adjusted cuffs.

The other one set out a pipe, a kit holding its cleaning implements — reamers and whatnot — and a tin of tobacco on the table in front of him. Elliot caught a whiff of the bowl's figgy pong. The man's woollen suit was antique; a wispy comb-over underlined (in pencil?) his baldness rather than veiling it.

Cuffs gave Elliot a flash of dentures.

"Sandra" — Cuffs gestured toward the woman from Barnaby Vesco — "confesses to having been lucky."

"Oh?" said Elliot.

"That someone such as yourself should happen to be in town now and willing to come in for an interview on such short notice."

"How they found me . . . I can't even venture a guess. That I am in Toronto at all is complete coincidence."

"Kismet," said Pipe.

Cuffs gestured that they should be seated.

More than for what Elliot might do as vice president of the CBC, the panel mostly plumbed him for war stories from Hollywood. They induced him to drop as many names as he knew. Elliot obliged and, having exhausted those actors and directors with whom he'd had direct professional dealings, retold tales he himself had been told of big-name A-listers. To mask the origin of these, he played cagey with details as if, the model of discretion, he didn't want to reveal too much. Cuffs and Pipe, in turn, reacted knowingly, implying "enough said."

His interviewers were familiar with *The Centuri Protocol* and knew Elliot was involved and probably in on the action. Elliot modestly deflected inquiries in this vein, stating, truthfully, that his participation in the project wasn't such a big deal.

They dispensed early with the question of why a man of such professional accomplishment as Elliot should, in effect, take a step down to work at the CBC. Elliot said that it had not been an easy decision but that after reflection, he felt it might be time to come home and give something back. He hinted that he no longer needed money so could afford the token $400,000 per annum, but would insist that he be given latitude in terms of the time he spent at the office. While he would put Hollywood behind him, he would never let his beloved vines suffer.

They danced around the topic of the actual making of shows. This was either shop-floor detail or too vulgar for the executive realm. They responded well to his implication that the role of "the talent" in the creative process was oft overstated and that executives held a more critical function than was commonly recognized. He implied that he himself was much more a producer than a writer, having crossed the river from worker to manager some years ago.

After about twenty minutes there was a change in tone. There were issues that, however unseemly, must be addressed.

"The Internet. New platforms. Your thoughts there?"

Elliot had a few: that it made more crap more widely and readily available, that writers saw only puny residuals on the action, that it was content's Kali, erasing the value of mechanical reproductions of every sort, and that it would supplant broadcast television. He thought he'd fudge this last bit.

"I'm neither threatened nor seduced by evolving technology," he almost purred. Though meaningless, this answer was, judging by his interlocutor's slight nod, the correct one. Elliot stayed the course. "Computers, phones, the next thing and the thing after that: they are part of a continuum for television."

"So do you see making content specifically for these platforms or —"

Elliot was confident enough of what they wanted to hear that he interrupted.

"I don't see the economics. While the CBC is a public broadcaster, it must, surely, be mindful of sound business practice."

All three panellists were nodding now.

"Let's look at the first television broadcast as the ur-platform," he continued. "That content can then be redistributed either as is or broken down and platform-purposed. It's really an opportunity to alter, to re-engineer content so as to expand its audience. It's media ecology: reuse, recycle. People say that a network can't serve everyone, every way. I say it can, and for less." Perhaps this was pushing it.

"I have to say it is heartening to see such optimism," offered Cuffs. "Perhaps it's an American thing."

"Yes, there are a lot of doomsayers at the CBC," added Pipe.

"I have nothing but optimism for television. What else are people going to do? Read?"

"Indeed," said Pipe. "Literacy figures in Canada are television-positive, half the population can't understand a newspaper."

"Now . . . when you say 'everyone, every way'. . . ?" Cuffs wanted to back up.

Yeah, Elliot had gone too far.

"Well, obviously not certain elites. But was television ever their medium?"

Pipe and Cuffs almost smiled.

"It's schedule architecture and design," Elliot improvised. "Are you familiar with the book *A Pattern Language*?"

"The title is familiar." Pipe scratched a note to himself.

"Think of the various entrances to the programming day. It's been the practice to plan and place those gateways before we see where people are going. My notion would be to put the shows out there, see how people are approaching them, and then reorganize their placement to accommodate viewing patterns. Let's see what people are watching, when and where, and *then* build the schedule. Three-sixty-degree management." Elliot was losing track of the incomplete thought that had spawned this line of reasoning. Three-sixty-degree management? What the fuck did that mean? "Appointment viewing is dead anyway. We've too long been doing it backwards."

"Yes, backwards, at the CBC, very much so," Cuffs said.

"We have to bring them in and keep them with us through the schedule. The television audience is relatively passive; we should capitalize on audience inertia."

"What of metrics?" said Pipe.

Elliot didn't have a clue what he was being asked. Thankfully, Cuffs interjected. "Not benchmarks now but . . ."

"Yes, perhaps I shouldn't have asked," said Pipe, chastened. "We've had some disappointments in terms of measuring the audience. I mean, you set a target, inevitably you'll miss."

"Even the bigger, more nebulous ones," added Cuffs.

"I'm not sure I . . ." Elliot felt safe in saying.

"A previous VP rather impetuously said that if shows didn't reach a certain viewership, defined numerically, well . . . then he would cancel those shows."

"And it didn't work out —"

"— the way anyone anticipated," Pipe finished for Cuffs.

"Desired," clarified Cuffs.

"So . . .?"

"So, we had to hastily change the terms, bring in softer, more qualitative measurements of success."

"We moved to the ROOB 6 system."

"Which is a great system."

"It replaced the metrics recommended in *Television Canada 2015*," said Pipe.

"TVC-15 was such an amazing study." Cuffs sounded wistful.

"Classic consulting, TVC-15 — longitudinal, a keeper."

"People couldn't appreciate TVC-15 early on. It was complex, wasn't going to show its potential until a few years out."

"Yes, complex but elegant. Everybody wants consultation that they can use right away,"said Pipe.

"But a good analysis, it has to be for the long term."

Cuffs and Pipe sighed in unison.

MBAs were the Mayan high priests of Elliot's time. They needn't possess any actual knowledge of a practice to pronounce, from on high, about it. They used systems of complex divination, known only to themselves, in concert with calendars and schedules and rudimentary mathematical models to determine when should be the planting and the blood offerings. They did it all from within the temple. They would, in time, destroy their own civilization. Elliot, needing refuge in

Canada and possibly some sort of signing bonus, was not in a position to point this out.

"I am prepared to live or die by the ratings," interrupted Elliot. "Remember, my background is American television."

Those words, "American television," were dirty talk for his audience, irresistible and pornographic. They were stirred by the words, but felt guilty in taking pleasure from them.

"Just a few more questions," said Cuffs. "I've heard all I want. Something I'd written down . . ." Cuffs searched his papers. "Oh yes, here it is. I know this sounds trite but . . . Which television programs do you like?"

"Like"? How many times had Elliot been asked which Châteauneuf-du-Papes he "liked"? He could never bring himself to answer, and now, being asked this question about television shows, he finally knew why. He didn't "like" any of them, just as he didn't *like* any Châteauneuf-du-Papes — he liked the concept of them in the abstract; he was in love with a memory of a perfect sip of wine that was no doubt impossible to revisit.

What television shows did he like? He was hypnotized by the primitive magic of storytelling. He was transported by the well-spun yarn, the telling details and then the detours and feints and mostly the lies, the anticipation as the teller took a sip of rum and a drag off a fag and considered, reconsidered, where next would turn the truth. When he first saw Godard's *Vivre Sa Vie* he realized that the machinery of cinema, moving pictures in montage, had reinvented story for the age. It was self-aware and self-referential, at once tale and essay — we are all prostitutes in the Western capitalist system, it said, brazenly, and then proved it with photomechanical poetry.

If a picture was worth a thousand words, how many were said when they were churning past the lamplight at a speed of twenty-four per second?

"Like"? If you liked something, it couldn't be very good, could it? It would be enough, just enough to satisfy. And maybe that's why network television worked. It was enough to keep you there, unmoving, on your couch so that you were a stationary target for the commercials. It didn't have to be any more than that.

If one cared deeply for something, was truly devoted to its beauty, one saw only its potentiality, its possibility of perfection. Surrounded by only those examples that, at best, strove for the absolute expression, you came to wear, in joyous agony, in masochistic ecstasy, the failures as trophies. If you loved something that much, you necessarily hated it. Elliot hated all television shows and all movies, but, in the abstract, he loved moving pictures.

Which television shows did he like?

"I have to return to what I said earlier," Elliot finally answered. "I'm not afraid of the numbers. I don't mean to be rude, or evasive, but in truth I don't think it's the job of a vice president of the CBC, or a person in the same position at any network, to like television at all."

Across the table was sunshine. Elliot sensed they wanted to applaud. Cuffs used the energy coming from his enthusiasm to launch himself from his seat and bound around the table. He thrust a hand at Elliot with the speed of a punch.

"I can't say anything, of course, there are some procedural things . . . but if you could plan on being here, in Toronto, next month . . . I appreciate that this is sudden."

Pipe couldn't restrain himself. He clapped his hands a couple of times before reaching for his smoking kit. "I know it's completely inappropriate to say this but . . . you're the candidate we've been waiting for."

"It's the truth," said Cuffs.

Elliot took only a moment to feel good about himself. This whole performance had been a brazen gambit, and he'd executed it with élan. He had not flinched or varied; he'd set upon his goal and he'd achieved it.

But were they not too anxious to hire him? And surely, in all of Canada, there must be at least a few dozen candidates for the position who were genuinely qualified. Why were these people not vying for the post? Elliot would now have to do the job, which, on consideration, didn't seem all that appealing. He was going to be running the English-language television service of the CBC. Why would anyone want to do that? Who had fooled whom?

"Once all the terms . . . even before, I feel that once this is put in front of the president and the board —"

"A formality," added Pipe.

"— they'll be asking that you start right away."

"Right away."

"There's next season to program and schedule."

"Lingering morale issues from the strike."

"Budgetary issues."

"Issues relating to declining ad revenue."

"Coming from the issue of the increasing age of our audience."

"Definitely a pressing issue."

"I think issues related to the bid to continue hockey."

"Issues regarding the Brier."

"Lot of issues that require immediate attention."

Yes, though Elliot, a trap. Setting traps was the foundation of British North America, was it not? In gratitude, Canada had gone so far as to put a beaver on its currency. The Brier? Curling, wasn't it? It was. The men's, no? And the ladies held the Tournament of Hearts. Yep, that was it. Every minute, more of Canada was coming back to him.

"I understand the urgency but . . ." Elliot said. He heard all three, Cuffs, Pipe, and Sandra, the chick from Barnaby Vesco, draw in and hold their breath.

". . . but I will have to come up to speed, familiarize myself with the files before . . ."

Pipe and Cuffs laughed. Sandra allowed herself to exhale. Elliot could not fathom what was funny.

"Don't worry," said Cuffs.

"You'll have Hazel," said Pipe. "No worries."

"Hazel?" wondered Elliot.

"Hazel Osler," Cuffs and Pipe both said at once.

"She's your second," Cuffs detailed, "though that seems an unjust diminutive. I believe her title is . . ."

"Executive in Charge of Production?" guessed Pipe.

"Something like that. She's been at the CBC for years and years. She's a genius."

"A genius," agreed Pipe. "Polymath, mind like a steel trap."

Trap?

"She's the institutional memory."

"Started here as a tot. Fresh out of U of T . . . at nineteen years of age!"

"Production assistant on the later years of *The Friendly Giant*."

"And she took his advice."

They were talking about a CBC show that Elliot knew, a children's show from his youth.

"She looked waaaaay up?" ventured Elliot, quoting from the show's opening sequence.

"Exactly," said Pipe.

"She sounds like the ideal candidate for this job." Elliot might as well have farted.

"Yes, that . . ." said Cuffs.

"Auditor General, I'm afraid," said Pipe. "Gender imbalance, you see. Air on the seventh floor rather thick with estrogen. Entire executive with the exception of the president himself and Leo Karek in News are women."

"And an even higher percentage of middle management," said Cuffs. "At the same time our technical staff is overwhelmingly male. It's a climate thing, there is this sense these days that boys are being left behind. So . . . to be politically correct . . ."

"Hazel, being the progressive type, felt, in the light of the AG's report, she couldn't put herself forward." Pipe was obviously saddened by this. "Awful, this equity business."

"I sure hope the windows open over there," Sandra said, organizing her papers.

"Sorry?" said Elliot.

"When they all start going through menopause at the same time the place is going to be bedlam under a broiler."

The three men stood mute.

"Sorry." Sandra now looked at them, face flushed in full mortification. "That was inappropriate. Going through it now with my mother and . . . Please, I wish I'd never said it."

The silence continued until, trying to crack a joke, Pipe turned to Cuffs and said, "You get Jerome."

"And I'll call Rusty," answered Cuffs. "Expect to hear something official in a week or so, Mr. Jonson."

Sandra was smiling at Elliot. It was a professional gesture, something practised in a mirror and devoid of real meaning. Her whites were indeed pearly, though her central incisors, her "two front teet," seemed, somehow, oversized.

TWO

THE CBC HEADQUARTERS was a featureless block in Toronto's downtown Anywhere. It could have been the Frankfurt offices of a Swiss underwriter: there was a (likely inadvertent) pattern of red crosses, like those of the Knights Templar, repeated in each of the windows. In the parts of France Elliot frequented, people would have spotted the religious symbol. But Canadians were not reflexively on the lookout for marauders back from the Crusades . . . yet.

Hazel Osler was there to greet Elliot on his first day in the building. She was a tall woman, in her slight heels just inching out Elliot. Her hair was silver and black, with a Susan Sontag skunk stripe of white. Wearing it back and up, as she did, one could not help but think, after a time, of the Bride of Frankenstein. She wore a smart woollen dress to the knees, with a fine belt to show off her waist. It wasn't a female executive's power suit: the earth-and-green weave made it too English-country-living for that. She wore tortoiseshell specs that vamped with restraint on a cat's eye. She did her best to confine and thus deflect attention from her breasts. She was all business. Elliot guessed she was a few years older than he, but he could not be certain. He put out his hand and she, with a hesitation Elliot noticed, put out hers.

She was doubtless self-conscious, for they were crooked, swollen, the knuckles raw.

"They are making you a temporary pass," she said.

"Not being given a long tenure, am I?"

Hazel laughed.

"Until we get your picture. I will take you to the security office at the John Street entrance later."

A security guard appeared with a plastic identity tag. Elliot's name was spelled "Johnson." Not for the first time: CBC's communications department got it wrong in the press release announcing his appointment. They also somehow managed to confuse a number of the details from his CV, giving him more profile and influence in Hollywood than he held. Hazel apologized for the mistakes over the phone, offering that the communications department of the CBC was a sort of internal exile, a gulag of incompetence for employees who might have been overwhelmed by more onerous responsibilities in other departments.

Elliot's new passport was similarly in error, issued in his birth name, "Wesley Elliot Johnston." Elliot called the office and explained that it had been legally changed. The response was that while that might be the case, the change was made before the "centralization of services." A computer program refused to associate Elliot's social insurance number with any other name. Remedy, the gent on the other end of the line assured him, was available in the form of yet more forms and affidavits from consular officials in Los Angeles, a justice of the peace, and a clergyman.

Scant coverage was given to the CBC in the press. What little there was, Hazel warned Elliot, tended, for reasons just and otherwise, to be negative. Elliot recalled the article he'd fallen asleep reading on the plane from Los Angeles. But Elliot's appointment was being heralded as a positive one, in that he was the first VP in memory to possess any experience in film or television before taking on the job. The scribblers in the trade rags and the back pages of the papers would grant him a brief honeymoon. A couple of blogs pointed out that Elliot's oeuvre was hardly one to inspire confidence, but they were read mostly by their own authors.

Elliot lifted his valise so that he could pass through a locking turnstile. "The security seems . . ."

"Since 9/11, and then the Mississauga 13 . . . or however many there actually were in the end," said Hazel, beckoning Elliot forward.

"I wouldn't have thought the CBC would be a target of . . ." Elliot hesitated; he had never heard of the Mississauga 13. ". . . jihadists. I wouldn't have thought it — *we* — would be on their radar."

"I doubt we are," said Hazel. A natural toe-to-heel gait gave her a bounce, recalling for Elliot coyotes retreating between the rows of vines. Her bum was lovely. "That said, we have a fair number of disgruntled former employees as well as a few hundred nuts that hate the CBC."

"What are their reasons?"

"Most of them perceive us as having a liberal bias and an

agenda to match." Hazel looked back over her shoulder at Elliot. She kept a step ahead of him.

"Some truth to that, I suppose," said Elliot.

"Not at all," Hazel laughed. "Maybe at one time but not anymore. And then . . ." They were walking into an atrium that rose the entire height of the building. "There are people who hate some of our shows so much . . ."

"I hate a lot of shows," said Elliot. "I change the channel." In truth, Elliot's last changing of the channel had been absolute. In a fit of rage over the paucity of watchable programming, he had yanked the cable from the wall of his Los Feliz home and, in the process, shredded several feet of (as yet unrepaired) drywall.

"Yes, I'm afraid most people do reach for the remote," she said, pushing a button for the elevator. Elliot saw she wore no rings, perhaps because of the condition of her hands. Elliot guessed she suffered from severe arthritis.

So as not to stare at Hazel's bent joints, Elliot looked up, measuring his new place of work. The lofty interior hall was clearly supposed to make the building soar, to buoy it, but the dimensions diminished its inhabitants. High above, the employees trudging the balconies trimming the void went unsmiling. It begged, as though it were some Incan shrine, ritual sacrifice, bodies tossed off the precipice and into the cavern, into the pit; but it was modern, in the Stalinist sense of the word.

On the seventh floor, Hazel stuck to the wall as she walked. Elliot couldn't resist the rail overlooking the atrium. Even if it was only for a brief interregnum, this was now his domain. He was a tourist who might as well enjoy taking it in.

"I'm sorry," said Hazel, "but I can't stand to look down there. Vertigo."

"Right."

"First, your new office, and then it's almost an entire day of reviewing the troops."

Elliot was disappointed with his new digs. They were spacious enough, a corner suite with room for a couch, chairs, and a coffee table and a sturdy-looking empty bookcase. There was a tiny private bathroom, and four television monitors hung from the ceiling to be viewed from the desk; a floor model serviced the casual nook. Still, it was not as luxurious as something befitting a vice president. And there was a distinctly acrid note to the air. Hazel must have seen his hound-nose twitch.

"There was a . . ." She had not hesitated in speech until now. It underlined how fluent and easy a conversationalist she normally was. " . . . an accident. A few years ago there was a long strike — actually, a lockout."

"Yes, I knew about that."

"And . . . the vice president at the time, Bernard Hunt, he was putting a videotape in the player . . ." Hazel pointed to the television on the floor. "There was something wrong with the wiring and he was electrocuted."

"You're not saying that the smell . . .?"

"Some of the carpet was burned."

"Oh."

"The carpet was replaced. The room has been repainted. The furnishings are new. It's just . . . the building is sealed, you see. There are no opening windows. You get used to the smell. I hardly notice it anymore."

This *was* the public sector, Elliot reminded himself.

"Seems incredible . . . a VCR," was all Elliot said. "You never know what it's going to be."

"There was a thorough police investigation. They ruled out tampering, or there wasn't sufficient data to make that determination. I never believed the story that was floating around. It would have taken a lot of ingenuity and enterprise to booby-trap the thing. And poor Mr. Hunt, because of the terms of the contracts in that era, wasn't allowed to put a tape in a machine himself, he was obliged to ask a technician to do it for him, so he probably never really learned how it was done."

"I'm allowed to pop in a DVD now, though?"

"Absolutely. I think it's generally perceived that management won." Hazel needlessly lowered her voice. "Leadership at the union . . . not of the highest standard. But, strictly off the record, I'm of the view that this was one of those instances where everyone managed to lose."

"Hardly a personal triumph for Bernie?"

"No. And he was one of the best we've had." She shrugged. Another woman entered, portly, in a deliberately drab grey skirt-and-jacket combo. Hazel seemed to be expecting her. "This is Stella Neary, your personal secretary. Best in the building, so you will want to keep her."

"Ms. Neary."

"*Mrs.* Neary. And please, 'Stella.'"

"And you can call me Elliot."

"No, I'll stick with Mr. Jonson, if it's all right with you."

"As you wish."

"There have been a number of letters for you, Mr. Jonson,

mostly congratulatory notes and welcomes. This one was more personal," Stella said, handing Elliot an envelope that had been opened with a blade. "Should I vet correspondence in the future?"

"Please, would you?"

"I'll give you ten minutes or so," said Hazel. "Then we can meet some of the managers who report directly to you."

Hazel escorted Stella out. Elliot sat at his desk. His first? He surely must have used a proper secretaire, of polished wood, with drawers, sometime in his professional life — but if he had, he could not remember when. He worked on a computer on a wide table in his home in Los Angeles. What was supposed to have been his desk at the vineyard office, a utilitarian metal thing, had been taken over by Bonnie before he'd put so much as a bottle of cognac in the bottom drawer. There was a laptop on a bench in the winery, in the room with the fermentation tanks, which he used while standing. No, he supposed he'd never ridden a desk.

He opened his valise and took out the contents: a blank pad of legal paper and a toothbrush, a tube of toothpaste, and some dental floss. He had no idea what he was supposed to do. He remembered the envelope and withdrew from it a single sheet of paper. Had he seen a handwritten letter in a decade? The author's hand appeared tremulous.

Elliot,
Was sure it couldn't be you when I read that an Elliot "Johnson" got that gig at CBC but they named a few pictures and shows I knew you worked on. Never figured they'd have the sense.

Let's get together soonest. I've got a play opening at the
Theatre Passe Muraille backspace end of the month. I'll
have a pair of comps in your name at the box. Drinks!

Lloyd Purcell

The return address was Delaware Avenue. Somewhere
just left, in every respect, of the city's soft centre. It only made
sense that old Lloyd had landed in Toronto. It would be good
to see him.

❧

HAZEL HAD BEEN correct: his entire day was taken up with
meeting those directly beneath him in the corporate hier-
archy. Elliot met fifteen of nineteen "Creative Heads." He did
not comprehend why there should be three people with the
title "Creative Head, Variety" when the broadcaster carried
no programs in the genre: "variety" had been pronounced
dead twenty years earlier. Yet all three claimed to be terrif-
ically busy — taxed, in fact — mostly with shooting down
pitches from producers who hadn't read the obit.

But for one lippy chick stinking of booze, cigarette smoke,
and failure who took their first meeting as an opportunity
to quit, each Creative Head greeted Elliot with an apologetic
sycophancy. They forced smiles, laughed uncomfortably in
the wrong places, and visibly braced themselves for a dressing
down. It appeared his predecessor was a tyrant; Elliot's comparative disengagement would be welcome. Probably, over
time and in spite of himself, Elliot would become a better

exemplar of the dickhead they expected. By their nature, most bosses were bullies and assholes. (There were so few full-time employees back at the vineyard that Elliot had been afforded only the opportunity to be a part-time blowhard. The Mexicans brought in to pick the grapes got away with pretending not to understand him.)

Elliot signalled his waning interest in the meetings by looking over the Heads and up to the four muted monitors hanging from the ceiling; this did nothing to stop them from talking about all the projects that were coming down the pipe. He decided he should take comfort in their blather. So what if he was responsible for programming the upcoming television season, an enterprise for which he was unqualified? He commanded an army to do it for him. As the last appointment of the day — the acting Creative Head, Commissioned Unscripted and New Media Initiatives Regions (Content Planning) — backed out the door, Elliot felt more at ease in his role.

Elliot thought there might be time to scan some of the show proposals and scripts the Heads had stacked on his desk. But Hazel was back.

"I will be candid if you can be discreet," she said, closing the office door behind her and walking to his desk.

"Of course," said Elliot. "Please speak freely." He was relying on her doing so.

"I liked Bernard Hunt. He was not a brilliant man and he made mistakes. I believed his heart was in the right place. His intentions were good. He believed in public broadcasting —" Hazel stopped for a moment. She splayed her fingertips on the desk so that her hands, with their swollen joints, looked like scorpions. She rocked, her heel probably up out of one of her shoes. "But I held a different view of Stanford Heydrich. I was on the verge of resigning when he was forced out by his indiscretions. I'm speaking in strict confidence."

"Yes."

"And I volunteer this only as a necessary preface for the explanation as to why there are so many Creative Heads."

Could Hazel read his mind? They'd only spoken on the phone a few times before meeting today.

"I wondered," said Elliot.

"Appointing senior managers was Stanford's way of deflecting and shifting blame, as well as a kind of displacement activity."

"Displacement activity?"

"*Übersprungbewegung*. When animals are put under stress, they perform certain actions out of context. When you steal an egg from gull's nest, it will start pulling out grass with its beak."

"Scratching your head."

"Exactly. Whenever there was problem — ratings, mandate, labour relations — mostly ratings — Stanford would make an appointment, create a new position. All to say . . . you will have to filter some of the noise."

"Could we not cut their numbers significantly? Terminate the contracts of the least useful half?"

Hazel shook her head.

"The severance packages, the optics. If someone's performance was terribly poor, Stanford would send them to a management training course at the Niagara Institute. And they are useful for keeping pitching producers from your door."

"Okay."

"I suppose . . . it might be worth firing a few of the most incompetent. If only to send a message."

"Could you run me up a list of the five or six worst?"

"Absolutely," said Hazel. "Now, I thought we might take a stroll, give you a tour of the plant, meet some of the worker bees."

"Sure."

"If you'd rather not, right now . . . I've been presumptuous . . ."

"Not at all. That's the way I'd like to keep it, at least until I better know the lay of the land. Presume away, and stay close."

⌐ 🙾 ♉

ELLIOT KNEW TO expect low morale stemming from the recent labour troubles. Wages were middling and the CBC, subject to cutbacks imposed in an earlier era and never reversed, didn't have enough money to do things the way they should be done. What surprised him, moving through the expansive, unwalled newsrooms and open-concept offices of the other units, was just how dreadful the conditions were. Employees, even those of standing, were allotted a tiny working space. They were organized to lay eggs on an industrial scale, not to invent anything. Here was the handiwork of MBAs, thought Elliot: it wasn't a workplace issue as much as a human rights matter. No wonder that his hand was shaken with so little enthusiasm and even, in one instance, refused.

That the mood was black was reinforced by the nagging omnipresence of posters for the EAP, or "Employee Assistance Program." It was enough to be reminded, at every turn, that the people around you were in almost constant need of assistance, but it was worse to have that message conveyed with the aid of lurid graphics. One poster showed office workers, arms by their sides, morphed into matches in a book; the head of the employee farthest to the right was bursting into flames, dooming the conjoined to the same incendiary fate. The faces were all in a terrified, screaming rictus. The caption read, "Don't get burned by the office hothead. Call EAP." A banner in an elevator showed CBCers being hustled into boxcars by Gestapo, with the caption, "On time and under budget." A sallow, beaten jobber nailed to a cross that rose from a cheery cocktail party of suited managers exhorted its audience, "Don't die for their sins. EAP." Elliot resolved to deal with the situation by staying, as much as possible, in his own office.

The tour was concluding with a quick recce of the studios, the shooting floors. A sketch comedy show was being made in the first of the hangar-sized rooms. The crew had obviously been alerted of his visit, for they were executing a technically demanding shot, using some sort of certain-to-break-down robotic jib arm, when Hazel and Elliot entered. Elliot pretended, as best he could, to be interested, but he was well enough versed in the mechanics of show making to know its tedium. The operator of the jib device was controlling it far from the action with a joystick. When Elliot offered his hand to shake, the technician took his own from the control. They finished their how-do-you-do's just in time to see, on a monitor, the camera crashing into the wigged noggin of one of the goofmeisters on set. The funnyman was knocked senseless. Elliot could imagine the playback, the actor's eyes and mouth wide as the lens bore down on him. Now that would be truly amusing stuff: definitely a cut above any of the witless gags crawling up the teleprompter.

Elliot was dreading having to repeat these meet-and-greets with "the talent" and so was relieved, if perplexed, to discover that all the other studios were rented to outside concerns and consequently off-limits. From without, as they passed, these appeared the busiest spots in the building. Actors milling about one sound stage were in period suits and dresses from the 1930s. "Some film out of Hong Kong," Hazel explained. Farther down, a couple of tiny Southeast Asian tarts, sexy young things in skimpy body stockings and thigh-high boots, approached. "Vietnamese television over there," said Hazel. As they passed, Elliot saw that the southern deltas of the performers' suits were stretched and lumpen on account of the packages they carried.

In preparation for taking his post, Elliot had familiarized himself with — well, scanned — the Broadcast Act, the yellowing Canadian legislation that first established the CBC. As Elliot recalled them, the organization's objectives and terms of operation, however fuzzy, did not include the goings-on he was now witnessing in these public facilities. Before Elliot could get his question out, Hazel was answering it.

"The real estate division of the Corporation is tasked with finding money, and their authority is absolute. They determined that the studios were being underutilized, so they put out the 'for rent' sign. It could be worse. Out in the wilds, in St. John's and Edmonton, they sell the joints."

Liquidating assets was always a last resort, a desperate measure. Elliot thought of his Mackintosh set, his snooker chairs.

"So all the vice presidents are not . . ."

"Equal? Heavens, no. It's understood that, while you are on the same tier of the management committee's organizational chart, your office is, in practice, more elevated than, say . . . VP English Radio. Similarly, the real estate division, despite their official standing in the bureaucracy, effectively outrank you. The CBC is broke, you see."

BEFORE LEAVING AT six thirty Elliot stuffed his valise with a selection of show bibles and scripts from the pile on his desk. Rather than comparing one hapless sitcom to another, he decided to mix it up, grabbing a couple of half-hour comedies, a movie of the week for a family audience and another that could probably air only after midnight and even then only on cable, a reality show, a sketch comedy show, two hour-long adult serial dramas, and a twelve-hour documentary series about "Reason."

In finalizing his contract with the CBC he'd implied, discreetly and disingenuously, to those drafting the terms that the compensation was considerably lower than that to which he was accustomed. To lessen the blow they threw in a company car — an Audi — and a condo off King Street, walking distance from the Broadcast Centre. He would just as soon have stayed on at the Four Seasons, but it was too costly a proposition and would betray his lack of commitment to the job.

The forbiddingly named Liquor Control Board of Ontario turned out to be a well-stocked source of wine (though they did not carry Locura Canyon), with an outlet conveniently located at the nearby Queen's Quay. There was a Loblaws supermarket there, too. He got what other grub he needed delivered from a tony local victualler, Pusateri's.

He couldn't be bothered to cook so threw a frozen President's Choice rogan gosht in the microwave and opened a bottle of lager. He checked his email.

From: wstuckel@locuracanyon.com
To: matou@aol.com
Cc: bonorg@locuracanyon.com
Subject: ATF
Pickers freaked by uniforms in the Grenache. First pass on the east block and five dudes in the trees with sidearms, guys thought it was immigration. Miguel went up to see what was going on. Guys flashed ATF badges and told him to fuck off.

From: matou@aol.com
To: wstuckel@locuracanyon.com
Subject: Re. ATF
Don't copy Bonnie on this stuff. No email at all. Call me on my cell.

From: bonorg@locuracanyon.com
To: wstuckel@locuracanyon.com; matou@aol.com
Subject: Re. Re. ATF
What would the ATF want? Should I call them?

From: matou@aol.com
To: wstuckel@locuracanyon.com;
bonorg@locuracanyon
Subject: Re. Re. Re. ATF
I'm sure it's nothing. I will deal with it.

And indeed that was his intention. The when and how still eluded him.

If 80 percent of success was showing up, was there not a corollary that said there was a 20 percent chance they'd forget about you if you failed to appear? Sure there was. Lucky Silverman was playing just such a game in the matter of the wiretaps. If nobody was around to answer, the questions wouldn't get asked. Maybe, if Elliot stayed out of reach long enough, the ATF and USDA would let the matter drop.

In the meantime, the new job meant Elliot was going to avert — just — a couple of disasters. With his first few cheques he'd catch up with Lucy, allow Bonnie to deal with the most pressing bills, and make a symbolic payment on (but still not dent) the winery debt. The wolf would no longer be at the door. He'd be in the parking lot, finishing a cigarette.

The microwave timer sounded, signalling that his prefab curry was ready and that he was alone.

The best he could do was to turn on the television, obliged as he now was to be conversant with the medium in Canada. The new couch gasped as he sat on it. All his furniture smelled of the factory, the synthetics still venting.

What was this show he was trying to watch? It was another medical drama, something set in an emergency room, but no, now there were guys in raincoats flashing badges, so a police procedural; one of the cops was placing a call on a cellphone; cut to a far too beautiful woman drying herself, having gotten out the shower again, one towel in hand, the other wrapped around her breasts — this was the troubled home life to which the dedicated investigator was not paying enough attention; having received the exposition, the woman slammed the portable handset back into its cradle. Next our hero was at the morgue, attending an autopsy. The audience was witness to it all, the incisions, the viscera, the close-up removal by forceps of some invidious foreign object.

Elliot knew why these shows were so popular these days. They told the viewer that murder and mayhem could all be decoded. Crime on the street, the random victim, the blood-drenched colonial war in the desert, the alarming biopsy results . . . it would all be explained away by an expert. Another agency of the hypnotic box: giving answers, even if entirely made up. And, of course, anything involving the police and gun violence was a gift for the lazy screenwriter needing to up the dramatic stakes — the "Guy with the biggest gun" merely had to point it.

Elliot changed the channel to the CBC. A horse opera? No, too many trees. A . . . well, you would call her "handsome" — a handsome lady was riding a horse. She came alongside a fence to talk to an RCMP officer. Cut to her coming home. She hung up her cowboy hat and walked into the kitchen, where a man was at the stove. She gave a tween girl a maternal kiss on the head; the house husband got one too. Elliot checked his jacket pocket and found Hazel's business card. He dialled the number she had written on the back. It was answered after a single ring.

"What am I watching?" he asked.

"Hold on, what time is it? . . . Okay, it's *Banff 911*."

"Right."

"Don't blame the creative team. They have something new on your desk now and —"

"Why wouldn't I blame the creative team?" Elliot asked, though he hadn't yet decided, having watched only a couple of minutes with the sound off, whether he liked the show or not.

"Originally there was going to be a lot more skiing and resultant injuries, more helicopter medivacs from the mountains, that sort of thing . . . but it was too expensive. And the lead didn't have the kid, she was leaving the husband. We had to have an Alberta show and it had to feature traditional family values. Stanford insisted on the horse angle; he felt if the show was from Alberta it had to have horses."

"Are you watching it now?"

"No, but I've seen them all. And look, there was a notion, noble if antiquated, that the CBC could gather the whole family around the television together. It was wishful thinking. I don't think you should be concerned about what's gone on in the past."

"How are this show's numbers?"

"In the range of the survey's error."

"So we won't be renewing it?"

"Unless we can't get another show from Alberta."

"There's a regional quota?"

Hazel did not answer right away. Elliot was learning to be mindful of any hesitation in her speech.

"Not officially. Never acknowledged. It is certainly not the way I would do things."

"Understood. Thank you, Hazel."

"Any time."

"By the way, what were you watching?"

"Watching? No, I was reading."

"That's what I'd like to be doing. A book and a glass of wine."

There was another silence. Elliot felt a need to fill it.

"What are you reading?" he asked.

"Me? . . ."

"Is there a show in it?"

"God, no. Leastways not for us."

"Shame." Elliot did not know what else he could say.

"Don't . . . Try not . . . It would be best that you not mention that I was reading."

"Of course. I understand."

"Thanks."

"Well, goodnight."

"Yes. You too. Meetings tomorrow — with News."

"That should be straightforward."

"News? Oh, no. Leo Karek, the editor-in-chief . . . he really doesn't like you."

"But he's never met me."

"He hates what you stand for."

"I don't stand for anything, I'm in entertainment."

"Exactly. See you tomorrow."

❧

HAZEL KNEW IT ALL. Elliot arrived in his office perhaps three or four minutes late to find a cube in a suit staring at his watch. Karek was all right angles, boxy head on a steamer trunk, limbs jointed assemblies of blocks. His was the pained and flushed visage of a constipated man struggling for relief. He rose stiffly and shook Elliot's hand.

"I hope you weren't waiting long," said Elliot.

"Big news day."

"Right." Elliot wondered why. He'd scanned the *Toronto Post and Leader* over breakfast and nothing had registered.

"The financial statement. The federal government is tabling a mini-budget today."

"Of course. The mini-budget." Elliot worried that he sounded as though he were making fun. "Coffee?"

Karek shook his square head. Squared hair, too, razor-straight lines across the back of the neck and the bottom of the sideburns. In need of caffeine himself, Elliot called for coffee anyway. He tried looking relaxed, smiling, leaning back in his chair in the hope that his mood, even if affected, might rub off. From the unchanging expression on Karek's face, Elliot saw it would not.

"Let me say first," Elliot said, taking his cup from Stella, "that my immediate concern is next fall's schedule . . . as it pertains to everything *but* news."

Karek grunted something Elliot could not make out.

"And, you know, realistically . . ." — Elliot was grasping for something to say — "where the news is 'new,' I mean, how much planning can you do? How to . . . anticipate? If there's a big disaster, we want to be there. If we have to bump an episode of . . . *Banff 911* . . . because shit is blowing up and people, especially Canadians, are throwing themselves out windows, so be it."

This did not put Karek at ease. Elliot could see it would take more time than he was willing to waste to win the Cube's trust.

"Budget?" Karek asked. "Have you looked it over?"

"I have," Elliot lied. He was sure it was among the hundreds of pages of incomprehensible financial statements and projections he was supposed to have read by now. "And while this may be a disappointment . . ." He could actually hear Karek tense, the fabric of his suit gather with a crackle of static. ". . . there will be some adjustments . . . but I'm really obliged to . . . freeze it at last year's level."

Karek had drawn insufficient air to yell at Elliot so said only, "I see," rather too loudly. Cube had expected cuts.

"I want to take advantage of the accumulated knowledge in this building."

Karek held his breath.

". . . and in the regions."

Karel exhaled with relief.

"You, for instance, it's what . . . ?" Elliot said, gambling with confidence that Karek had been around the Corporation for years.

"Started in the newsroom in Regina. Radio. Sports."

"Wow."

"Local sports. Summer replacement. 1972." Karek said it as though the dimensions of his tenure at the CBC were only now dawning on him. He was doing life.

"I want to leverage that sort of investment." This sounded great, thought Elliot, despite being unsure what it meant. "I've made my notes on my copies of the budget. Why don't you have a look at your copy, tell me how you imagine resources being reassigned, and I'll take that into account."

"Done. What about consolidation of radio and television news?"

Elliot waved a hand vigorously over the papers on his desk as if shooing a fly.

"Radio? I mean, really, who gives a shit."

"Right," said Karek. "Fuck them."

"Absolutely," said Elliot, wondering if this stance was a bit bold considering he knew nothing about radio. The imposture Elliot had undertaken came easily, but it was still exhausting. "Great to meet you," he said, pushing his chair back from the desk.

"One other thing. There are rumours you plan to move the evening news."

"Where do these rumours come from?"

"Probably something you said during the hiring process. I don't know."

"Well." Now Elliot stood; Karek couldn't but follow him to his feet.

"So? No?"

"Everything is under consideration. Let's talk about it after I've seen your budget revisions."

Elliot saw that this offhand avoidance of the matter was, however unwittingly, a vicious sneak attack, gamesmanship in the power dynamics of the office. Karek was winded by the statement, pushed back against a wall by a stronger combatant. The chunky sap limped from the room. Elliot could get the hang of this. He made a mental note to ask Hazel what was up.

"THE TIME SLOT for the evening news, at ten p.m., cuts into prime time," Hazel explained.

"Yes. Yes, it does. It's crazy."

"But say we moved the news to eleven and had an extra five hours of prime time every week."

"Yes?"

"We would have to program it with prime-time shows," said Hazel.

"Expensive."

"Very. You haven't solicited my view, but I think moving the news is exactly what has to be done if we are going to program the shows we should."

"Karek said he'd heard that the rumour came from my interview . . . but I'm sure the scheduling of the news never came up. They hardly seemed like gossips, the panel."

"Rumours defy physical principles of the universe, they can come from nothing."

"The universe did come from nothing," said Elliot. "That's the conceptual leap that people have such a hard time making. That's why they invented God."

"Existence is a rumour?" Hazel laughed. It was a high-rolling, convulsive, and entirely winning whinny.

"Mine, anyway," said Elliot.

"Not a believer?" Hazel asked. She seemed genuinely interested.

"No. Yourself?"

"I've heard rumours of stuff you said in the interview. Men in suits, in my experience, gossip as much as schoolgirls."

"What have you heard?" asked Elliot.

"You made a tremendous impression. Perhaps they couldn't keep their tongues because they were so excited."

"Specifically, what am I supposed to have said?"

"That the CBC could serve everyone, every way."

"I think I did say that. It's . . . inclusive."

"You've set the bar high."

"We've got audience research people, yes?" said Elliot.

"They profile the viewer?"

"So they allege." Hazel was amused by this, and Elliot wasn't sure he liked that.

"Then I'd like to get a picture of *everyone*," he said, before thinking.

"Sure you don't want to start with a list of 'every way'?"

"You're right."

"Every way as it relates to broadcasting, right? Not a list of every way anything can happen in the rumoured universe."

"No."

"And in terms of 'everyone,' you meant, I presume, all people who comprise a potential audience. Not *all* people."

"Of course, I mean the people who watch television, otherwise, fuck 'em."

Hazel made a performance of taking down the directive in a notebook.

"The scheduling of the news is germane to the discussions of the coming weeks," she said.

"Why?"

"Almost your entire calendar for the next two weeks consists of meetings regarding the next season."

"Shit. I was hoping to take a brief trip home."

"Home?"

"My vineyard in California. It's been so hot this year they're harvesting early, some stuff is already in vats fermenting. I really need to be there."

"Is it nice?"

"It's the land."

"I don't follow."

"As opposed to the office."

"I see."

"The earth and seasons in a glass, and it makes you feel good, it's great stuff."

"Unless you can manage to get back and forth in a day, you're probably not going to be able to go."

"We'll see."

"You'll have to take me sometime."

"I'm sorry?"

"To your vineyard."

"I would love to."

⤙ ❡ ⤚

From: wstuckel@locuracanyon.com
To: matou@aol.com
Subject: Counoise
I think maybe no cunny in the blend this time round.

From: matou@aol.com
To: wstuckel@locuracanyon.com
Subject: Re. Counoise
No. Must. Why??

From: wstuckel@locuracanyon.com
To: matou@aol.com
Subject: Re. Re. Counoise
Weird barnyard notes.

From: matou@aol.com
To: wstuckel@locuracanyon.com

Subject: Re. Re. Re. Counoise
I like some of those.

From: wstuckel@locuracanyon.com
To: matou@aol.com
Subject: Re. Re. Re. Re. Counoise
Not these.

From: matou@aol.com
To: wstuckel@locuracanyon.com
Subject: Re. Re. Re. Re. Re. Counoise
Horsey?

From: wstuckel@locuracanyon.com
To: matou@aol.com
Subject: Re. Re. Re. Re. Re. Re. Counoise
Miguel says donkey.

From: matou@aol.com
To: wstuckel@locuracanyon.com
Subject: Re. Re. Re. Re. Re. Re. Re. Counoise
Bad yeasts in the mix? Like Brett?

From: wstuckel@locuracanyon.com
To: matou@aol.com
Subject: Re. Re. Re. Re. Re. Re. Re. Re. Counoise
No. But microflora under the scope. Someone at
Davis?

From: matou@aol.com
To: wstuckel@locuracanyon.com
Subject: Re. Re. Re. Re. Re. Re. Re. Re. Counoise
NO! Nobody at Davis. I'm going to see if there is any
way I can get down there.

Even as he clicked "Send" Elliot knew the trip could not happen. His predecessor's television season was now being born with such horrible deficits and defects that it would be left to die without intervention. As the attending physician, Elliot couldn't leave until he'd broken the news to the weary and teary mothers and signed the certificates. Hazel was filling his schedule with discussions about the coming year as a way of changing the subject and moving on. A Daytimer, Elliot saw, was a shackle.

THREE

MEETINGS AND MORE meetings, meetings always concluding with the assembled consulting agendas to determine when they should next meet. Elliot was no stranger to the drill: Hollywood loved its meetings. The majority of those Elliot had been obliged to "take" were to receive notes on scripts. These would come from the many disparate parties participating in the making of the film or television project. In recent years, this meant the additional contribution of multiple middle managers from the media conglomerates consuming the trade like flesh-eating disease. Often — no, always — notes from different sources prescribed mutually exclusive or contradictory actions. Thus Elliot was often sent away from a meeting with the command to make it shorter and longer, funnier and more serious, with characters who were at once older and younger than they'd been in the preceding draft. There was only ever one universal note from all chiming in, none of whom had a clue about storytelling: the entreaty to make the protagonist more sympathetic. If screenwriters did what they were told, the lead in every flick and program would be a puppy dog.

Now, barely three months into his post at the CBC, he found himself slogging through meetings, called on his behalf, of exactly the sort from which bad ideas originated. The hydra of Creative Heads brought forward proposals for new shows but, lest they be blamed for their failure down the line, did what they could to find fault with them. This was not a demanding task: the shows had been worked over by so many notes and hands by the time they got this far that they were indistinct enough to have no possible chance of exciting an audience. Frustrated, Elliot wondered about the hundreds of pitches that were not reaching him. If the ones he was see-ing were so poor, then . . .? "Only worse," was the response.

There was a fatalism informing every presentation. The CBC, Elliot was informed, was doomed — as was, in fact, all of television, art, and entertainment in the Canadian con-text. The CBC had it worst, naturally, because its audience was so old as to be resistant to change. The hope of attracting new, younger viewers was futile; they were abandoning the medium. The Corporation could not yet deliver them material made specifically for the Internet — it had limited staff and infrastructure for doing so, no agreements with content providers over fair compensation, and no effective commercial model. (Content, they said, was king. But Elliot discovered there were only six writers among the entire staff of the CBC.) It was all so discouraging and confusing that Elliot decided to use one of his cards and fired the Cre-ative Head, Movies and Miniseries. The poor bastard cried at the news, claiming a mentally ill wife at home and limited prospects in the ageist job market of showtainment. Alas, his unit's recent output, mostly clunky historical dramas, while costing many millions, had attracted audiences of many thousands. A subhead from the documentary division took a message on his BlackBerry while Elliot was speaking. Elliot sent the guy to a leadership seminar at the Niagara Institute in the hope they taught manners.

A yet more lachyrmose display was offered by Jill MacDonald, the in-house girlfriend of Elliot's predecessor. She claimed she was now a pariah at headquarters for her *collaboration horizontale* with the tyrant Heydrich. Elliot gave her safe passage to the supper-hour news in Calgary, a sort of internal exile. Someone, whether they liked it or not, was getting a co-host.

On top of these meetings, Elliot learned, he was expected to fly all over the country to meet with his soldiers in the provinces and with the whiny, threadbare independent producers living in the huts outside the battlements. Everyone wanted money — every region, every city within every region, every genre, every department, everyone. The government support for television production was balkanized, Hazel explained, so regions continually argued their cases against the others. The CBC was favouring the Prairies, with three shows (all terrible) on the network, at the expense of the West Coast. The depopulated East Coast was overrepresented compared to the expanding Centre. Stuff proposed by Newfoundland was too scat for the national palate. There was nothing from the North, and everybody on air was too white. The process sounded too wearying to endure, so Elliot excused himself from the first, eastern leg of the tour and sent Hazel in his place.

Quite improbably, she departed for Moncton, Halifax, and
St. John's with enthusiasm.

From: hazel.osler@cbc.ca
To: el.jonson@cbc.ca
Subject: Terra Nova
Good series of meetings Hfx and NB, even if prod.
community feeling hard done by. Staying on in St.
John's extra day.

From: el.jonson@cbc.ca
To: hazel.osler@cbc.ca
Subject: Re. Terra Nova
And pray do what?

From: hazel.osler@cbc.ca
To: el.jonson@cbc.ca
Subject: Re. re. Terra Nova
Hike Signal Hill AM, play I want to see at LSPU Hall,
late supper bar at Raymonds

The trails around Signal Hill could be treacherous in
December, gales whipping up spray and polishing the ice it
left. Was it his place to warn her? Would that be presumptuous? Paternal? Patronizing? And, more important, with
whom was she dining?

Before leaving, Hazel had answered his call for a portrait
of everyone in Canada and all their "ways," leaving him to
study a voluminous document, in a three-ring binder, of sta-
tistics and analysis. Elliot, who'd hoped his impulsive request

had been forgotten, failed to open the thing. He was learning that as an executive it was all too easy to set whimsical notions, embryonic ideas, into motion, and all too difficult to whistle them back. Hazel also left Elliot with notes in preparation for a pending meeting of the Board and the Executive Committee. Elliot did begin these but, finding himself in disagreement with many of the points Hazel was making, put them aside. It wasn't Hazel's job to direct policy; most likely she'd created such a provocative document only to stimulate some thought.

His condo was equipped with a pool and a gym, which Elliot tried but soon gave up using. At first he appreciated that the facilities were undersubscribed by the building's other inhabitants, but quickly began to feel, whenever he went in there, like Dave Bowman at the end of *2001*. Alone in his private white Louis XVI digs, beyond the end of time.

Force-fed processed air in his office (the entire Broadcast Centre shared one consumptive artificial lung) and the condo, he pined to draw a breath in his vineyard. "The air is wine," Jack London once said of his plot up in Sonoma. In Elliot's free time, which was being consumed by ever more of less and less discernable significance, he availed himself of the only alternative — he took to the hoof on the chilly streets of Toronto, telling himself that he was discovering the *Volk*, and so the CBC's audience.

The nearby lakeshore should have been appealing, but the tainted slush on the beaches was not borne by tide and seemed, to a man born by the sea, lifeless. The vistas there were not of openness but of emptiness. The vicinity of his condo was by day a characterless concrete canyon and by night a sewer into which drained the waste of the street-level nightclubs. The city was essentially without pedestrian malls or warrens of narrow alleys. It was a car town, evidence that its European settlers had been determined to make a clean break, to leave the good ideas behind with the bad when they crossed the pond. Protestant Toronto clearly understood renewal to be a culling process and was self-loathing in its compulsion to smash its material history, as idols, to dust. There were fewer old buildings than in any other city Elliot had visited.

For no particular reason Elliot enjoyed perambulating the tiny Vietnamese neighbourhood around Broadview Avenue. This street lead him to the Danforth, which, while only a mixed commercial strip, was rooted in something older than its years. Had Elliot any intention of staying in Toronto, he would much prefer to buy something off Danforth Avenue and not, as the grand social plan would have of a man of his station, in swish Rosedale or the Annex. But each day he was more and more resolved not to remain. The level of dysfunction at the CBC was such that leaving would be a mark of achievement, the right move by an executive not afraid to do the brave thing. It would also be a demonstration that Elliot Jonson was a man with options. No one would admire his courage at deserting so early in his tenure so much as those left behind.

Initially chuffed at having pulled off the job interview, he'd briefly thought he could stick it out for three or four years — by which time the winery would be profitable. But now that he'd seen the situation up close, he was thinking a couple of years, max. And two years wasn't enough time for his incapacity to perform the job to become evident to the people who had hired him.

There was no one keeping him in Toronto, no woman. Not Hazel. Yet Elliot realized that even after the short time they had known one another, he would miss Hazel's company. If she could be coaxed to come down to Los Angeles she would do well — though there was something hopelessly Canadian about her, attachments to antiquated ideals about the country that would probably keep her forever bound to Fort York.

He wondered again — with whom was she gallivanting around St. John's? There was never any mention of a partner or a lover in Toronto; maybe she kept one out there, some enchanting pirate. Maybe she occasionally indulged in a little sex tourism in the colonies. They said she was married to the CBC. Someone in such a relationship would have unmet needs.

⟅ ♣ ⟆

OWING TO HIS chronic labyrinthitis, Victor Rainblatt, the president of the CBC, had, for Elliot's first two months on the job, communicated only by phone. Rainblatt was confined to bed and couch; if he stood up, the room spun and he fell. What was more, it was impossible for him to watch television without becoming nauseous, so he deferred to Elliot's opinion of existing or piloted projects. He was "a manager of people, not a programmer," Rainblatt said. In this way, Elliot and Victor had become almost friendly.

Now, under a new pharmaceutical regime — something called Nelfex — and therapy, Victor Rainblatt's condition had improved. His coming out, his return to the helm, was a series of meetings: first, an all-day affair with the Executive Committee of the CBC, on which Elliot sat, and then, the next day, a shorter, half-hour session with the Board of Directors followed by an informal mixer for the two bodies. Elliot guessed it would be not unlike an intersessional meeting between the Presidium and the (symbolic) Supreme Soviet.

All the executives were towing their attendant seconds. Owing to her extended stay in Newfoundland, Hazel was coming straight from the airport. But at 9:45, fifteen minutes before the powwow was to begin, there was no sign of her. Elliot called Hazel's EA, a bright young man named Troy.

"I've called Ms. Osler's cellphone, Mr. Jonson, but I'm getting that message saying the phone is off or out of range."

"Was the flight delayed?"

"I have the arrivals board on the screen in front of me, sir. It says the flight arrived early . . . at 9:09."

Hazel was mad! Even assuming that morning traffic would be ebbing, this was cutting it too close. It was at least thirty minutes from the airport. Add the wait for the luggage. Elliot dashed to the elevators and went downstairs.

He was about to quit pacing the sidewalk of Front Street and try the John Street entrance when a Crown Vic pulled up. A back door opened. It was Hazel. Her complexion was transformed by salt air and wind, and even behind her specs Elliot could detect a cold sea's clarity in her eyes. For all its deficiencies, for all its torments, the atmosphere in Newfoundland was a cure. Either that or she had indeed enjoyed the comforts of some rogue.

Hazel had put one heel on the pavement when Elliot, forgetting himself, took her hand and pulled her up and out of the car and toward him and kissed her cheek.

"Oh my," she said. "I shall go away more often."

Elliot looked to see if any staff were about. His inexplicable indiscretion would surely be reported in one of the poxy blogs hosted by his disgruntled employees. No one was staring, at least. A couple of shivering yobs smoking by the entrance seemed scarcely conscious.

"Just glad you made it in time for the meeting."

"I left you notes. You would have been fine."

"Actually, I'd wish we'd had time to go over them together. The direction they take, in terms of programming, it's not what anybody at that meeting wants to hear."

The smile went from Hazel's face and much of the colour in her skin with it. Just out of the car, fresh from a restorative and brief break, just the other side of a surprising and, Elliot saw too late, welcome kiss, and he pushed her nose into her work. He showed her who was boss.

"Some of it was bold," Hazel said. "I was getting the impression that you were . . . Well, we will have to talk about it, won't we. And it was wrong of me not to have anticipated your needing time in advance of the meeting. Let me put my bags in my office."

RAINBLATT'S DIMINUTIVE STATURE was exaggerated by the stance his condition forced him to adopt. He explained to everyone that he'd been instructed by his doctors and therapists to always lean on something. As his semicircular canals no longer gave him any sense of where he was in space, the medical team was attempting to retrain his brain to gather the information it required from touch. Standing to talk, Rainblatt leaned against a wall. Sitting in his chair, he pushed himself up against one arm. He joked that he tried to favour the right, lest the president of the CBC be accused of being "left-leaning."

Rainblatt was tic-ridden — constantly bringing his hands together, knitting invisible threads, blinking and stammering. Aggravating his unfortunate circumstances were arms too short for his body. Elliot thought that if he spread them for balance he might only spin like a top.

The time until coffee was occupied entirely by some opening banter and the introduction of the nine vice presidents and the fart catchers they'd brought along. The next interval, until lunch, was taken up with narcotic presentations from the VP and Chief Financial Officer — despite some one-time money from the sale of real estate assets, they were still broke — and the VP Strategy and Business Development — sales of CBC shows and formats in other territories were (there being none) behind projections. However, the plan to sell off many of the transmission towers owned by the Corporation to cellular telephone outfits held promise. She ended her submission by saying, incomprehensibly, "Go Leafs, go!"

A light lunch of sandwiches, woody fruit, and weak coffee was served in a lounge next door. Elliot spoke in person with some of his fellow VPs for the first time since taking the job. They all expressed hope for the new season he was supposedly engineering and took the opportunity to cautiously diminish his predecessor Heydrich, by noting that the man didn't have the requisite experience in the production end of the business to make good programming decisions. Elliot gave them all a funny Hollywood anecdote (he was now recycling the few he had) and they were happy. Only the VP for Radio, Caroline Bonham, seemed immune to his charms. Elliot worried that perhaps Ms. Bonham was on to him.

Elliot made his way to Rainblatt, who was wedged in a corner, munching an egg salad sandwich with a tilted head.

"Elliot, good to um um see you in the f-flesh."

"You too, Victor."

"It's um-an-nah a good meeting today, no question."

"Yes." Elliot supposed that when meetings were your life you became a connoisseur.

"We've scheduled you to speak last, you're the um um h-headliner, no question." The pitch of Rainblatt's voice rose until reaching a girlish laugh.

Elliot was beginning to gather that Rainblatt's view of his billing was not an overstatement. The assembled would be disappointed, for he had not studied the pitches with anything like the attention demanded to make a call. In all honesty, he didn't have a clue what next season, his season, might look like.

Maybe this meeting was the time to announce his departure. Rainblatt pushed himself off the wall and grabbed Elliot's arm, now using him as his anchor.

"Don't give too much away. Keep them, um nah, guessing. You want some drama at the rollout, no question." There was something paternal in Rainblatt's manner; Elliot didn't like it. Rainblatt dropped his voice. "Keep next Friday evening open, having a dinner thing at home."

"I will."

"Do you need to go anywhere?" Rainblatt held a pinched thumb and forefinger to his lips.

Was Rainblatt suggesting that Elliot and he go outside for a toke? They prescribed marijuana for nausea, it was plausible the dizzy old dude was on the weed.

"Maybe later," Elliot said.

Immediately after the break it was Bonham's turn to speak. Hers was a substantial and focused presentation. Canadians apparently cared as much about the CBC's radio service as they did not about its television service. She confessed to continuing failure in the two-to-four-p.m. slot but could speak with pride about other parts of the schedule. There was also a problem with the demographics of the radio audience: they were even older than the TV audience and were, quite literally, dying off. There had been some new shows that attracted younger listeners, but these tended to alienate the geezer core. Perhaps it was the soporific effects of lunch, perhaps it was the unaccountable disdain for the radio service, but scarcely anyone around the table seemed to care.

After tepid applause Bonham gave the floor to the VP and Chief Technology Officer, who then passed it to the VP Communications, after which followed the Executive VP French Services, the General Counsel and Corporate Secretary, and the VP Human Resources. On and on they went with meaningless palaver about mission and branding pyramids and new platforms and new Canadians and five- and ten-year plans. Nothing of substance was put forward, but it was all said in the ornate poetry of management nonspeak. The very air in room became shit mist.

Elliot could think only that here, in essence, was the

reason for the decline of the West: its leadership class excelled only in its ability to obfuscate and occlude, to appear to take responsibility while never doing anything for which there was a risk of being held to account. Accomplishment was less important than the running of things: the primary objective was the continuation or advance of one's position in the bureaucracy. The world, in short, was being managed out of existence. Product was insignificant; process was all.

It was soon Elliot's turn to speak. What could he say to get these people on his side? Elliot had been in the company of some powerful figures in Hollywood; there was a science to their influence. They suggested sociopathic cruelty, that they would use their clout brutally. But they were bullies in whose company you were safe, not ever their friend or equal but, as long as you agreed with them, not numbered among the enemy. Lucky Silverman was one of those men, respected because they were feared.

But who was the enemy in this circumstance? The production community? The writers? The private broadcasters? The audience? Elliot scarcely knew which his "side" was. He thought of his most recent pitches back in Los Angeles: abject failures. He hadn't told those listening what they wanted to hear. That, in the end, was the secret, wasn't it? That's what he needed to do. Jesus, Rainblatt was wrapping up his introduction, they were applauding. Elliot got to his feet.

"Thank you. Everybody has made me feel welcome, made me feel at home. After all, this is, as most of you know, a homecoming. I've spent my entire professional life in the entertainment industry in the United States." He watched Hazel move to an empty seat closer to him.

"I've had a lot of success down there," Elliot lied. "My experience should have prepared me for this position at the CBC. But even in my first weeks here I saw that we faced a unique challenge. There is one master in America: the market. The situation in this country is more complex. The CBC has a mandate that is almost impossible to meet. We have a viewing public that is also a shareholder, and one that is vocal about its stake in the operation. We have to be mindful of regional representation; our programs have to reflect the diversity of the new Canada; we have to entertain but also, in some ways, to educate. If we provide programs that are too populist, we are accused of dumbing things down. If we do shows that are sophisticated but appeal to too small an audience, we are accused of being elitist." Hazel was smiling — was she buying this? Encouraged, he went on.

"We are accused of having a liberal bias and of being too accommodating to the right as a way of countering this criticism. We are asked to be all things to all people. How can we possibly do this? As much as the television business in the United States is driven by stars and money, by glitter and ambition, the business of public television here is driven by the very lack of those things. This is a broadcaster whose mandate is dictated by an act of Parliament. That is why, unlike a private broadcaster or a studio, it has to be led not with bluff and bravado by risk-seekers but with caution by professional managers." Now Hazel's eyes popped, sparkling, and he saw her suppress a bark of laughter. Poor gal was the smartest person in the room, but not smart enough to realize that no one else got the joke. Elliot guessed she'd suffered thus her whole life, in school, in love, in work.

"It is too easy to overstate, to romanticize, the role of creators in this process. Decisions regarding content cannot be impulsive, but have to be weighed. And the people making those decisions have to be conscious of all the mitigating factors. I'm happy to say that I feel I am in the company of just those people."

Elliot saw that a couple of women opposite were about to applaud. He gestured, pontifically, that they should wait.

"As I put together the coming season I am going to be in a process of continual consultation with all the knowledge in this room. I am going to prevail upon you to take more meetings than you might usually, there might be more analysis than you've been used to in the past, there's going to be thorough planning in advance of any action. It's going to be all hands to the bridge. There are a couple of executive decisions I'm going to have to make, mostly obvious things like putting better-looking people on the screen, only because there isn't time to gather input. But otherwise I'm counting on you."

Now Elliot let them rise to their feet and clap. How much time had he wasted in Los Angeles trying to get his point across, trying to convince, trying to make the producers see things his way? All this time he should have been telling people what they already believed.

⟿ 🎭 ⟾

From: bonorg@locuracanyon.com
To: matou@aol.com
Subject: Bank
45 large was less than they said was min so I am amazed they aren't calling it. You owe Loschem 17 for spray.

From: malvoise@aol.com
To: bonorg@locuracanyon.com
Subject: Re. Bank

I can forward another 17 in two weeks.

FOUR

WHEN HAZEL HAD given Elliot her address in Forest Hill, he'd understood it was a tony quartier. But the Edwardian brick edifice in front of which he pulled his car was a mansion. It was surrounded by an iron fence, on top of which rested light snow like a line of piping on a cake. He was curious and about to get out of his car and make for the front door when, by remote control, a gate barring a long, wide driveway opened. Hazel, pulling on gloves, was high-heeling it from the rear of the main building, or perhaps from a smaller carriage house he only now noticed hidden among trees in the back.

Hazel was from money?

Climbing into the passenger seat, Hazel had only to glance at Elliot to divine what was going on behind his eyes.

"It's in the family."

"The house?"

"Yes. And other things."

Driving to Rainblatt's Rosedale home, Hazel told Elliot what she knew of the president's set. The guest of honour was

Thorsten Marshall, former editor of the magazine *Toronto, Toronto, Toronto*, now the director of the Toronto Symphony. Hazel once saw him at a Halloween party at the end of a dog's lead held by his much younger boyfriend. The leather collar had looked shiny from wear — new dog, old tricks. Hazel said Marshall was a wine snob and a bore and would therefore probably latch on to Elliot. This meal was a public rapprochement between Marshall and Rainblatt. They were both on the board of the Royal Ontario Museum and they'd feuded over the design of an extension. Rainblatt felt that Thorsten had hoodwinked the board, promising them a design that looked nothing like the exploded baby barn that was finally rammed into the structure. Rainblatt never ceased telling anyone who'd listen about how much he loathed the look of the addition, saying it had "more wonky corners than the cabinet of Dr. Caligari."

There would also likely be in attendance, Hazel continued, one Joanne Johanson, a theatre actress and director, now a leading culturecrat at the Canada Council. After a few drinks Johanson could not be stopped from tallying the leading men she'd bedded. Johanson was a friend of Rainblatt's wife, Helga. Helga was a permanent fixture on the board of the Textile Museum (was "positively mad for textiles," said Hazel) and always invited along a prominent Canadian textile artist who never lent anything to the conversation. The financier Delmore Reitman was a regular, as was Patrick Cahill. Cahill was a defrocked Catholic priest who, many years earlier, when television was an altogether different beast, produced a CBC program about faith and spiritual issues called *Glory Be*. In St. John's, when Elliot was a kid, people joked that, in the case of the local station, CBC stood for Catholic Boys Club. Hazel said that Cahill held a Rasputin-like influence over Rainblatt, a Jew, that nobody could understand. She herself found Cahill disagreeable; he stood too close and held too tightly to outmoded ideas about telly. As well as these usual suspects, there would always be two senior partners and their spouses, one each from a leading Tory and Liberal law firm. There would be a few new faces, people with some profile in Toronto, and there would be "an exotic," someone visiting the country or from the far-flung colonies.

"And from the CBC?"

"Rarely anybody. It would poison the atmosphere. I haven't been myself in many years."

Turning off Yonge Street into the maze of luxe Rosedale, Elliot wondered if his bringing Hazel as his date was a faux pas.

It didn't seem so as Helga and Victor greeted them as the door. The zaftig Helga even gave Hazel a hug once the maid had taken her overcoat. Again Victor shifted from the wall to Elliot for support. Elliot found himself tensing at Rainblatt's grip and forced himself to relax. He was grateful for the clamour and chatter of a large group inside. He could hide among them.

The Rainblatts' dwelling, two storeys at the end of a crescent, would have felt spacious if it were not so cluttered with furnishings, many of which were collectible antiques. They were serious pieces all, but too many. Moving up the hallway to join the other guests, one navigated two intruding benches, one simple, the other backed. The former was so plain Elliot guessed it was a genuine Shaker piece. Hazel's brief on Rainblatt said he was from modest Montreal beginnings. Before his term at the CBC he'd managed the equity fund of a family fortune from his hometown and achieved notoriety for being one of the few to lose big in the bull market of the 1990s. The worn maple Shaker bench was the sort of object acquired by the most well-to-do, which Rainblatt was not. Helga, then, was the dough. Perhaps that was how she knew Hazel.

Farther into the house could be seen a similar taste in pictures, uninteresting work by names. There was a murky Tom Thomson that looked to have been painted through a veil of blackflies. There was even a small Bonnard, a supine nude on a bed that conveyed not indolence but somnolence. It was the collection of someone with the means but not the taste. Perhaps Helga gravitated to textiles because she could at least feel what she could not see. Elliot resented not her affluence, or her profligacy, but the fact that her bad eye made him think, as he was trying never to do these days, of art.

There were fifteen or sixteen guests in all, an ambitious party. An extra table was set and ran into the living room. This pushed the Champagne-sipping guests tightly together and gave a sense of boho fun to the fete. Elliot sniffed his bubbly — it was a brand, Veuve Clicquot, he thought.

Hazel had the guest list right. Rainblatt introduced Elliot to a circle containing Thorsten Marshall and Joanne Johanson. And while Reitman, the financier — a potential investor in Locura Canyon and so the one person Elliot looked forward to meeting — was not in attendance, the former cleric, Cahill, could be heard sermonizing from the other side of the room. Here also were the "exotics": a young playwright called Steven Harris and his girlfriend, Abby Amstoy, who, by their dress at least, looked to live much farther south and west in the city. Johanson reacted as if Elliot's introduction was an ill-mannered interruption of her hungry study of the young dramatist.

"Vice president English television?" She wondered aloud. "I used to listen to the radio until it became . . . what? Thorsten?"

"I'd say 'common' if not for the risk of being called a snob or an elitist."

Everyone chuckled but the young playwright and his girl.

"There was a day," Johanson said, addressing Elliot by way of young Harris, "when a play such as your little thing at Tarragon — satire, historical themes — might have ended up on the CBC."

"I'm sure," Elliot said to Johanson, "you are too young to remember when we broadcast stage plays."

"You flatter me," she said. "It wasn't that long ago."

"Opera. Experimental film. Theatre," said Thorsten. "Time was you could find it all on the CBC."

"Did you, um um, ever really, um, watch any of that stuff, Thorsten?" Rainblatt asked. He was standing back from the group, against the nearest wall, and so needed to raise his voice.

"Rarely."

"But still you um a-ad-advocate for it."

"I can see more value in it than in some dire situation comedy or cop show that tries to ape the American equivalent." Thorsten was one of those snobs who dismissed television without ever watching it. Elliot was one of those snobs who defended television without ever watching it.

"So it's um um, important what's on, even if you're not, um-nah, seeing it."

"Absolutely. It's a public institution."

Johanson still hadn't taken her eyes off the playwright. He was a rail, over six feet tall with a mass of carefully uncombed blackest hair. He was wearing an elaborate western shirt, with pearl-buttoned pockets and florid embroidery.

"What sort of television do you like not to watch, Mr. Harris?" Johanson asked.

"I don't own a television."

"What a surprise," said Hazel. She must have escaped Helga and silently sidled up to Elliot. She held in her swollen hands a glass of bubbling mineral water, lemon floating atop. It was Elliot's first good look at Hazel since she'd taken off her coat. She was wearing a mod kilt-like skirt of an unusual emerald-coloured material, scaly like the skin of a snake, fastened by a punkish, easily weaponized, raw metal pin. Her ivory blouse was tightly tapered and flirted with transparency. Hazel had buttoned the shirt so that the ochre and orange stones hanging from her long neck played support to her décolletage. It was almost audacious, but by richness of fabric and precision of cut stayed just within the line of respectability.

"Like a television *set*, I mean. I watch a lot of shows, on my computer," said Harris.

"We usually bring the laptop to bed and download a torrent," said Abby.

"There's an old show that I find really funny," Harris added. "It's called *Get Smart*. Have you heard of it?"

"Elliot is more than a, um, t-television executive, you know," Rainblatt said, mercifully changing the subject. Shop talk was a bore, and if the shop was the CBC then all the more so. "He has his own vineyard back in, ahhhh, California."

Johanson raised her glass to this news.

"What's it called?" she asked.

"Locura Canyon."

"Can't say that I've heard of it," said Thorsten Marshall.

"It's not available in Canada. Production is modest, a thousand cases a year."

"A hobby, then," said Marshall.

"No," said Elliot. "It's a business."

"I like some Ridge and Caymus wines but must confess to having gone off New World lately," said Marshall.

"Ridge and Caymus are good. There are others. You're missing out."

"There is something unsurprising about California wine," Marshall said. "Do you think it's because it's grown by graduates of agricultural colleges rather than by farmers?"

Was there anything more humbling, more poisonously and profoundly humbling, than hearing oneself in an idiot? How else to respond than to protest too much?

"Slagging UC Davis was fashionable once," said Elliot. "I see a lot of science in the fields of France these days too; even the most dogmatic *biodynamie* freaks are mindful of it. And I have never met a race so convinced of the healing powers of the latest potion, whether it's an antifungal from big pharma or an ox horn filled with dung from some witch doctor, as the French. There aren't so many hunched old vignerons out pruning the vines as people like to think."

"Those California Cabernet Sauvignons, they all taste the same."

"Yes, but the left-bank wines in Bordeaux are now trying to taste like the ones they make on the right, so . . ."

"I don't follow you."

"Those California Cabs taste that way deliberately," said Elliot, warming to the task of giving smug Marshall a lecture. "They made those wines to ape what they loved in French Bordeaux. Something plummy, something like black currants, something like licorice allsorts, smell of a cigar box . . . They got land in California that was close enough climatically to grow the same grapes they grew in Bordeaux, and they made wines. They made wines that hoped to mimic the famous Frenchies: the Latours, the Lafites, the Moutons."

"Yes, and?" said Thorsten.

"But those winemakers realized that the one thing they could not taste in the French wines they were trying to make in California was France."

"The terroir thing, yes, and you're making my point."

"Let me finish. By the time they'd realized this, their fat, fruity, juicy wines, made from grapes that were too ripe, had found success in the market. The wines they made were easy to like." Was the young playwright rolling his eyes for his girlfriend? "They could not very well go back and change the taste of the consumers, a taste they had fostered. So now the Bordelais, the garagistes, and even some of the classed growths have started to make their wines taste more like those of California. The imitated now imitate their imitators' imitations."

Elliot could tell he'd bored both Marshall and Johanson. The only person who'd been paying him close attention was the playwright's date, the tiny Miss Amstoy.

"You can't ask that people learn how to like a wine," she said now. "People like what they like."

"Not even if knowing more means they will get more out

of it?" Elliot said, no longer wanting to talk about it. "I'm just saying . . . I don't know . . . you can chase taste all you want, you'll never catch it."

"I know there's a corollary in there somewhere," Hazel said, "for television."

"You own one of these Napa wineries, I take it?" asked Amstoy.

"No," said Elliot, "I'm doing something slightly different, much less successfully, somewhere else."

"You don't seem to enjoy it much."

"Don't I? I've given the wrong impression, because I miss being there every day."

He turned to look at Hazel and found she was already looking to him, wanting to meet his eye. Elliot wanted to tell her that she had made too big a leap in conflating two different sorts of taste; that one could not simply substitute television for wine in his argument because television was always, by definition, in the broadest taste. However, Rainblatt, choosing this moment to launch himself from the wall, tackled him.

"C-come Elliot. I'd, um, forgotten about it but I wanted to show you my, aaah, wine cellar, get your views, show me how many of those terrible Californians I've salted away," he said.

Rainblatt hung off Elliot until they reached the steps to the basement. By comparison, locomotion down the stairs in the narrow passage was comparatively easy. He held a rail and, with his shoulder pressed to the wall, more or less slid down.

The cellar was large for a home. Perhaps an earlier owner was a serious wino. Rainblatt's collection looked, at first glance, to be typical of what you saw in basements: wines that had been kept too long under the mistaken impression they would improve, the occasional trophy label received as a gift with a transparent cash value. Elliot had been asked to perform this same task on several occasions. Sometimes you found a gem or, better, an oddity with a good story. Rainblatt got purchase with an elbow on an empty shelf as Elliot started, with some dread, to give the bottles his attention.

"I don't know who else to to t-talk t-to, Elliot," said Rainblatt, his voice pitching up involuntarily.

"Oh *no*," thought Elliot, keeping his eyes on the wines to avoid Rainblatt's. So this was the reason for all the chumminess: Rainblatt had some personal problem, a disgruntled mistress, money woes, a secret he wanted to unburden himself of or, worse, was seeking assistance in solving.

"I still have a few friends in Ottawa," Rainblatt began, "but most of those I'd call allies have been pensioned off or shown the door." In the lower reaches of the rack Elliot thought he saw a Châteauneuf-du-Pape by Henri Bonneau. He withdrew it. A 1978. Gentle Jesus in the garden, a '78 Bonneau.

"The current government, well, they are no friends of the CBC, I mean ahhhh philosophically they would be opposed, but it is much more than that. They really believe that we have some sort of v-vendetta against them."

"Yes," said Elliot, noting that there were two bottles of the Bonneau, a ferrous blood tonic, a sap with the polish of vintage port that, without residual sugar, challenged fundamental perceptions of dry and sweet. ". . . the Liberals, I see," he murmured, in response to something he'd not quite heard.

"No, no," said Rainblatt. "*Neo*-liberals, as in the global economic movement, in an unholy alliance with evangelical Christians, at least while they have a shared agenda."

"Of course," said Elliot.

"And I'm sure you've heard these ahhhh conspiracy theories about Stanford's reign, how he bungled things on purpose, that he was a saboteur acting on behalf of some sinister right-wing cah-cah-cabal in Ottawa."

"The conspiracy theory, yes . . ."

Next to the Bonneau, Elliot saw, there were at least six bottles of the 1990 Rayas. There was an unopened case of 1998 Pignan on the floor. Someone with a sophisticated palate, knowledge and connections, and wads of cash was buying the best of Châteauneuf-du-Pape. It could not be Rainblatt. "These wines from the southern Rhône, Victor . . .?"

"I never bought it, I took Heydrich's mistakes for conventional incompetence," Rainblatt continued. "But now —"

"There are some exceptional wines here."

"There's always been talk of privatization, but I never bought it. I never thought it could fly, ahhhhh, politically. The Canadian public wouldn't stand for it."

"No, of course not," said Elliot. "The Canadian public, never." Now he saw several bottles of Beaucastel's 2005 old-vine Roussanne, a veritable *confiture* of figs and white flowers. Whoever had acquired these wines was intimate with the region.

"But we have to accept that after the past few years, with ahhhh viewership down, the radio audience aging, the old platforms maybe coming to their end, maybe the public has less invested than they, they used to. And immigrants, I mean

New New Canadians, the CBC means ahhh nothing to them."

"I wouldn't say that," said Elliot, now rooting through the bottles with fervour.

"These friends of mine in Ottawa tell me that the Prime Minister's Office has commissioned a study, all very huh-huh-hush-hush, secret, to investigate the sale, in whole or in part, of the organization. They've gotten it into their heads . . ."

It was in shifting a very *vieux* bottle of Vieux Télégraphe that Elliot saw them, just two of them, beneath dust icing, the only adornment on their labels a rough line rendering of a single key. The thought first occurred to him that it was some common symbol on labels from the region, a now meaningless crest signifying loyalty to some sub-sect of . . . but then he saw the word *Isabelle* and, without hesitating, with a grasp that was ginger but sure, withdrew the bottle from its iron cuff.

". . . perhaps he was being p-paranoid." Rainblatt's speech was now racing, as if he needed to get everything out before being found out. "But at the same time there was a meeting, with only the Minister of Heritage himself, with representatives of CCTV."

Elliot placed the bottle upright on the floor. The cloudy green glass container, unlike the contemporary bourguignonne version for Rhône wines, was in the normande shape, with steeply sloped wide shoulders atop a tapered cylinder. Elliot knew that the type of bottle used by the estate could be variable, that they had even, being both economical and contrary minded, put it in cheaply acquired Alsatian flutes in the 1959 vintage. The fluid within was level with the shoulders.

"With CTV, that's terrible," said Elliot.

"No, CCTV, the Chinese national broadcaster. I know this seems incredible but there are other indications . . ." Rainblatt was panting.

The label on the wine bottle was crumbling but clear. There it was, in flowing script: *Isabelle d'Orange*. In the lower left-hand corner in another typeface was the indication of vintage: *année 1961*. Elliot was about to say something, tell Rainblatt that he was in possession of a most unusual bottle of wine, one that Elliot coveted, but he stopped himself.

"These are . . . startling revelations, Victor." Elliot hoped Rainblatt would repeat them another time, so he could actually hear what they were.

"I can't substantiate any of this. I can't even tell you who told me, and I am still unsure about their motives. We cah-cah-can't stay down here too long, I don't want anyone to think . . ." Without finishing the thought, Rainblatt cocked his head, put his cheek to his shoulder, and launched from the shelf, through the door, and onto the rail of the stairway. Elliot realized that Rainblatt's method of propulsion could best be described as one of controlled falling.

To his right, as he exited the cellar, Elliot saw a door, presumably to the backyard, and considered making a dash to unlock it. This would allow entry from the outside, necessary to facilitate his returning later and stealing a bottle of Isabelle d'Orange. He was aware he'd come to this decision rashly. From the moment it was clear that Rainblatt was ignorant of the cellar's inventory, Elliot had known he was going to take one of the two bottles. Perhaps he needed only to ask for one, but the tiny risk that he might be refused, that Rainblatt might claim he'd received it as a gift and must keep it for sentimental reasons, was simply too great.

But a few steps up the stairs Rainblatt turned to look back at Elliot.

"Say nothing of this to anyone. Once I've learned more . . ."

"Of course, Victor." Elliot could not get to the door.

"You had a question about one of the wines?"

"No, nothing, only that there was a decent selection of stuff from the South of France."

"Pat Cah, Pat Cahill brings them to me." To get up the stairs Rainblatt had to pull himself, hand over hand, by the rail. "He has some business in Avignon and often comes back with something."

"Are they any good, Mr. Jonson?" boomed a voice from above. Cahill. Elliot could see his scuffed, heavy-soled black shoes at the top of the stairs.

"Speak of the devil," said Rainblatt, hauling himself upwards, shoulder into the wall as though he were trying to push the house free of its foundation.

"You're a man with good taste," said Elliot to Cahill.

"No, sir. I am a man with many friends and acquaintances with good taste. Helga wondered where you men had gotten to. She would like us to sit."

Cahill and Elliot stood next to one another waiting to be assigned their seats.

"Victor said you are back and forth to Avignon," said Elliot.

"Yes, I am," Cahill answered, in way that pre-empted further inquiry.

Helga beckoned Elliot to come forward and sit next to some Tory lawyer's wife.

Elliot wondered if he might be coming undone. A bottle of wine, however great, however full of associations, was just that. Did he imagine that tasting it again, swishing the fluid around in his mouth, would provide him with the information to reverse-engineer it? Anybody obsessed with anything — a painting, a car, haute couture, a boy or a girl — obviously fantasized that finally having that which they desired would solve their problems. All it could provide, at best, was the memory of why they'd pursued it in the first place. All it could do was put their decisions along the way into some sort of context. All it could do was give the choices they had made in their lives meaning. Only that.

THE LAWYER'S WIFE turned out to be named Carrie. She was an executive in professional figure skating. Elliot was genuinely surprised when she informed him of the considerable audience the "sport" drew on television, and he made a mental note to scan the pitches piling on his desk for something featuring it. Though he expertly managed to deflect queries about his own family, Elliot knew he was doing a poor job of pretending to be interested in Carrie's.

He was dually distracted: by the thought of the bottles in the basement, and by Hazel's décolletage. She was seated on the opposite side of the table, three chairs north of Elliot, and as she turned to talk with Abby Amstoy next to her, the panel of blouse shielding her breast folded and fell back from the flesh. He was buzzing in the sex-crime tendrils and jellies. He'd not thought that Hazel might ever be sexually available, and knowing that he relied on her skills to prop up the charade that he had competencies, he knew that to consider her so would be a mistake. All the same, the allure of Hazel's boob was strong enough to befuddle his calculation of how to get the wine out of the house.

He was confident that Victor did not know what he had down there. But perhaps Cahill did. Still, even if Cahill asked after the wine some time in the future and Victor could not account for it, it could easily be that Victor had drunk it without knowing. The wine was so obscure . . . it wouldn't be missed if Victor didn't know that he possessed it.

His first plan, to unlock the basement door near the cellar and return in the dead of night, was, on consideration, ridiculous. The door could easily be relocked by his hosts before they turned in for the night. And there were certain to be alarms. No, what Elliot had to do was get one of the two bottles outside the house *during* the party. He remembered exactly where he'd placed the one he'd taken from the shelf. Once people got a few more drinks in and someone got up for a piss, he would follow. Finding the washroom occupied, he could claim to be going downstairs in search of another. He'd snatch the bottle, exit into the backyard, and then stash it just the other side of the fence or hedging. Easy.

The course of watercress soup had been finished by all but a few of the more vociferous when the playwright, Harris, excused himself. Harris was likely looking for a respite from the table, planning to close the bathroom door behind him so he could free a trapped sigh of despair at the tedium of his evening and reflect on how he'd become so toothless that these sorts of people would invite him. His peers were probably having a grand old time over jugs of draft at some dive downtown while he was listening to (Elliot had caught snippets floating over the table) Friar Cahill expound on schism arcana.

Elliot watched Harris shuffle into the john before he ducked for the stairs. He took all twelve in three bounding strides, like a student late for class.

Only when the Isabelle d'Orange was in hand did Elliot calculate the cost. Utter disgrace was disproportionately high in relation to the possible reward. But it was in hand. His flight commenced.

He was pleased with the confidence and stealth with which he conveyed the bottle out the back door and into the night. He was calm, even poised. Elliot had always assumed himself to be the sort of person who performed poorly under pressure, but having so rarely put himself in such a position he might have been mistaken. His sang-froid was impressive.

Leafless branches caught light from windows above to lay a net of shadows on the lawn. There were patches of snow on the grass but not enough to be reflective. Elliot slid slightly on the wet stone walk beneath his feet. Heading to the rear of the yard he worried whether the fence, when he found it, might be electrified, or outfitted with motion detectors or such. A forward step felt not turf or pavement but deep air.

His first, right, foot was immediately joined in the atmosphere by its trailing partner. His left heel catapulted toward the stars. Thrown into a cartwheeling motion, his head was thus thrust downward even as it dropped under its own weight. The skull would have continued in accelerated descent, perhaps all the way to Hades, if not for its colliding with frosty, perfectly firm, terra. The weight of his carcass above felt, for a moment, as though it might bend his neck to breaking, but the load was relieved as his body continued its unstoppable tumble, his arse now foremost.

Instinct drew him into a ball. While this did the trick of protecting his organs, it also made him tumble faster. He was rolling, bouncing, into a crevasse. That he was plunging into a ravine over which the Rainblatt shack was cantilevered became known to him only in retrospect. His endless falling was so unexpected that Elliot judged, even as he was being pummelled along the way, that he was actually experiencing not a physical event but some cerebral catastrophe, some stroke or embolism that made him feel as though he was falling into a cut in the earth.

Coming to rest, abruptly, on his back, winded by the unyielding planet, he thought about the barranca at the end of *Under the Volcano*. He looked up, waaaaaay up. Unlike Lowry's consul, however, he was alive, and no dog appeared to have been tossed in after him.

What sort of tithead built on the edge of a ravine? The answer smirked down from the crown of lights a hundred feet up: a Rosedale tithead with more money than sense. He sat up. Nothing broken, but — for as Elliot looked into the gloom he saw a hairy, semi-erect ape clutching a bottle of wine — perhaps head trauma.

No. No. There was a very real creature not six feet from him. It studied the treasured Isabelle d'Orange for a moment. It looked at Elliot. It pointed its index finger at him like the finger was a pistol. It drew back the hand, as if starting to put the weapon back in a shoulder holster but stopping short. It employed the rigid digit of the gun hand to push the fragile cork easily down the neck. The pressure propelled a gush of

scent into the air. Elliot could smell the wine, its celestial violets, only the length of a man away. Cautiously, Elliot stood.
The creature put the bottle to his head and chugged. He was
thirsty. The cork within the bottle was tossed about by the
currents made by the rapid emptying of the contents and
the consequent backwash of breath and spittle. It brought to
Elliot's mind the old flow indicators on the sides of gas pumps,
the balls dancing around in their transparent dome. The creature downed a third of the liquid in one go, ceasing with a
smack. It then held the bottle out to Elliot as an offering, a
suspension bridge of saliva from its lips to the bottle's own
mouth. Elliot was tempted but finally shook his head, declining what was surely a hot herpes Slurpee.

"Who the fuck," the creature asked, hot breath condensing
into billows in the cold air, "are you?" The hairy thing was
inadequately dressed in a wollen lumberjack shirt that might
once have been red and black. Its trousers were lacquered stiff
and shiny with oily grime. The head was shaggy, the mop
morphing into natural dreadlocks, face bearded. It wasn't
nearly as tall as Elliot but was considerably more muscular —
twice Elliot's width at the shoulders.

"My name is Elliot Jonson."

"Johnston, hey?" The creature took another pull from the
bottle. He held it back so as to scrutinize the label and said,
as if reading from it, "What's your business with that cunt
Rainblatt?"

"I'm a dinner guest."

"I pass by every so often, wait for that dizzy motherfucker
to come down that bank like you did."

"You've not thought of calling, leaving him a message?"

"Out for a smoke, were you?"

"Yes," said Elliot, thinking that a cigarette would actually be a plausible, if frowned upon, excuse for his absence. He could say it was pot; people were usually better with that than tobacco. Certainly no one would believe that he had been detained by a sasquatch.

"Wait . . . Elliot Johnston . . . I know that . . ."

"There were notices regarding my appointment in the papers. It's 'Jonson,' by the way, J, O, . . ."

The creature started, going into a slight crouch — whether an offensive or defensive posture, Elliot couldn't say.

"YOU!" growled the creature. "You're the new Heydrich!"

"I'm the new vice president of English television, yes. But I'm not a 'new Heydrich,' I've got my own agenda," Elliot said, thinking again that it was really time he did get some sort of agenda. "And you are?"

"Benny Malka. I'm an entertainer."

Malka . . . Yes, Elliot recalled reading about him in the paper on his ill-fated flight from LAX to Paris. Show cancelled, rumoured to be living as a wild man in the ravines . . .

"I've heard of you," said Elliot.

"Seen my act?"

"No. I've lived in California for many years. You wouldn't have a reel, would you?"

This angered Malka, who lunged at Elliot. They were less than a foot apart.

"I don't keep one with me in the goddamn ravine! The raccoons could give a shit." Malka smelled like Spadina on garbage day. "There should be tape at the Corpse. But if it turns out they've been bulk-erased, you could try my agent."

He took another deep pull of wine. "I don't know whether it's because I've been drinking the dregs from blue boxes but . . . this wine, it's . . ." Malka could not find the words.

"I should be returning to the party. I promise I'll look at your tape," said Elliot, with no intention of ever doing so.

"You wanna hear my pitch right now?" said Malka. "Talk-show format but —"

Elliot turned to the steep incline, beginning his climb back up to Rainblatt's. "I would love to but . . . I don't want to be rude to my host. Look, why don't you send me a one-sheet," he said.

"I just might do that, Johnston." Elliot heard Malka finish the bottle and toss the empty into the bushes. "I warn you, no one has ever left the CBC on good terms. I'll keep a spot warm for you."

There was distance between them now, so Elliot thought it safe to call out, "Have you considered radio?"

"Been there, fuck that," shouted Malka.

THE SOUP BOWLS had been swept away and a course of fish, skin-less and white, was being set in place as Elliot returned. Hazel was putting her hand over her wineglass, declining a Saint-Aubin. She caught Elliot's eye and with a most discreet flick of her chin indicated that he should look down at his jacket. There was a terrific tear in the left panel, no doubt sustained in his fall down the ravine. He took the jacket off and folded it to conceal the rip. Hazel managed to grin at him quizzically in such a way that only he was aware of it. Willed light in her eyes implored him to be careful. Yet the corners of her mouth twitched, betraying delight that he was up to some secret mischief.

". . . isn't that so, Elliot?" she said, once he was seated. "Programming next season right now." Her phasing suggested he'd been there all along. She knew her social witchcraft.

"Thinking about it constantly," Elliot said.

"It would be impossible," said Marshall to his fish, "to do worse than your predecessor." He looked up at Elliot. There was suspicion in his gaze. He, perhaps alone, had noted Elliot's lengthy absence. "Unless one tried to."

Some of the dinner party took their coffee in the living room while others stayed at the table. It was relaxed. Elliot had finally cooled down from his ravine adventure. During the main course he could feel his shirt wet against his back. Only Hazel and Marshall seemed to suspect he'd been up to something and so, to avoid the latter, Elliot took a seat on a couch next to Patrick Cahill. Alas, now, when Elliot would rather the matter forgotten, Cahill deigned to answer Elliot's earlier questions about the wines.

"So Victor told you that my order have a presence near Avignon."

"A monastery?"

"Yes, though I am not a monk myself."

"Get out more, do you?"

"We also maintain a cottage, formerly a hermitage, near Uzès. Do you know the town?"

"Know it well," said Elliot. "Lovely spot."

"There is a caviste there. He recommends the wines to me. I am not a man of means. Our order still has several hectares under vine. We make some sacramental wine; otherwise, the grapes go to various winemakers. I don't know the details.

We get so much of this and that in compensation. There is some bartering."

"Your caviste is knowledgeable." Elliot knew he should drop it but could not resist. He saw from whence the Isabelle d'Orange came. "I noticed some obscure —"

"Like?" Cahill said, too quickly.

Elliot was going down a dangerous road. He veered. "What does one look for in a good sacramental wine?"

"Smooth transubstantiation." There was nothing in Cahill's tone to tell Elliot whether or not he was joking. The Farinist nutters back in Paso were big on transubstantiation, believed the dough they donned could turn, like the host, into the flesh of Christ, and so protected them like godly armour.

"Your order, your religious order . . . ?"

"The Clementines."

"I've not heard of them. Mostly found in France, in the South? Or the Maghreb?" Elliot said, thinking of the source of much of the tiny citrus.

"We've a centre, for study, here in Canada. In Niagara. We had vineyards there as well, but I'm afraid we had to liquidate them to cover court settlements with . . ." Cahill hesitated.

"I'm originally from Newfoundland."

"So you know."

"I understand a St. Pat's dancer could be hard to resist."

"Patent leather shoes, short pants, and a tartan sash. Lucifer himself could have tailored such temptation."

"I've been meaning to drive down to Niagara, see some of the wine country here. I myself —"

"We're having a retreat in three weeks' time," said Cahill.

"I couldn't."

"No?"

"Well . . . 'wouldn't' is probably truer."

"Do you not have faith?"

"Faith? No."

"I should have thought that would be a qualification for your position. It was in the past. I have personally given counsel to many senior CBC executives. I was for a time a consultant for religious programming."

"The slack has been picked up by cable."

"No, sir. Cable is not to blame."

"I thought cable was always to blame."

"The cause is adoration of the devil, and the consequent decline of the West."

"Oh."

"Granted," Cahill said, expelling a breath, "the fractionalization of viewership has some role."

"That's all I was saying."

"It's not like having some spiritual programming on Sunday mornings is going to bump a hot new show." Cahill's tone had changed completely: he was now another petitioner. "We'd only be displacing shows about gardening and house renovation."

"The new, secular religions?"

"I think you will find that Canadians are becoming more pious, not less."

"You're a Catholic, so you would be inclined to —"

"I'm no Roman!"

"Oh . . . I am so sorry, I thought . . ."

"I belong to the true Catholic Church, not that of the Roman antipopes."

"I don't follow." Elliot was genuinely lost.

"We do not recognize the papacy that returned to Rome from Avignon. We remain faithful to the church of Clement VII and the popes of that line."

Elliot smiled and nodded, trying to show that he took all this as interesting but not terribly significant. Cahill, though, was staring at him with undisguised menace, as though now, having revealed a dangerous secret to Elliot, he might need to ensure his silence.

ELLIOT RELATED HIS conversation with Cahill to Hazel as he drove her home.

"So nothing to do with fruits at all," he said. "Clementines after Clement VII."

"He *is* a most disturbing man. You said as many words to him tonight as I have in my entire life," she said.

"I've spent years looking for this lost grape variety, Matou de Gethsemane, and I think there is a chance that Cahill's order of monks cultivates it. I might have been looking on the wrong side of the Rhône River."

"How nerdilicious. What's so special about this . . . Matou de . . . ?"

"It's thought to add elements that are . . . cranky, in a good way; it lightens wine that can be too heavy, works against the sense of sweetness that high-alcohol examples can have. It's a difficult grape and brings all the wrong things, but it gives the whole picture a kind of asymmetry that makes it more interesting."

"Where the hell did you go?"

"The Vaucluse, mostly, between Avignon and Orange, but —"

"No, I meant during dinner. You disappeared."

"I stepped out back for some air."

"I told Victor you'd snuck out for a cigarette. He does all the time. Or did, before his inner-ear thing." Hazel said, looking out the window at the city. "I could go for a smoke about now."

Elliot wished he had one to offer.

They arrived at Hazel's immodest digs. One of two swinging gates opened, suggesting that Hazel had pressed some remote control device in her clutch. Elliot was curious about the house and Hazel's domestic arrangements and hoped she would invite him in. But she was half out of the car before she said "Thank you, Elliot."

"You are welcome, Hazel."

Hazel was standing on the pavement. She bent down so she could look within Elliot's car.

"What happened to your jacket?" she asked.

"I slipped on the grass when I went outside." Elliot gave her the answer he had prepared.

"See you at the office, boss," Hazel said and closed the door.

FIVE

AFTER A THIRD attempt to call Soledad failed he tried Lucy. It was early morning in Los Angeles and her not answering suggested she and Ascension were travelling. Hazel could not be raised at any of her phone numbers and did not respond to his text.

He went to an afternoon screening of *The Centuri Protocol*. Sure enough, Elliot was credited as a producer. He was in for points. Given box office reports, this was going to be a significant chunk of change.

It wasn't a drama in the old sense, with story and character; it was rather a purely visceral entertainment experience. It played not on the eyes and the ears and the mind but rather the kidneys. It was a new kind of loud for Elliot. He supposed maybe that *was* what it was like to be inside an explosion, or to be incinerated. The actress Virginia Whalen, who also had a turn in Elliot's *The Nevada Girl*, was raped, noisily, by an angry metaloreptilian alien.

Elliot left before the end and walked to Lai Wah Heen Chinese Restaurant for Christmas dinner.

SIX

THE BUREAUCRACY of the institution was virulent. Elliot's desk, which he'd once feared was suspiciously empty, was now so cluttered as to be impossible to navigate. The credenza at his back was a dumping ground. Both were off limits to Stella, as Elliot claimed, falsely, that there was order in the teetering stacks.

Sorting the potentially worthy proposals and show pitches from the piles would have taken him days. Instead he called for fresh copies of those he could remember and took them home. Too many distractions at the office to give them the attention they deserved, he said. He knew that somewhere in his office were another half dozen or so worthy projects of which he could not remember the working title and which, therefore, would not move forward. This seemed arbitrary, but Elliot reassured himself with the thought that if the titles or concepts weren't catchy enough to have lodged themselves in his head, they probably wouldn't do so in the ever-shortening attention span of the viewing public.

Consideration of the population's generalized ADD helped him recall the audience profile Hazel had worked up at his request, the "everybody" he was going to make the CBC serve "every way." He was able to find this fat document amidst the mess because she'd enclosed it in a memorable shiny red binder.

Once home, with a second glass of decent Bourgeuil, Hazel's survey was the first thing he reached for.

Canadians, he saw, liked to think they were more liberal and more cosmopolitan than they were. Their tastes in all things, from coffee (they liked it weak and milky and sweet; the double-double was their brew) to potatoes (they liked them in a variety of plain preparations, and often) were described, kindly, as simple; less generously, as pedestrian. Elliot flipped through the pages. Easily embarrassed, they couldn't stand to see even a nipple on display. Though they went to church less and less often, more of them than seemed sensible remained "believers." Cahill had this right. The exception was the burgeoning evangelical population, who, if their numbers continued to grow as they had, would soon be a powerful minority. These people worshipped a lot, and hard.

He paged ahead to "Economics." Contrary to what the citizenry imagined, the gap between the wealthiest members and the less fortunate was widening. And in numbers, the poor and destitute were large for an industrialized society. The treatment of the Native population was a horror show, an apartheid system where the townships were so remote they could forever be ignored.

Backwards a dozen pages to "Health and Welfare": Canadians were overweight, but not in the gross manner of their southern cousins. A quarter of adults were depressed enough to seek treatment, usually in the form of medication.

"Demographics": once of English, Irish, Scottish, and French extraction, they were more and more of Asian stock.

"Education": Most of them couldn't read and comprehend a newspaper.

"Self-Image": They felt a connection to the land, to the wilderness, but few of them ever went. They were small-town people living in cities.

The most puzzling aspect of the national personality was its self-satisfaction. This was strange, because it was twinned with a persistent self-doubt. Despite evidence placing them forever in the middle of every scale, they held that they were better in most things than other peoples. They thought their health-care system a model, for example; ditto for their tolerance and peacefulness. They were proud to be polite. At the same time, they never felt themselves good enough, as individuals, to meet international standards.

So it was that, despite holding the view that they were culturally distinct and wanting such reflected in public policy, they overwhelmingly liked their television and films made in Los Angeles. The pages relating to entertainment consumption were the gravest of the portrait as applied to the business at hand, and here Hazel could not resist an editorial comment. A handwritten note paperclipped to the top of a page read, *While it is generally the case that Canadians prefer American television to their own, there are notable exceptions. Programs that are demonstrative in their "Canadianness," that are jingoistic — especially those critical or mocking of the United States — have been successful. I don't entirely understand this unless those programs are a symptom of low national self-esteem. This may be a protest against the more common practice of adoring all things from the United States and, in the neediest way, seeking the approbation of Americans. This is a cycle of abuse that I think we can change with a new approach to programming. Much to talk about in this regard.*

Elliot sighed. One thing one should never do in entertainment, he knew (having watched Lucy cock it up), was make shows to service an agenda. Hazel was implying that television programming might heal the nation's self-image. Could Elliot accept that entertainment's function as a brief diversion from life's worries was as worthy as art's project to challenge and engage? Alas, he could not. So what was the shame in giving the crowd what they wanted? He had done just that speaking to his fellow VPs, and they'd loved it. He put aside the binder.

The trick to it, he saw, was knowing what the people wanted *before they themselves did*. This was the first time Elliot had been in the position of making that call. His part back in Hollywood had always been that of an unconditional advocate, a zealot for the cause of the story he thought should be told — the one he had written. Over the next few days and nights he would, instead, judge the appeals. He reached for a bound document, a show called *The Wonderfuls*. It was supposed to be "warm and wry," it was set in Winnipeg, family fare; a showbiz dad was finally retiring from a life on the road as a popular illusionist. During his first look at the pitch, Elliot remembered, he was taken with a funny subplot of an ongoing, not entirely good-natured, competition between the father and a retired psychic — based clearly on the Amazing Kreskin — living down the block. Did the show have what it took to capture the imagination of the nation? Knowing that was not a science or an art but pure divination. "Fade in," Elliot read.

ᐧ ᐧ ᐧ

ELLIOT LOCKED HIMSELF in the apartment. He did not shave, ordered in, worked naked for a time. He made coffee at three a.m., drank whisky in the morning. He did not answer the phone (it rang twelve times in four days). He programmed his email to issue an out-of-office reply.

Imagining an entire fall television season — a suite of dramas and comedies and information programs and reality shows — was, it turned out, something akin to a fever dream. He lost himself in the process, fitfully moving from script to script, scribbling notes that he later found incomprehensible, sketching diagrams and schema, flow charts inside calendars stitched with arrows. To each of the programming week's days he assigned characteristics and traits — Monday was "clammy and grim"; Thursday was "hopeful"; Friday, "giddy."

Early in the process he imagined an ideal viewer, a composite Canadian, a young professional woman he dubbed Geraldine. But he realized that programming for such a specific niche would cut the CBC off from more than half its potential viewers, a violation of the mandate and a patently dimwitted business decision where advertising was concerned. So instead he considered a family, the Canadian version: 2.3 children, three-quarters of a pet, English-with-a-dash-of-Slav dad (stressed weekend binge drinker, slightly overweight), Irish-French-Métis mom (stressed and coping with depression, slightly overweight). Tim Hortons. KD. Canadian Tire. New Toyota Camry, old Ford Escort. *Hockey Night in Canada*. Florida vacation. But this didn't work either, because when he started factoring in the children, he realized the generational divide was too great. It wasn't just that his family were all ordering different things from the menu; they were all going to different restaurants.

But what about people in an office? He got to work on a prototypical workforce. It had to consist of people of various ages — though none of them so young as to get all their programming via their laptops and phones. Some of them would use the new media, of course, but not to the exclusion of the old. The group should represent a range of incomes, gender, ethnicities. It would be a modest collection: not three codgers in a rural post office, not a bank tower in downtown Toronto.

A weather office? A group of meteorologists, the clerical support and the bosses, the janitor! What could be more Canadian? A weather office, formerly· government employees, now privatized — their hours and workload were heavier than before and they had less job security; some were forced to move to the new location to keep their jobs when their former office was closed due to cutbacks. Thus, some of them were outsiders. Their incomes were in the middle of the range, but they didn't make enough to get ahead. Elliot saw them all . . . the janitor who nobody in the office but the boss (an old pal) knew was a disgraced lawyer, a disbarred jailbird. Two of the metereologists were, like Rainblatt and Hazel, secret smokers, and Gerry — this janitor, he'd call him Gerry — allowed this pair to sneak puffs in the basement . . . There they fell in love. Frank and Betty and George and Kulvinder and Linda were all there . . . working away, looking at satellite images, worrying about the bills, not getting enough sex or sleep, commuting forty-two minutes to work . . . and they'd go home exhausted and drop on the couch and turn on the tube.

Elliot was going to be each and every one of them. He was going to inhabit the skins he'd drawn. What did they watch? What would they watch that they would talk about the next day at work? And what of Alice, the obese receptionist, with legs the size of barrels, whose life was an utter mystery to her colleagues, whose husband, Fred, had never once come to the office Christmas party, who kept a picture of her pet Lhasa Apso on her desk, who never talked about what she'd done last night or over the weekend? What did Alice watch?

Yes, *what*? The shows, Elliot knew, must have the capacity to take one away, out of oneself, out of the day. They must provide easy, unambiguous answers, deliver truths and never pose difficult questions. They would be an invariable habit, a ritual . . . devotional? Television would be their god! No. No, it probably wouldn't be God. And definitely shouldn't. Or should it? No. Elliot was tired.

He did not bother to go to his room, thinking it was his obligation at this point to lie on the couch and fall asleep with the set on. Women's curling. The Scotties Tournament of Hearts already. Jesus, how long had he been back in Canada? The next day he called Hazel to tell her the draft schedule was complete. He wanted to celebrate and booked them a table at a restaurant, Canoe, which someone had told him was good. There, over a meal, he would tell her all.

ᕙ ❧ ᕗ

From: bonorg@locuracanyon.com
To: matou@aol.com
Subject: Spray
Loschem will not provide Rubigan on credit. Cash sale.

From: matou@aol.com
To: bonorg@locuracanyon.com
Subject: Re. Spray
Why not?

From: bonorg@locuracanyon.com
To: matou@aol.com
Subject: Re. Re. Spray
Late payment last year.

From: matou@aol.com
To: wstuckel@locuracanyon.com
Subject: oidium & other fungus
Inclined not spray this year, get a lot of air in the canopy.

From: wstuckel@locuracanyon.com
To: matou@aol.com
Subject: Re. oidium & other fungus
Suicide

ᕙ ❧ ᕗ

THE RESTAURANT'S LOCATION — or rather, its situation — came as a surprise to Elliot. It was on the fifty-fourth floor of an office tower in the financial district. Given the restaurant's name, he expected wilfully kitschy Canadiana, a room dressed like the set of *Forest Rangers*, smoked bison jowls and beaver cheese on the menu. But this was a modern spot. The expansive view out the windows on the south and west sides of the establishment, above downtown and far out over Lake Ontario, was spectacular. The patrons were dolled up and ebullient, having a blast. The whole place was, appropriate to Elliot's mood, flying.

A gracious young woman unburdened Elliot of his coat. Hazel was already seated. Elliot spotted her immediately, as her chair was pushed away from their table, into the traffic lanes of the wait staff. She appeared to have taken this position to better examine a metre-high floral arrangement at the room's centre. So engrossed in the flowers was she that she did not see Elliot enter.

This allowed Elliot to study Hazel unobserved as he was escorted toward her. The grey skunk stripe in her hair gave away her years, but the deep crow's feet pointed to positively girlish eyes. Her dress, while conservative, always came with a funky, rebellious accent — a saucy belt, an almost too loud piece of vintage jewellery. Her legs, emerging from a short skirt and curled to one side of the chair, were long. She often showed arms with noticeable musculature, hard biceps the shape of an egg, and ropey triceps. But then everybody went to gyms these days.

Hazel noticed Elliot only when he placed his file folder on the table.

"Oh," she said, "you really did mean this to be business?"

"Was I unclear?" Elliot accepted the window seat offered by the waiter.

"No." Hazel moved gingerly from her chair, on the aisle side of the table, to the seat opposite Elliot. She still seemed distracted by the flowers.

"It's gauche, I know, bringing papers to dinner but . . . to be perfectly candid I can scarcely contain my enthusiasm. Next fall is going to be a fantastic season of television."

"A first."

"Anything to drink before you order?" queried the waiter.

"A double gin martini, please," said Elliot, "not too dry, olives."

"Could you half-and-half cranberry juice and club soda?" asked Hazel. The waiter nodded and left.

"It's a radical shakeup. Some of the returning news and current affairs shows aren't going to like it," Elliot said. "Wanna hear the week?"

"Please," said Hazel.

"Monday. Blue Monday. Back to the grind. The first day of the rest of your life."

"I think you're misreading that expression. I think 'the first day of the rest of your life' is a statement of optimism."

"No, no, no. Really, you think?"

"Confident."

"You're sure it's not a situation like with that song 'Don't Worry, Be Happy'?"

"How do you mean?"

"People missed that it was meant to be read ironically. People took that at face value."

"I sure did."

Elliot shook his head. "One of most plaintive things I ever heard. I'd hear that on the radio and I tell you . . . the darkest sort of thoughts. At least we can agree that Monday is no one's favourite day."

"Well . . ."

"You like Mondays, Hazel?"

"I find my work fulfilling."

"Most people don't."

"Most people? You sure?"

"Confident. So Monday is *the* day for comedy."

"You want to move it from Tuesday?"

"What's Tuesday? It's serious, Tuesday. It's acceptance. It's not funny. If Monday is the first day of the rest of your life, then Tuesday, well, Tuesday is all the rest of the rest of your life. Stick with Monday for a second. Comedy. *501 Pennsylvania Avenue*?"

"I know it well," Hazel beamed. "I love that project."

Elliot held up his hand. "Not exactly as presented."

"The writing, I thought, was sharp."

"Rather too. Dialogue in the pilot script drew attention to itself and not the characters."

"I'm surprised you chose it."

"This all comes from that demographic profile you gave me, Hazel. Of the many things I took from it was the Canadian obsession with America. With *501* we throw the regulators a bone while doing what's essentially an American sitcom. A comedy set at the Canadian Embassy in Washington: it's perfect."

"I thought maybe *The Border* served that purpose."

The Border was a broad half-hour comedy about a unit of Canadian Border Services. They were predictable misfits, always running afoul but finally getting the better of their over-equipped, trigger-happy, paranoid American counterparts down the road.

"No, I like *501 Pennsylvania* more than *The Border.* I'm thinking of Kulvinder Singh."

"Who?"

"I imagined a bunch of people working in a weather office as the audience," said Elliot. "Kulvinder Singh is one of them. He's a New Canadian. To him border security is a serious matter. Since 9/11 he's had trouble crossing into the States despite the fact that he's Sikh. And horror stories dating back to the partition of India are family lore."

"You've lost me, Elliot. This Sikh guy you've imagined?"

"Kulvinder Singh."

"Right. He's not going to find abuses of power at the border funny."

"Exactly. In defence of *The Border*, his kids could find the whole thing hilarious. They might eat up the show precisely because it so obviously transgresses a feeling held by their parents. But this is the CBC, young people don't watch it."

"You've imagined this Kulvinder Singh's family too?"

"Not yet," said Elliot. A shimmering martini was set before him. Hazel took a sip from her juice and turned back to the floral arrangement. "Is there something about the flowers, Hazel?"

"Oh, heavens, no. Don't think me rude, Elliot, but the windows . . ." Hazel glanced at the view and then made a gesture of pushing it back with the flattened palm of her hand. "My vertigo."

"Of course. You mentioned that before. I'm sorry — I had no idea when I booked it. Do you want to change tables, or go somewhere else?"

"No, no, no. I've heard only good things about this place. It's not that serious, just a tingle."

"I'm sure they would understand."

"No. This is wonderful."

"You're sure?"

"*501 Pennsylvania Avenue* is a very — what, 'barbed'? — satire," Hazel said, making it clear she wished not to discuss her phobia. "The character of the ambassador — I mean, he's venal, he's almost criminal — and you know I love him, he's funny. The embassy staff are *so* jaded. His wife, she's screwing half of Washington. In the past it would have been considered too much for CBC."

"I said it would have to be changed. Number one, satire is not on. Critics love it, real people turn it off. *501 Pennsylvania* as currently imagined is too scathing, too ironic." Elliot tasted his martini. It was delicious. "Do you realize what portion of our audience is on antidepressants? The medication makes their world literal; they take it to see and accept things only as they are. The inability to comprehend irony is a side effect of the drugs."

"So change it to . . . ?"

"Lighten it up, make it a broader comedy. The ambassador, make him a hapless but well-meaning goof. Give him and the wife some kids. The chief of staff — do you remember a show called *Benson*?"

"The creative team behind *501* — they're pretty attached to the satirical aspect of the show, I mean, for them that's the whole point. I don't know if . . ."

"Hazel, I have some experience on the creative side of this business and I think I can say with some confidence that if we say, 'Make it *Happy Days* or we're going with *The Border* instead of your show,' then they'll change it."

"I know that Jeremy McManis is going to want to discuss it."

"Who's Jeremy McManis?"

"Creative Head responsible for the project."

"Oh, right, I'd forgotten all about him." Elliot snapped his fingers. "I'll get Jeremy to read the writers the riot act, that'll be much easier. Next —"

"What time slot are you thinking about?" Hazel sipped a bird's portion from her glass of juice.

"Nine o'clock."

"Okay . . . and . . . what I'm getting at is the news. Are you going to leave it at ten o'clock?"

"I am."

"You don't know how relieved Leo Karek is going to be. He's been phoning me at home. Having not heard anything, he assumed the worst."

"It's not that I didn't think about it. I mean, it's stupid to be blowing that slot on news. But in the end, given our limited dough, I thought we might as well stick with fewer of the better shows. And I've figured out another way to address the news-in-prime-time problem."

"Oh?" Hazel sounded worried.

"Yep. If you're going to have news in prime-time, then *make* it prime-time news. These guys are always starting with the grimmest shit, the biggest disaster. 'It bleeds, it leads.' Or worse, 'the deepening crisis in Ottawa.'" Elliot made a gesture of hanging himself. "What about the entertaining human-interest stuff? Let *it* lead for a change."

"They will resist that."

Elliot waved off Hazel's caution.

"The last half-hour can still be a wrist-slasher. It's not like it's been trenchant analysis in a long time — everyone knows it's showbiz. They're the worst sort of ratings whores in News." Elliot waited for a rise but Hazel said nothing. He continued. "Another thing we need: national weather. How can we have a national news broadcast and not have a national weather forecast? There should be a short hit at the top of the hour. And we need some weather celebs too, a team with, like . . . a goofy, affable guy, a hot babe . . ."

"Leo will —"

"I've anticipated his reaction. I have a plan."

"Yes?"

"When he sees the alternative he won't complain about having to do a bit of lite in his first half-hour."

"Are you going to bully him? Blackmail?"

"I think he'll respond to both."

"You're really taking to this senior management role."

A waiter was standing next to the table. He handed them menus and told them the specials. As Elliot had anticipated, there was gustatory Canadiana on the menu, even something with bannock, but on the whole it looked good. He ordered sweetbreads, she the bison. She wished to skip the appetizer. Elliot insisted she share some of his foie gras. The wine list was perfunctory and Elliot wondered if he might speak with the sommelier about alternatives.

The sommelier, eager as a puppy, was soon at Elliot's side.

"What do you have in the way of Californian wine?"

"Are you thinking Napa, Sonoma, a Cab?"

"Do you know Locura Canyon?

"I'm afraid not."

"From around Paso Robles."

Elliot must have said the right thing, for the sommelier's excitement leapt.

"You know what we just received today? The Haldeman Estates Toujours Prêt. It scored ninety-seven points in *Wine Advocate.*"

"Oh." Elliot's voice dropped an octave.

"Announced yesterday."

"I guess you've got some leading Canadian wines?"

"Of course, sir."

"Just the best Canadian red you've got, then."

"Very well," the sommelier said, before shuffling off with evident disappointment.

That Haldeman's beastly cough syrup had received the high score grated on him. It was predictable, he supposed, given the publication's taste in things.

If Hazel had noticed the souring of his mood, she didn't let on. "Okay," she said, "if Monday is going to be all comedy, I want to advocate for another show."

Elliot already had another one picked out, but he said, "Go on."

"*Les Les.*" Hazel pronounced it, as was the intention, "Lay Lez."

"You're joking."

"No."

"Point one: a title that requires a tutorial for the audience . . ."

"It's the funniest script I've read. No exaggeration, in all my years at CBC this is the funniest. And the two women that play the leads, I've seen them on stage —"

"Like, the theatre?"

"Yes, and they are hilarious."

"It's about a lesbian couple."

"So?"

"In their forties. Catty. Cynical."

"Skeptical. A lot of the humour comes out of that."

"You've seen *The L Word*. Those girls live on cable, in West Hollywood." Elliot knew his aversion to the *Les Les* script was partly to do with some similarities he noted between its principal characters and Lucy and Ascenscion. If Lucy merely suspected he'd used even a moment of her life as fodder for a sitcom on Canadian television, she would murder him.

"Granted, the characters on *Les Les* are not happy, well-adjusted people," said Hazel. "They are marginalized. Sometimes they're angry."

"One character is a Québécoise, the other is from Newfoundland."

"Yes?"

"Those people have nothing, nothing whatsoever, to do with Canada."

"They're part of Canada."

"Politically, for now," said Elliot. "Nobody in the populated areas of English Canada really cares about what's going on with Newfoundland or Quebec or women. We need people of colour. Have you walked around this town? How about fiscally conservative Sri Lankan or Korean dykes? That's much more the Canada of today." How loud had he said this? Elliot wondered.

"I agree we've been too white, but you can't order up a 'show of colour.' One will evolve organically."

"Not at the CBC it won't."

"I want you to look at *Les Les* again, please."

"These two girls get drunk and make out in the pilot episode."

"Was that not a funny scene?"

"I guess. Yeah, it was. But. I know that at another time in my life I would have said, 'Let's challenge the audience,' but maybe they don't want to be challenged." A thought came to Elliot. "Do you think that the taste of an entire society can change at once?"

"How do you mean?"

"It's seemed to me that one day, people are, I don't know, eating butter- or cream-based sauces, and then another day, all at once, people don't like them."

"I'd not noticed."

"It's the same with shows, you know. A sitcom that every-body found funny one day becomes ridiculous the next. I mean maybe the culture gets saturated with police procedur-als or Cabernet Sauvignon or hip hop and then turns from it, but what's important is that the culture behaves as a single organism."

"And you're suggesting that . . . ?"

"That maybe the comedy of *Les Les* is of a different time. One where people were perhaps more . . ."

"More sophisticated?"

The sommelier returned. He held a bottle of wine out for Elliot's scrutiny.

Elliot gave a perfunctory nod, still pissed at the man's fawning mention of the *Wine Advocate* review. If Elliot's wine had achieved same, he would have worried that he had completely compromised his principles. And yet it would be nice to occasionally get some approbation, a meaningless score or an award of some sort for a screenplay or the wine, even if the people making the call didn't have a clue. Wouldn't it?

The sommelier uncorked the bottle and poured a sample. It was closed, not showing as well as it would with some air, but promised fresh thyme rubbed between your fingers and the rare figgy thing of an unlit Gauloise. Better than expected.

"That will be wonderful," said Elliot. The waiter went to fill Hazel's glass but she put her hand out to cover it and decline. "Hazel," protested Elliot, "this seems decent stuff."

"I don't really drink," she said. She glanced out the window. "Half a glass, then." The waiter poured and left the bottle. Hazel tasted her wine.

"It's nice," she said. "But perhaps wasted on me. My father drank wine, got the bug while he was a student at Oxford. He was an interesting man, fabulous storyteller — with many to tell. Quite funny. Only when he talked about wine did he manage to become a bore."

"Is that a warning?"

Hazel took a great draught of the wine and swished it about her mouth with the same vigour she might Listerine. "What about Wednesday?" she asked.

Over three courses Elliot explained the rest of the schedule. Hazel voiced her disbelief with an animation, and volume, that attracted the attention of the neighbouring tables. It wasn't that Hazel did not drink but, Elliot saw, that she could not. His hitherto decorous second was, under the influence, voluble and blousy.

"If we aren't going to carry *Reason*, who the hell else will?" Hazel was pitched up on the table by her elbows, leaning over empty plates toward Elliot. Her right hand, clutching a lipstick-rimmed wine goblet, swung loosely, yet she spilled not a drop.

Reason was twenty eponymous television hours dedicated to the discussion of its advance. This was without precedent on television. The documentary series' writer and host was an eccentric academic, Dr. Jurgen Palme. The scholar was motivated to make a public case by what he saw as a return to irrationality in contemporary society. Palme's producers provided not just a proposal but the entire run in first and second draft, as well as a fifteen-minute pilot. The show was engaging and — this should not have been a surprise — well considered. It was even entertaining, was never stuffy but always, always demanded the full attention of the audience.

Elliot weighed how the show would play at the weather office. Two people there were religious: Kulvinder was a devout Sikh and Heather, from HR, was a recent convert from non-practising Catholic to enthusiastic Pentecostal. They would be offended. Elliot could see a few of the other guys and gals maybe staying with it for a few minutes, but when it got challenging, and they were tired . . . only Felix, the clarinet-playing, cross-addicted information technology dude, would stick with it. And in Elliot's reckoning, Felix's tastes flagged trouble. Felix would love *Les Les*.

"It might have once been the CBC's function to carry shows no one else would," Elliot finally replied, "but I made some commitment regarding performance when I interviewed for this job."

"Forget about those dorks. I mean, really, Elliot, think of the sort of mind that can measure things only in quantitative terms. Jesus, bring in Robert McNamara and instead of bodies he can count viewers." Hazel put a finger to the corner of her mouth to wipe away a drop of wine. She checked the spot with her tongue. Elliot watched this with what must have been too close attention, for she looked back at him and laughed. "If people are stupid enough," she continued, "to judge whether the CBC is serving the nation only by how many people watch a show . . . you can't listen to that. Everything isn't quantitative, doughnuts aren't better than lobster because more of them get eaten, you don't buy your dresses because they're cheaper by the dozen, bigger is not necessarily better . . ."

"No, but bigger *is* bigger." Elliot did not like where the conversation was going, or, more accurately, where Hazel was holding it.

"You know, when I was younger, when I was doing my communications theory in university, I completely bought into that po-mo notion that there was no essential difference between high and low culture. WRONG!"

Heads turned toward Hazel's raised voice.

". . . Because . . ." Hazel hoisted an empty bottle. "Elliot, do we need more wine?"

"Maybe a glass of a sticky with a shared dessert."

Hazel made a face like a baby rejecting a spoon, muscling her lips into a moue and crushing her eyes shut.

"Not partial to sweet wines, Hazel?"

"Make mine a Cognac . . . and no dessert for me. What about late-night? The audience is gonna be tiny no matter what we put on. We can't pimp enough A-list celebs to compete with the American slate, so why not chase an entirely different part of the market, one that's younger and smarter?"

"They are mutually exclusive." Elliot needed to piss. He excused himself, hoping that Hazel's drunkenness would help her forget what they were talking about in his absence. He looked back from the door to the washroom to see her waving down a waiter. Too much was made of wine, Elliot thought. In the end it was just booze.

He planted himself in front of a urinal. Finishing the schedule gave him a sense of accomplishment, one without the protracted anxiety that came with finishing a script. Scripts went on to be judged, and, despite all the hands in their realization, the author always assumed the ultimate responsibility for failure. Never mind that directors or actors would be credited for success — a bomb was the scribbler's fault. These shows and pilots, on the other hand, would be commissioned with conditions, and Elliot would simply sit back and wait to see whether they met expectations. Finally he was the ultra-audience, sprawled on some elevated couch, like a Roman emperor, in judgement. As an executive, it would be he who assigned blame, even if the mistakes were his own.

Surely, though, there must be an upside to being in the creative end of the business. He was trying to think what it was when a man stepped up to the urinal immediately next to his and noisily unzipped. This was strange; there were four other pissoires available. Elliot turned to get a quick look at the man and found that he was staring straight back.

"Beautiful evening," the man said. His white hair was combed back over a wide head. The ghostly mane was long for a man of his years, running to the collar of a bespoke jacket.

"'Tis," said Elliot.

"So we meet. Fortuitous, us being in here alone."

"How so?" Elliot was putting himself back together in what he hoped didn't appear to be a panic.

"We don't have much time." The man looked over his shoulder and then back down toward his dick. "So I will be direct. You've had a hand in the privates."

"Before you continue . . ." Elliot saw that in his haste he had captured a corner of shirttail in his fly. It was stuck.

"I want you to —"

"Look, no offence, I'm flattered, but —"

"Nobody has to know. The offer is there. I trust you understand me."

"I —" Elliot pulled the fabric free, tearing it, and closed his trousers. He rinsed his hands, shaking them dry as he dashed for the door.

"I'm not asking that you do anything you don't want to, certainly nothing unlawful, merely that when you're done there . . ."

"Thanks . . . but no thanks."

Hazel was slurping from a snifter when Elliot returned to the table.

"I saw that!" she said.

"There was a guy in the john."

"Yeah, that's what I'm saying. I didn't notice he was here."

"Who?"

"Janeck Klima. He must have seen us."

"This guy . . . I think he was trying to proposition me."

"The man who runs CTV?" Hazel now whooped. It was a hillbilly holler; Elliot felt the wait staff bristle. "Klima what? Offered to blow you? Not likely. You must have got the signals crossed. That is too rich."

"He runs CTV?"

"The corporate parent, these days. I saw him scurrying to the washroom after you went in. He must have been waiting for a chance. What did he say to you?"

"I . . . geez . . . I'm not sure. I assumed he was, you know, toilet trading."

Hazel threw her head back and let laughter shake her. Her neck made Elliot think of a tall birds, herons or cranes, and he wanted to kiss her. She buckled a bit, so funny did she find the thought, bringing her knee in across her body as if to stop from peeing.

"Perhaps we should get the check," Elliot said.

"Yeah," said Hazel. "Let's go to your place."

EN ROUTE TO Elliot's apartment Hazel made the cab swing by a 7-Eleven so that she could buy, she said, "a deck of fags." She tried lighting one up in the taxi but was stopped by the driver.

Once in the door, before Elliot had even removed the key, Hazel made straight for the kitchen and lit a cigarette off the toaster. She wasn't much practised in smoking, holding it away after a puff and yet somehow still managing to get smoke in her eyes. There was three-quarters of a bottle of La Gramière, a wine from the southern Rhone that Elliot admired, on the kitchen counter. She helped herself, pouring a hefty measure in a tumbler, and called for Elliot.

The hand holding the cigarette was around his neck and she pulled him in with all her weight. Her kisses were ravenous; she shoved her tongue against his and he could feel her teeth. As abruptly as she was on him, she pushed him away and stepped to lean against the counter. She took another graceless draught of the cigarette and tossed it in the sink.

"I don't smoke," she said. "But sometimes I feel like I want to."

She grabbed him by the belt, using it as a lead to yank him closer even as she rushed to undo it.

Making their way to his bed, shirts were shed. It seemed imperative to Hazel that they be stripped naked, and once they were on the sheets she slid her whole length over him, getting an urgent fix of skin to skin, as much as she could at once. With her crooked arthritic claws she hauled on his cock as if it were a rope.

She was full to bursting with desire. This Elliot knew because Hazel said so. She was the most garrulous lover he would ever know, only ceasing her shameless talk if her mouth was full of him.

"I soooo need a good fucking, Elliot," she said. She shoved his shoulders flat to mattress and climbed atop.

Not only did she demand her needs, she narrated the act. "Now you've got your fucking cock right fucking inside me, Elliot, now you're driving it. Hah, now you've got your hands on me, don't you!"

This let Elliot take his pleasure twice, having it and hearing it again. They were commands and congratulations at once.

Her voice grew hoarser and more tremulous as she drew closer and closer to coming. The language fell apart — first into strands of words: "this like this, to me, yes, here in me here," and then to guttural dissociated animal sounds: "tum-tum," she said, and "wasssawass," then *grrrrs* and grunts and purrs leading up to a swallowed scream that took all her air and dropped her, limp, onto his chest. The cry finished him; he could wait no longer, and the rope went over the side, racing over the gunnels as the anchor sank back to the bottom of the sea.

She rested for no more than three minutes and then began to vibrate like a motor. She pawed at him for more, but he wasn't capable. She crawled off and walked to the kitchen, giving him a show of exquisite ass on the way. He could hear the cupboards opening. She came back with a teacup full to the brim with Cognac; with her mouth half full of it, she kissed him. She pulled his hair and said, "You fuck me again." That was enough to bring Elliot around.

And once more after that, after which she seemed to go into a faint and then a half-sleep of content and satiation. She murmured and whispered, nothings, incomplete thoughts, licks of the unconscious. "No wife? No family?"

"Divorced," he said, and then, perhaps because he knew Hazel was falling away into brandy-drenched dreamlessness and would never recall, "And one kid. A son. Named Mark. You've probably seen him on television. He played the adorable Little Ricky on *Family Planning*. Unfortunately, with puberty . . . It wasn't just him, the show was winding up, there were enough episodes for a syndication package. That kind of thing, for a kid of that age . . . and after that his life got sort of out of control. He blamed television, the whole industry, and me for landing him the gig. He's in Soledad Prison now on drug and robbery charges."

Hazel was asleep. Her head was on his chest, a good place for it. Elliot closed his eyes.

HE WOKE A few hours later to the sound of Hazel retching. She was curled around the toilet in the en suite. She refused help. "Please, Elliot, I am so sorry, please leave me alone. I'm allergic to booze. I can't, I can't." He fetched her a glass of water and set it on the bathroom floor. She shooed him away again and, showing considerable pain, closed the door behind him as he left.

Elliot thought it best to leave her alone but after twenty minutes or so got worried and knocked. The door opened and Hazel brushed past him, making for her clothes on the floor.

"Hazel, please get into bed."

"I can't, Elliot. I can't. I can't believe what's happened. I am so sorry." She already had her skirt on and was looking around for her blouse. It was in the kitchen, Elliot knew.

"Sorry? No, that was wonderful, Hazel . . . I mean making love. It's terrible you were sick but . . ."

"No, Elliot, my behaviour was totally inappropriate."

"It was not. It was . . . much appreciated."

"This has happened before . . ." Hazel was now in her bra. Another piece of the night came back to her; she made for the kitchen to retrieve the shirt. Elliot followed. ". . . I simply cannot drink because I become an instant slut. I'll sleep with anyone."

"Well, now . . ."

"I am your subordinate, Elliot. Even if I wanted to have sex with you, which I don't —"

"You did."

"Even if I did, it couldn't happen. I feel terrible."

"You're a little hungover maybe."

"I'm still drunk." Hazel fished through her purse and found her cellphone. "What is the address here again?"

"Don't leave."

"I can just go downstairs."

"It's 272 Arrabal Avenue."

Hazel called a taxi.

"Elliot, this was entirely my fault. Don't feel bad about yourself."

"I was feeling great about myself, about you . . . about the both of us, together, until now. Stay. I'll sleep on the couch. We'll get breakfast in the morning."

Whether it was the thought of bacon or sausage or spending another few hours with Elliot, Hazel choked something back.

"Breakfast? No. Not breakfast together. Fucking you was bad enough."

"Really."

"Not like the sex was bad, just that . . . we will have to talk about it in a few days. I'm sorry."

She left.

⟅ ❧ ⟆

ELLIOT WOKE THE next morning before dawn, not emptied of desire, not satisfied and spent, but full, bloodily full, of want. He considered what Hazel had said about the inappropriateness of their having such relations and conceded to himself that she had a point. It probably was wrong, and would surely be awkward at the office. But the apartment seemed, in her absence, for the first time since Elliot had moved in, empty. Her laughter, her bawdy talk, her growls of delight, even her tearful protests and apologies had changed the place, seasoned it somehow, so that it needed her. He walked to the living room and the window that looked down on Wellington Street. He felt lonely. Sitting down to send an email to Stella to schedule a meeting with Hazel, in his office, that afternoon, he detected signs of life in his personal inbox.

From: lucy@kinokind.com
To: matou@aol.com
Subject: Jerry
Do you know anything about Jerry Borstein?

From: matou@aol.com
To: lucy@kinokind.com
Subject: Re. Jerry
He's a dick?

From: lucy@kinokind.com
To: matou@aol.com
Subject: Re. Re. Jerry
He's missing.

From: matou@aol.com
To: lucy@kinokind.com
Subject: Re. Re. Re. Jerry
WTF?

From: lucy@kinokind.com
To: matou@aol.com
Subject: Re. Re. Re. Re. Jerry
Drove to test screening in the valley three days ago
not seen since.

❧

HAZEL ARRIVED AT Elliot's office, as scheduled, but with her assistant, Troy, in tow. She was doing her best not to look hungover but moved with caution. Her outfit was layers of mourning charcoal over middle grey. Troy wore canary yellow stretchy jeans and a brown T-shirt with a picture of a man's flaccid pierced cock on the front. People were taking this casual Fridays thing to an extreme. Wait . . . it was Thursday.

The presence of Troy and the fact that Hazel carried Elliot's programming document from the previous evening was a clear announcement that she did not wish to discuss what had happened between them. Elliot was prepared to talk about nothing else.

"Troy will take notes," she said.

"I'm excited about the new season, sir," Troy offered.

"I'm glad to hear it. So, Hazel, do you have . . ."

"Yes. While I'm not sure I fully comprehend this 'weather office' model of the audience, I think the shows you've chosen to develop speak volumes."

"Where should we start?"

"Before we get to specifics there is a larger concern we should address. All of the projects you chose have been put forward by Toronto producers."

"Have they? I didn't notice, but I suppose that's to be expected."

"I know you've found some of our discussions about the balkanized funding regime for Canadian film and television less than interesting —"

"Yes. Much less than interesting."

"We still have to face the fact that some of the shows are going to have to be produced in the regions. And besides the funding, there is the organization's national mandate."

"Mandates are sort of wish lists," said Elliot, "don't you think?" And with the exception of *501 Pennsylvania*, I didn't see many of them as being set particularly anywhere. Tell the producers they have to make the show in B.C. I know they were forever shooting projects out of Los Angeles up . . . er . . . over there."

"We could do that."

"Some establishing exteriors and b-roll from Washington and the rest is shot in a studio outside Vancouver . . . Jesus, it's a three-camera —"

"And at some level we will have to reflect the country."

"Okay, okay, like what?" Elliot didn't want to talk about programming television, he wanted to discuss how he and Hazel could find a way to continue having sex.

"In *The Wonderfuls*, Winnipeg plays itself," Hazel pitched.

"Why would it want to do that? Don't write that down, Troy. And didn't you find . . . the family name is 'Wonderful'? Isn't that a bit cute, a bit 'on'?"

"It seems the sort of show you are looking for."

"I liked parts. I loved the Amazing Kreskin but had to ask . . . why would a guy who can see the future move to Manitoba?"

"Excuse me, sir?"

"Yes, Troy."

"Just a point of information? Kreskin is not a psychic. He's a mentalist."

"Thank you, Troy."

"Another concern," said Hazel. "Before you put any of these shows into development, the producers should know that the CBC is going to have a proactive role in casting."

"Yes, I'd assumed we would be consulted, have approval . . ."

"More than that. The shows are going to have to reflect Canada's diversity."

"Isn't that what you just said?"

"In terms of the cast, not the locations. Ethnicity. The shows you picked are very white, and you've said yourself that's a problem with the current season."

"My mother's father was of Roma descent," said Troy. "And my father's grandfather was part Cree."

"Look," said Elliot. "And don't write this down, Troy. I could give a damn about race, creed, colour, sexual prefer-ence. It bores the shit out of me. I didn't particularly see any of these characters as being white or black or brown. You're picking a fight. You're writing, Troy. Stop that!"

"These are my own thoughts, Mr. Jonson. Talking about my Cree ancestry just opened something in me."

"All right." Elliot turned to Hazel. "We can take those con-cerns into account, but within reason. Obviously the Wonder-ful kids can't be Chinese with a black mom and a Turkish dad."

"I think we would get in trouble assuming that," said Hazel. "They could be adoptive, or they might be from ear-lier unions . . ."

"Right." Elliot thought of Ascencion: his estranged son's stepmother was a Salvadoran lesbian.

"It's not just people of colour. We've had complaints that there haven't been enough Ukrainians."

"That's absurd," said Elliot. "How would you know?"

"You say that and you can expect the Congress of Ukrainian Canadians to intervene at the next CRTC licence renewal," said Hazel.

"Funny, you used to have to change your name from Levitch to Lewis, now it's the other way around."

"Can I write that down, sir?" asked Troy.

"No," said Elliot. "What I'm getting at is, regardless of all that, you simply have to cast the best actors."

From the silent glance exchanged between Troy and Hazel, Elliot judged this was a dramatic departure from practice.

"But," said Hazel, "when we have exhausted the supply of good actors available to a particular project . . . ?"

Elliot looked away and out his window. Freezing drizzle made the view gelatinous. A slice of milky lake was visible beyond the convention centre. He knew from experience that network meddling never made a television project better. But Hazel was making it clear that if Elliot were to have his way, he would have to take a hand.

Spring was always so far away in Canada. At Locura Canyon the cover crop between the vines would be green by now, the occasional wildflower showing. Walt would be squinting at the canes, anticipating and worrying about bud break. Hazel was consulting her BlackBerry.

"Leo Karek is apoplectic."

"Why?"

"I sent him an email earlier, giving him the broad strokes of the changes you are proposing —"

"Are you punishing me for what happened last night?"

Troy looked at his sneakers.

"I had better go see him." said Hazel. "Put this fire out."

"No," said Elliot, standing. "I'll sort Leo."

LEO WAS WAITING for Elliot in the middle of the television newsroom. It was a vast space, open concept taken to ridiculous extremes. (There was a report on Elliot's desk detailing how this workplace design was proving to be a complete failure. The CBC had been warned it would be, by a number of highly paid consultants. Elliot had asked, in a widely addressed email, why the Corporation had gone ahead with a plan it knew would fail. Nobody responded.) By positioning himself in the centre of this forum, Leo was showing that he desired a public confrontation. Elliot, soured by Hazel's conduct, was more than happy to give it to him. The asshole was standing with his hands on his hips and his chest out, like a gunslinger, when Elliot finally reached him.

"Hazel tells me you're having a kitten."

"What the hell do you know about news!"

"That it's on a lot and is generally a downer."

"A 'downer,' Hollywood? Is Afghanistan a 'downer'?"

"And how. Mostly it's a mystery. You guys certainly can't explain it."

"I will not have the flagship news program of the national public broadcaster turned into another A&E circus."

Leo was speaking loudly, almost shouting, and had drawn the attention of the nearby cubicle workers, whose heads were popping up out of their boxes like prairie dogs.

"Nothing has happened yet. These are proposals."

"Move 'the depressing stuff' to the back half of the show?" Leo scoffed.

"Why not? What's the urgency, Leo? When was the last time news broke at ten thirty? Have you heard of the Internet, Leo? Twitter? BlackBerrys and iPhones? *Cable* news is obsolete, and you're in network. And as for editorial opinion or analysis, I can get that, custom-made for my particular bigotry, at any of a number of blogs."

"I won't see the news service, which is at the very heart of this institution, reduced to just another TV show."

"You've been living with the illusion that it was ever otherwise?"

"You've got your fist up Rainblatt like a puppet, don't you."

"I haven't even bothered to consult him. Nobody cares anymore, Leo."

"Bullshit. I care, and I'm taking a stand on this one."

"I'm sorry to hear that. You've contributed so much to this organization. While I'm sorry to see you go, I want to say I admire your principle."

Leo looked perplexed and then pained, as if stricken with a headache of tectonic proportions. Elliot raised his voice now and spoke to as much of the room as could hear him.

"This may surprise you, but I have nothing but respect for Leo Karek's view of the role of News at the CBC. If I didn't have to balance different aspects of the operation at a time when it, candidly, teeters on bankruptcy, I think I could even share them. Leo has chosen his own beliefs over professional standing." Elliot spied Hazel, Troyless, watching from the distant wall. "Leo has had the integrity to walk away from the top broadcast news job in the country knowing full well that in the new media environment and economy, there's likely nothing out there for him better than sessional work at Ryerson. That takes guts. I'm impressed. And I want to make it clear that I will understand if many of you now rise in solidarity and follow him out the door. Not only will you be standing on principle, you will be seeing to it that fewer of your colleagues will have to be let go in the coming cuts."

A few people who had stood in their cubicles to watch were now discreetly getting back in their chairs. Those in Elliot's line of sight pretended to get straight back to work, donning their headphones or clicking with theatrical import on their keyboards. Karek didn't even bother turning around. Elliot offered Karek his hand.

"Best of luck with your future endeavours, Leo. You'll understand why, given how this has ended, I won't, as much as I would like to, be able to recommend you."

Elliot was on the elevator returning to his office when Hazel appeared before its closing doors.

"Leo's still just standing there," she said, as the doors closed.

SEVEN

HAZEL MADE A last-minute decision to take a ski holiday with her sister and a large flock of nieces and nephews, who were on March break, in Zermatt.

When she returned to work, Hazel's organizational skills were such that finding plausible reasons to avoid Elliot was child's play. Elliot guessed that his personal secretary, Stella, was conspiring in it, sharing his schedule with her longtime ally. Hazel was only ever in Elliot's presence with human shields. She was there for the endless meetings with the innumerable "heads" of this and that. She was in the room to witness the easy capitulation of the creative team of *501 Penn*. She was there when Elliot expressed his disappointment to the group at the result of their revisions. She was there when script after script failed to live up to its pitch, when compromises about casting and location and story were discussed. She was never there by herself.

Moreover, whenever they did have a conversation — with Hazel using Troy as her ventriloquist's doll, or Stella as chaperone — they seemed always at odds.

Why was he beating himself up over what shows he, they, programmed? It was Canadian television: if they produced a bum season, it wasn't like the citizenry didn't have something else to watch. The dial was flooded with options. Why did it matter if Hazel put on a bunch of well-intentioned efforts that nobody in the frozen expanse watched? It would be, in essence, a government project that hadn't worked. A season of television on the CBC was just a community wharf. There was no audience — they were all watching American crap on the Canadian privates — and there would be no uproar. Besides, Elliot had no intention of staying on at CBC; he had no personal stake in the coming season. He'd been too generous, was giving too much of himself to the job, to Canada, a country he'd quit. Why should it be his burden alone?

His financial situation had improved. His plan was to return to California as soon as he could safely lay claim to a severance package, likely the end of the first season with himself at the helm. He'd shake up News to save the Corporation a few dollars, see a couple of decent new shows onto the air, and then split. Back home he'd sell his house in Los Angeles and move up to the vineyard, dedicate himself full-time to the effort. He might have to make compromises, sell some Zin, downsize, but with more modest needs he could make a boutique operation work. The programming meant so much more to Hazel, why shouldn't she have a greater say? She wanted to carry some of the load, let her.

He called Hazel and got Troy.

"Ms. Osler is in a meeting."

"Fuck off, Troy."

"Are you harassing me, Mr. Jonson?"

"No, I'd do that with a stick. Tell Hazel she can have the fucking season she wants but she has to come up here and talk about it with me in private."

"'. . . fucking season . . .' — I'm writing that down."

"If it shows up as the title of your memoir, I want a thank-you."

"If I ever write a memoir, Mr. Jonson, you are sure to be mentioned."

Within the hour Stella told him that he had a three-o'clock with Ms. Olser.

"BUT DON'T TAKE from this that I'll necessarily have sex with you again."

"As long as the 'necessarily' is there. Just so intimacy is not excluded as a remote possibility."

"I was drunk."

"And that could happen again."

"I hope not."

"I enjoy being with you, Hazel."

"Don't say any more than that."

"I will do my best."

"So we're going with *Reason*?"

"Despite having seen photos of the host, this Dr. Palme, I defer to your judgement."

"What about *501 Penn*?"

"The pilot sucked. I'm sending them back to remake it as a comedy."

"It was a comedy."

"So they said. They'll work on it for another year and then

you can tell them it doesn't fit with whatever new direction we are taking next season."

"*Les Les?*"

"Christian wingdings from Alberta are going to say we are encouraging homosexuality."

"Imagine if we could encourage anything."

"Dealing with that noise will be your responsibility."

"Done."

"I'm going to have to undertake some radical changes in News. Do you keep giving Leo Karek my cell numbers?"

"Just gave it to him once. There a problem?"

"Teary, pleading calls begging for his job back one night and then drunken railing the next. I gotta get a bag of new phones."

"'A bag of new phones'?"

"It's a Hollywood thing. Also, you personally will contact all the projects that aren't going to move ahead and say it was your call to kill them."

"This is how you're trying to get into my pants?"

"You're the one getting her kicks from being steward of the public trust. It comes with a cost."

"Agreed, with reluctance."

"And leave the late-night problem to me. I think I have a solution."

⌒ ❧ ⌒

TO STOP HIMSELF from pitching forward and tumbling, Elliot zigzagged, tree to tree, grasping low branches. He let the momentum aid, not rule, him on this descent. He was almost swinging, with orangutan style and pace, down the incline.

At the bottom of the cut it was dark enough that the funk of the rotting leaves and the rising damp from the thawing earth were his primary sensation. Smelled like a right-bank Bordeaux passing its best days. His eyes adjusted and he saw enough to advance. He feared that calling out for Benny Malka would alert other ravine dwellers to his presence and Elliot might end up bitten, bashed, or raped by something. But the ravines ran for miles. And so, once he started closing in on the general vicinity of Rainblatt's house, Elliot felt he had no choice and bellowed, "Bennnnnnnnny!"

He had done so only thrice before getting a response.

"Who the fuck wants to know?"

The voice came from above and to his right. Elliot looked up. There was Benny, hairier and maybe filthier than Elliot had last seen him, perched on a moss-covered log, reading the *Post and Leader*.

"It's me, Elliot Jonson, we met here before . . ."

"The fresh fuck from the Corpse. Which rich bastard's house you fall out of this time?"

"I came looking for you."

"I'm reading this article here, by Paddy O'Mara . . . Your numbers are fucked."

"They aren't mine. The current season was scheduled and in production by the time I got here."

"So the worse they do, the better your slate will look next season?"

"I don't have the resources to promote them. And you know what? That paper is three days old."

"So?"

"So the two people who would bother to read a newspaper column about TV have already forgotten."

"Why are you really here?"

"I want you back."

"Is this like an intervention? Did my wife put you up to this? Was it my sponsor?"

"The current late-night guy, he was supposed to attract a younger, hipper demographic and, well . . . he's getting old and his act even older."

"How long can anyone play the ingenue or the young turk? Entertainers should never paint themselves into that corner."

"You know the way out of that jam?" asked Elliot.

"I think James Dean took a Porsche Spyder to Cholame, California."

"No, you keep going, you keep driving . . . on and into the desert for a few years and come back to do character work."

"Yeah, sure . . . absofuckinglutely fascinating. You got any more vino?"

"What do you think?"

"About what?"

"Coming back to do a late-night show."

Benny threw down the newspaper. He gave his head a violent shake, flapping his lips the way Cheeta, the chimpanzee on *Tarzan*, would do when frustrated. "If you keep insisting on tormenting me, I'll come down there and fuck you up."

"I'm making a genuine offer."

"Then you're an idiot . . . Oh wait, right, you're the vice president of English services. 'Idiocy' in the job description."

"I'm serious."

"I live in the ravines. I haven't had a haircut or a shower in over a year. My last show was one of the most embarrassing bombs in the history of Canadian television. Surely you can get someone more qualified, even if it is a scale gig."

"Since you came down here, Benny, shame has died. It doesn't exist anymore."

"You *are* serious."

"The comeback is at least an angle to get some press attention, more ink than I could possibly afford. Think of *Entertainment Television* . . . it'll be the best story of their year. Cleaning you up, delousing and shaving you, it's the ultimate makeover. Nobody can do worse in that time slot than now and . . . yes, I had assumed, given your current circumstances, where you're indigent and your last show was a bust, it would be a scale gig."

Benny jumped from his tree and scurried with surprising speed to Elliot. His piss stink was strong enough to precede him.

"No fuckery from any amateurs or dabblers at the network."

"Done."

"Small cadre of showbiz pros."

"It will have to be modest, given the budget."

"No monkey costume, just a jacket and tie, no trying to be hip, no world music, a small, tight house band, a jazz trio. No nice writers, no writers that people at the network like. I want bitter, lonely old bachelors and fat chicks, or the new young guys with the talent and energy that scare the hacks shitless — real comedy writers. Anybody who's taken a drink with the head of Comedy Development at the Banff Television Festival — immediately disqualified."

"Old unemployable writers are good, and young guys with no credits or agents . . . as long as they are few."

"Simple set . . . Get Elwood Glover's desk out of storage."

"We're on the same page."

Benny scratched himself and smelled his fingers. "I *have* lost weight," he said. "And the beam is lower . . . not in terms of quality — how could it be? — but the sort of numbers a show needs to survive."

"Five hundred thousand is the new million."

"It's nice in the ravine." Benny shivered.

"Is it?"

"Yes . . . but everyone wants to be on television." Benny turned and strode into the shadows as if he were practising an exit from the stage. Elliot hauled himself up toward the lambency bleeding from Avenue Road. He'd go to that liquor store at Summerhill and score a decent bottle of wine.

Cholame, where Jimmy Dean bought it, wasn't twenty-five miles from Elliot's vines.

PART THREE

His winnowing fork is in his hand, and he will clear his
threshing floor, gathering his wheat into the barn and
burning up the chaff with unquenchable fire.

— Matthew 3:12

ONE

ELLIOT'S TORONTO CELLPHONE chimed at least five times before he realized it was his. With half the CBC on summer holiday, it rang only when Hazel called from a show in production with news of one crisis or another. She could have it — watching disappointing rushes, auditing hastily imagined story revisions . . . Elliot shivered at the thought of the *501 Pennsylvania* writing room: one-time stand-up comedians trying to force out the funny like old men straining at stool, trading sour quips, seeing who could out-blue the other with tragic accounts of indignities visited on their genitals or anus. Assuming the call was from Hazel, he didn't bother looking at the display before answering.

"Fire them, Hazel."

"No, this is Mike. Hazel your latest conquest?"

"No, she — she works with me." Elliot glanced now: 310 area code. "How did you get this number, Mike?"

"Allan, Lucky's EA, had it."

"How could he . . . ?"

"I'm flying in."

"To Toronto?"

"I'm on a jet right now. Good news."

"Which is?"

"I'm coming to talk with my newest client."

"Who is?"

"Barry Hart!" said Mike. "He ditched Herb Devine."

"Congratulations."

"It's a reshoot for that romcom *Indiana Wants Her*, a couple of scenes, the ending tested badly and they still want to release it before Christmas." Mike was chewing on something as he talked. "Barry needed to see me about some problems he has with the director concerning this sort of funny, sort of Mexican accent he wants to do. At this delicate stage of our relationship I want to be there for him."

"Speaking of testing, what's this about Jerry Borstein?"

"Clarification, please, Elliot."

"He went to some test screening in the Valley and disappeared?"

"That's the first I've heard he was going to a test," said Mike. "I never liked Jerry."

"'Liked,' past tense?"

"You said he had disappeared. Did you mean he's actually hiding somewhere?"

"No."

"But you'd tell me if you knew?"

"Why?"

"How about we say Fuck Jerry — there's something I need to talk to you about."

"Sure. When do you get in? What's your flight number?"

"Flying private, belongs to some Azerbaijani oil company — Lucky Silverman is on their board. He lent it to me. Barry's still shooting when I arrive so I'm meeting him on set at . . . Toronto is the same time zone as New York, right?"

"Yes."

". . . at around four thirty this afternoon. Maybe I could come by your new presidential suite on the way."

"Bad idea," Elliot said.

"Why don't you come by the set then, around four this afternoon? Barry's gonna be late anyway."

"Where is the location?"

Elliot heard Mike shout the question to someone.

"Queen's Road . . . no, what? Queen Street, does that make sense?"

"West or East?"

"West or East?" shouted Mike. "West."

"See you there." Elliot hung up, wondering why he had dismissed Mike's offer to meet at the CBC.

෧ 🟐 ෨

THEY WERE SHOOTING a couple of scenes of *Les Les* in a storefront on Queen Street West that day. The streetscapes there doubled easily for any in North America, so it was a commonly used location. Elliot decided to drop by the set unannounced, en route to his meeting with Mike.

Elliot did not enjoy film shoots. Inefficient enterprises, they tried his patience. The majority of the workforce did nothing for most of their long days. And though their job might involve little more than pushing a cart, the hype machinery of showbiz told them they were more skilled and worthy than someone doing the same thing at Costco.

What was more, atomizing the script into various shots sucked the life from the drama (film editors, unacknowledged as the most important agents in cinema, did their best to breathe it back in). The process had overtaken the purpose; it was the most managed of mediums. On a film set, storytelling was, too often, the last thing on anybody's mind.

Elliot found the location easily enough; seven long trucks, in Airstream silver, occupied the street outside the retail frontage. Beefy crew members fretted over a piece of hardware in the open back of one of the trucks, five men and two gals all wearing headsets and utility belts. They were studying a hinged joint on a heavy metal stand, for lights or accessories, Elliot assumed. Maybe they'd found it amidst all the other mechano but could not remember its function. Maybe they were trying to give it a pet name, dub it a "wingy" or a "ding flap" or a "treble futz." This sort of thing took many hours in the business of making movies.

So entranced were they with their pole they did not notice Elliot passing by them and walking into the location. They were between set-ups. Elliot gathered this from the presence of the rest of the crew around a temporary table set with snacks and coffee. No one stopped his advance, so Elliot moved toward the glow of the set.

The camera was a new-generation digital affair, and unattended. Hanging by a string from the arm of the tripod were the sides for that day, the script pages reduced to four-inch by five-inch cards. Elliot could not resist.

INT. A women's clothing boutique -- DAY

Betty is dismissively looking at items on the racks. Claudette enters from a change room off. She is wearing a green pantsuit. She stands, rigidly, waiting for inspection. She looks like Gumby.

> CLAUDETTE
> How do I look?

Betty stands and walks to Claudette.

> BETTY
> That is so hot.

> CLAUDETTE
> "Hot"? I don't want "hot," this is a job interview.

> BETTY
> You look just like the supervisor at my juvenile detention centre, Mrs. O'Leary.

> CLAUDETTE
> Had sex with her, I suppose?

                    BETTY
          Why else go to juvy?

Betty adjusts the collar of Claudette's
jacket.

                 BETTY (CONT'D)
          I'm proud of you.

                  CLAUDETTE
          Going for this job?

                    BETTY
          And doing so boldly as
          an out lesbian.

                  CLAUDETTE
          What do you mean?

                    BETTY
          I was going to insist
          you bring it up.

                  CLAUDETTE
          They're probably not
          even allowed to ask.

                    BETTY
          Regardless--it's not
          important. They see

```
you in that pantsuit
and they are going to
know right away.
```

It wasn't bad, Elliot thought. Preachy and polemic, true. Half the dialogue was superfluous and would have been cut by a good editor. Claudette didn't have to say "How do I look?" when a much better line in was "That is so hot." It was too "on"; you could taste nothing but the fruit. The temptation to state what should be seen was acute in Canadian projects because of their poverty. Since his arrival, Elliot had read seemingly infinite variations on "You'll never guess what just happened!" What had happened was always something they could not afford to shoot.

The cast was rehearsing the scene with the director, an excited middle-aged guy trying to dress like a twenty-year-old to stay in the biz. The set was not so much lit as it was exposed; there was an eerie absence of shadow. You could cook an egg in the darkest corner.

The proposal Elliot had read a few months earlier called for two large women, but these actresses were, if a bit hefty for film and television, surely a healthy weight. The actress playing the Québécoise was wearing an unfortunate wig. Elliot thought for a moment it was a gag but soon saw it was merely a poorly made and ill-fitting blond piece that would steal every scene in which it appeared. Budget, no doubt, as was the case with the rushed lighting.

From where he stood Elliot could pick up their cadences as they ran their lines. The woman supposedly from Newfoundland spoke without a discernable accent, the other with the faintest French Canadian lilt. The Newfoundlander seemed engaged and witty, the French Canadian placid. They seemed to be playing it straight, so to speak, naturalistically, not leaning on or pointing at the jokes. It was being shot with a single camera, without an audience. The performance would not accommodate a laugh track.

It would never fly. It was a modest, faintly charming, and forgettable stage play, not a television comedy. TV didn't challenge expectations, it reinforced them. The English Canadian audiences wanted their Québécois angry, their Newfies Irish, their lesbians shrill and cock-starved. And while tame, the script was still too racy to air early enough in the evening schedule to attract a substantial audience.

Elliot abandoned the idea of introducing himself; it would only put the cast and crew on edge. He left as discreetly as he'd come.

Halfway down the block Elliot glanced in the window of a used book store and saw, with a paperback just about stuck to his face, Lloyd Purcell. This stopped Elliot so hard he stumbled. Lloyd was standing near the store's front window, not ten feet away, his chunky spectacles riding the top of his expansive bald head. He was wearing a mustard and mauve lumberjack shirt, something only a younger man could get away with. His jeans were shapeless. Lloyd wore the expression, not unlike a scowl, of someone in deep concentration. Elliot was close enough to see Lloyd's beady eyes darting across the page.

Elliot had not gone to see his old friend's play. He asked Stella to gather what few notices there had been in case he wanted to pretend he'd attended. But none of the reviews, all good, gave much of the plot away. Elliot guessed, given the comparative freedom of the second space of an obscure indie theatre, that it would not have been a plot-driven piece anyway. Stella also let Elliot know that despite the positive reviews, the houses were only modest, and it closed, on schedule, with a whimper.

Elliot liked Lloyd. He was saucy and candid. His wit had won him many friends in the writing fraternity of Los Angeles. Yet Lloyd always took his work seriously, was quite the opposite of Elliot in believing that what he wrote meant something. In the good days, Lloyd had been a frequent dinner guest; he never failed to make Lucy laugh, had her holding her pee, with his stories. But he drank too much and could never limit himself to "a couple of lines." These character traits were the first links in the chain of bad decisions leading to the east-end takedown — and front-page fiasco — that got him kicked out of the United States. There was Lloyd in the *L.A. Times*, shirtless, moon-faced, whitest guy busted, so pasty he glowed, being dragged from the building. Fast-tracked deportation of some Canadian fatty wasn't what they'd meant when they sang "straight outta Compton," but that was Lloyd's fate.

What was Lloyd reading in there this quieter day in Toronto? *According to Queeney*? Whatever it was, it generated enough mental enthusiasm that Lloyd was unconsciously sort of chewing as he read. Was that ever an unfuckable look. In the end, here was Lloyd Purcell without a pot to piss in, writing plays, having grown old, his gums flapping involuntarily as he read from a page held four inches from his face. That's what happened. Elliot kept going.

The *Indiana* reshoot was a further ten-minute walk.

It appeared Toronto was under occupation. The line of trucks and trailers for the production ran the length of three city blocks. Elliot's name had been left at a temporary security gate, one watched over by an armed guard. Elliot was directed to a numbered trailer.

On his way he saw the greensmen hoisting, by crane, a large tree from the back of a truck. Once the tree was in position, an animal handler brought a basset hound alongside to piss on the base of its trunk. Elliot recognized the dog from a billboard that had hung over Sunset Boulevard last year. Big picture, that one.

Elliot knocked. Mike's assistant Blair opened the door. "Come in," he scowled. The trailer's interior was comfortably appointed with couches and chairs, a small wet bar, and a couple of large-screen monitors. Mike was standing, talking on a cellphone. On the floor between Mike's feet, as if guarded, was a leather Coach cabin bag — containing, no doubt, the dozens of fresh cellphones Mike would need on the trip.

"Look, I'm sorry, I have a meeting that I really must . . . Okay, I, or maybe Blair, will get back to you. It's truly brilliant." Mike closed the phone and pointed the device at Blair. "This is what happens when shit gets to me without coverage." Now the phone was pressed against Blair's temple. "You read every script we are supposed to be looking at! Every one!"

It occurred to Elliot that this was the first time Mike had ever terminated a phone call when Elliot arrived for a scheduled meeting.

"Elliot," said Mike. His arms were open, cunt was coming in for a hug. "You look handsome in that suit."

"Thank you." Elliot looked down. Yes, he was always in a suit now.

"I've been in Toronto before, you know."

"I didn't."

"No, neither did I. Blair reminded me. For the TIFF. I was at that once."

"The film festival?"

"Yeah . . . but plane, hotel, screening, reception, dinner, hotel, plane. I coulda been anywhere. Many positive developments to tell you about, Elliot. Blair, can you get me a coffee?"

"There's coffee in that Thermos," said Blair.

"I want a soy latte."

Blair made a face and left the trailer.

"I enjoy good news," Elliott said.

"Lucky Silverman is going to be named president of the Motion Picture Association of America."

"Why is that a positive development?"

"Not directly for you, but . . . we are all on Lucky's team now. That position, it's a Washington position, not a Hollywood position. It's got incredible power. Jack Valenti had more pull than most members of the Reagan cabinet. And, in case you didn't notice, we're in the middle of a culture war. The enemy has mobilized their hillbillies, they're coming down from their mountains, we're in deep shit. We need friends inside the Beltway."

"By 'we' you mean the liberal Hollywood, drugs-and-sodomy-positive crowd?" asked Elliot."

"Yes."

"When I left Canada, many years ago, there was an ambivalence about arts and culture. That's been replaced by open hostility. The barbarians may have already closed the gate behind them, Mike."

"I'm not willing to concede defeat. The thought of having to live in Europe is too much for me to bear. I'm a patriot, goddamn it, and my America includes drugs and sodomy. And please don't include film and television in arts and culture, it'll just make the situation worse."

"I need you to ask Lucky to get me out of this CBC job."

"What? You're kidding, right?"

"I don't know."

"Your job was one of the things I wanted to talk to you about."

"In what regard?"

"It's secure? You think it's secure?"

"If it were an American network I guess I would be judged on the success of the upcoming television season. Here, I don't think it matters. It's more like a government department than a real network. Why?"

"Speaking of government departments, ever hear of a Jasper Crabb?"

"Jasper Crabb? The name is familiar, I . . ."

"Are you aware that there is an active investigation into your vineyard by the U.S. Department of Agriculture?"

"Who told you that?" What the fuck was this? Elliot wondered.

"Lucky Silverman. Elliot, this guy is connected like no one you know."

"Why does he care about the USDA and the vineyard?"

"While there is no way you, a witness but not a co-conspirator, could be compelled to return to the States to testify about the wiretap, if you had broken laws by illegally importing rootstock to the U.S. . . . you could face extradition."

"I thought you said this was good news."

"Lucky is in your corner." Mike retrieved his bag and took it to a couch, where he sat. "He'll watch out for your interests. Lucky is with a group that has discreetly funded the protection of the Sixth Amendment."

"The Sixth Amendment, remind me."

"Rights of the accused. This is progressive stuff."

Mike unzipped the bag. Elliot assumed he was getting a fresh phone with which to call Lucky, but instead he withdrew two loaves of bread. They were hollowed out. Mike bent down and began untying his Bruno Maglis.

"Bread?"

"Yeah, Barry's a Farinist, so . . ." Mike put them on. "They're actually not that uncomfortable, but you don't get much wear. Lucky says he's grooming Barry for politics but he'll have to be born again. A Farinist might get elected in California, but Barry's got better chances in Texas. He was born — the first time, that is — in Corpus Christi." Mike stood and walked a circle, trying out his bread shoes. "So I can report that you are happy being home in Canada, giving back to the country you were born in, leader in public service, blah blah?"

"No. This is temporary and getting more so quickly. I want to go home."

"Canada is your home."

"My intention, all along, was to get out of show business and live full-time in my vineyard."

"That place, the CBV . . ."

"The CBC."

"Whatever. It's not really show business, is it?"

"Well, no, but . . ."

"And I thought you said that wine you make is lousy."

"I never said that."

"Somebody did."

"I really don't know what point you are trying to make to me, Mike."

"Lucky Silverman, a man who is much more powerful than you seem able to grasp, needs you to stay out of Dodge. This wiretap business has the potential to . . . People in Los Angeles, a few people, would like nothing better than if you permanently relocated."

"Permanently, never."

"Don't mess with these people, Elliot."

"Is that a threat?"

"No. It's advice."

❦

From: lucy@kinokind.com
To: matou@aol.com
Subject: Mark
Not answering your cell. Mark in a dust-up in Soledad.
Broken index finger and some bruising. Dreadful for
his parole.

From: matou@aol.com
To: lucy@kinokind.com
Subject: Re. Mark
Was in meeting. Can't reach you. What happened?

An hour and six calls later, after a single ring, "Hello?" It was Lucy, finally.

"What happened?"

"He got in a scrap. Something to do with his conversion to Islam. The atmosphere is extremely tense — there are over six thousand inmates in a place built to hold twenty-five hundred."

"Is he hurt?"

"He's not a fighter."

"Jesus. We have . . . There has to be something . . . Can't we have him transferred to a better facility?"

"They are all bad, Elliot. It's punishment."

"Is he in danger?"

"I don't think it was that big a deal, words exchanged, a couple of punches thrown. And I understand that there is some protection from his community."

"What community?"

"Muslims," said Lucy.

"Right, Muslims . . . Lucy, I should come down there."

"There's nothing you can do. He's in solitary confinement now, but just a week."

"Oh god. Tell him I love him."

"I do, every time I visit."

"I . . . the thing . . . the thing is . . . I feel . . . Jesus . . ."

"Are you crying? Don't cry, Elliot."

"No, I'm nasal . . . humidity here, goddamn lake. There has to be something we can do."

Elliot listened. There was cycling static, the pops and pings of outer space raining on the line, but silence from Lucy.

"I'm doing everything we can," she finally said.

❧

"LOCURA CANYON," Bonnie answered.

"Hi, Bonnie. Is Walt nearby?"

"Elliot, long time no see."

"I have made several efforts —"

"Elliot, listen to me. Nobody is going to extend us credit. Walt's telling me you've got the best grapes he has ever seen out there and you won't even have bottles to put it in."

"The best he's ever seen — he said that?"

"That wasn't my point. As it stands the bank is going to own the first decent vintage of wine this place has produced."

"I'll sort it out."

"From up in Canada?"

"I'll try to come down. Don't say anything to anyone. But I'll try. Is Bill Diehl still the branch manager in SLO?"

"He's called me personally," said Bonnie.

"I'll talk to him."

"Sure you will."

"I'll refinance."

"Again?"

"It's the American way, Bonnie. Where's Walt?"

"He and Miguel are in the vines, he's got his cell."

"BEST SYRAH I'VE ever seen grown in California," said Walt.

"You're shitting me."

"Nope. And because their sites were coolest and they had a longer hang time, something about the pace of ripening, they're more northern Rhône in characteristic, but the sunny side, you know, Côte Brune . . . those kind of tannins and iron too, shows as blueberry ink, but fresh ink, you know what I mean?"

"Yeah, I do." Elliot adored the fresh ink of the northern Rhône but placed it farther south, at Cornas.

"Grenache is a few weeks off but the fruit is spectacular. I mashed a bunch up the other day, no colour but terrific juice. The Mourvèdre got the occasional lick of fog, which worried me first, but with the exposures there and the daytime heat it seems just the trick. I picked at Pradeaux, in Bandol, in 1990, that's what it reminds me of . . . You there, Elliot?"

"Yeah. This is . . . it's wow."

"I'm looking at Miguel right now and he's doing a dance . . ." Walt laughed and then said something in Spanish that Elliot couldn't quite make out. "He just tasted the Counoise and, you know, it's tart. It's got serious zip, Elliot. It's all sort of coming together. I mean it won't be anything like a Châteauneuf, anything at all . . . but it's gonna be a good wine."

"I'm coming down soon."

"Good idea. Bonnie's freaking out."

"I know. Thanks, Walt."

Elliot put the handset in the cradle. On the first two monitors hanging from the ceiling were talking heads, one newsy with affected gravity, the next chatty and smiley; on the third screen, forced jollity on a working kitchen set, easy-nutritious-low-cal-fun-for-the-whole-grain-family-entertain-at-home-Prozac cookies being baked; on the fourth, some brown people dancing around a downed jet fighter, cut to them dragging the barbecued pilot through the dusty streets of a faraway shithole. Daytime television. He spun his chair around and looked out toward Lake Ontario. Making genuinely good wine was an accomplishment. Rarer than most people supposed but not unprecedented on the Central Coast. Given what Walt was saying, Elliot's viticultural practices were vindicated: he wasn't a dabbler or a hobbyist. And if he could replace the Zin in the mix with Matou, he could make more than good wine — he could make great wine. He was trapped in his bullshit gig at CBC. It wasn't on. If people got out of his way, if he could do things as he knew they should be done, if he didn't have to forever take notes from morons. Someday a group of people, friends, would be having supper, the evening might be warm enough, even with the breeze, to eat outside, and the food would be good and the talk better and the stories funny and they would have wine, a twelve-year-old bottle of 303 Locura Canyon that Elliot had bottled ten years from now, and someone would taste it and say, "My, that's lovely." As urgently as he had needed to get out of Los Angeles, he now needed to get back to Enredo, to Locura Canyon Road and his vines.

TWO

ELLIOT CHANGED HIS mind. It *was* wise of Rainblatt to throw a party on the first night of the new season. The alternative was to sit at home and watch, waiting for something to go wrong. (Technical hitches were commonplace at the CBC. Elliot had asked about this and was told there was a system of "fault reports" in place. These, it turned out, were kept in an archive maintained by three staff positions with no authority to do anything at all.)

The choice of venue was Rainblatt's: the bar on the top of the Park Hyatt Hotel on Avenue Road. It was of a decent standard for a hotel bar, and possessed some personality. It was bursting and boisterous. Booking it for a private function, which was rarely allowed, was a show of Rainblatt's pull, his Toronto bona fides.

It being an evening with his superior and many subordinates, Elliot guessed he'd be putting away the whisky in quantity, so he took a taxi. En route he saw a billboard for tonight's premiere episode of *501 Pennsylvania* and a poster for *Reason* on a bus shelter.

Hazel was pacing outside the front doors of the hotel, hauling on a cigarette.

"Camels?" Elliot recognized the scent.

"I suppose. I bummed it off some guy with an American accent. I'm going to have to buy a pack."

"There's not much that can be done about it now," Elliot said. "It's out there."

"What is?"

"The season."

"I'm not nervous about the season. It's that bar up there." Her vertigo. "The damn thing is open — the balcony, it's open."

"Have a quick drink."

"You'd like that, Elliot, wouldn't you?" Hazel said, looking him in the eye. "I don't think I can do this."

"It's really your party, Hazel. You have to."

Elliot presented his arm. Hazel crushed the last inch of cigarette beneath one of her snakeskin mules and, wincing, let Elliot lead.

MOST OF THOSE filling the room had only a passing association with the production of the new slate of shows. They'd bought those bus-shelter ads or signed off on some payments to the production companies. Nevertheless, they were claiming ownership, which Elliot reasoned was a good thing.

Rainblatt was anchored to the bar. He beckoned Elliot to join him. Hazel's breathing had become irregular as soon as they'd stepped into the elevator; now, looking across the room to its celebrated balcony, its view over the sparkling downtown and the great lake beyond, she was a clattering flag of tiny gasps. Her fingers were boring into his muscle. He dragged her along.

"Hazel," said Rainblatt. "Get you ahhh a drink?"

"Double bourbon," said Hazel.

"Do you have Woodford's?" Rainblatt called to the bartender. "And a glass of red wine."

"Are you sure you want a bourbon, Hazel?" asked Elliot.

"I thought I said a double."

"I dare say you've spent the odd evening h-here, eh, Elliot?" asked Rainblatt.

"Once or twice." Elliot sniffed the house red, supposing he had to drink it out of courtesy. Why did people assume that, being in the business, he must have wine?

"C-come, really?" Rainblatt grinned as though he was privy to some secret of Elliot's.

"I think so."

"I would have thought it was one of the last refuges."

"How's that, Victor?"

"The smoking. Out on the balcony. Isn't this the last venue in Toronto?"

"Is it?"

"Yeah," said Hazel, who looked to be weighing whether it was worth going out there to have one. She consumed the first half of her whisky in one draught. "Bartender?"

"I suppose you are even a greater pariah in Cah-California than here in Toronto. Don't worry, I smoke too, love a cigar." Rainblatt leaned in, stage-whispered. "When you ahhhh snuck out for one during that dinner party at our house I was desperate to join you." Rainblatt recounted several other occasions when, during meetings, Elliot had absented himself. Elliot supposed he would have to puff on a cigar later so as to continue to prop up the plausibility of Rainblatt's reasoning. In every instance but the one at Rainblatt's house, he'd merely been avoiding the man.

"And, ahhhh," said Rainblatt, "I thought this might be a half-pack evening."

"I'm not worried," said Elliot. "The promotion hasn't been the best, but the return to the core mandate bought us all kinds of free press."

"I have it on good authority," Hazel said, pounding back the remainder of her drink, "that *501* will be favourably reviewed in the *Post and Leader*. And I know the view that *Reason* is the best thing on television this year is held by every significant television critic in the country."

"Do we have those?" asked Elliot, getting a laugh from Rainblatt.

"I only wish I could watch the shows," said Rainblatt. "But this damn thing with my balance. I'm sure it's going to be a great season."

"Thanks to Hazel," Elliot offered.

"Top managers always take the blame and always assign the credit."

Hazel openly rolled her eyes.

"Nothing so noble, Victor. It really was Hazel's season. "

"Then I suppose you'll have to share this with her. Bartender?" Rainblatt pointed to something below the bar.

The bartender produced a bottle of Isabelle d'Orange.

Were Elliot's face and neck reddening like a boy's? Of course: it all made sense. Rainblatt's reminding him of his unexplained absence from the dinner party was the bait, and then that line of inquiry about the smoking; now, like a trial lawyer, he was entering the incriminating exhibit into evidence. Of course Rainblatt had noticed Elliot studying the bottles, of course he noticed when one of two rare articles went missing. A pair was a pattern.

"I thought I had two of these in the cellar, but when I went to fetch it there was only the one. I must have drunk the other one without knowing, though Pat Cahill says that's unlikely."

"Cahill?" said Elliot, unable to take his eyes off the bottle.

"He said I would have remembered it. I asked him what would be a good bottle to give you, and he said this one."

Elliot noticed tightness in his chest and let it go with a breath. "Thank you very much, Victor." Rainblatt hadn't a clue that the first bottle had been nicked and subsequently chugged. It was only some old wine in his basement. "I really do appreciate it."

"It's hardly much of a gift for me, though, is it?" said Hazel polishing off her bourbon. "I don't drink."

Rainblatt laughed, thinking Hazel was cracking a joke. "Stella tells me you're off to California?" said Rainblatt to Elliot.

"Yes, flight early tomorrow morning. Just for a couple of days. Things seem under control here."

"Business?"

"Pleasure, actually. My winery."

"At least you won't be in L.A. with those nutty Faranistas."

"Faranists. What about them?"

"They arrested one on Barry Hart's property, he was carrying a large bread knife and had a list of big Hollywood names. Don't worry, Elliot, I didn't see yours there."

"Any screenwriters at all?"

Rainblatt seemed not to have heard him. "Sure seem to be a lot of crazies out there."

"California's the last hope before you'd have to drown yourself in the Pacific," said Elliot. "A diet, a religion, a high concept . . . people out there are predisposed to believe."

"Come out to the balcony," said Rainblatt. "It's time for a toast."

"On the balcony?" said Hazel, and then rattled her empty glass at the bartender.

FROM UP THERE Toronto looked the perfect place. The concrete and steel of the city seemed borne on a sylvan cloud, a metropolis in the high canopy. A turboprop plane approached the airport on the near island in the lake. It was a Miyazaki movie. Elliot reflected that he hadn't really ended up in such a bad spot. He would come back here and visit after his permanent return to California.

Elliot was sure Mike was overstating the danger in his going back to the States, but as a precaution, he'd had Bonnie book him a flight through San Francisco. Nobody from Los Angeles would see him. What harm could come of a few days among his vines?

Rainblatt was crowded to the balcony's edge by his audience. Elliot looked back over his shoulder and saw that Hazel was nerving it, her back pressed to the stone wall nearest the passage back into the bar, readied for a quick escape.

"Please, everyone," said Rainblatt. "Don't worry, I will be brief." The chuffed murmur of the free-boozed diffused in the hope that Rainblatt meant it.

"Such an evening befits the launch of our new television

season," said Rainblatt. "Blue skies — the sort we've been talking about for a long time — above. I don't mind admitting that things were b-b-bad — I doubt that if Elliot Jonson had known how bad they were he ever would have accepted his position. Thank goodness he did."

There was a ripple of applause, faint and fake enough to tell Elliot that, for those attending, he was mostly unknown or disliked.

"The change in leadership brought bold changes in direction. We should all be thankful that Elliot Jonson chose to come home. I want to —"

"Can't hear back here!" called Hazel.

"Sorry," said Rainblatt. He pulled a chair from a nearby table and stood on it. "I want to, to toast . . ." Rainblatt raised his glass — which Elliot recognized, in retrospect, as the fatal miscalculation. "Ell —"

Elliot believed that he had started for Rainblatt, that he had made to save him. And there were others, too, who saw their Head in Chief teetering and reached out to help. But the accident, as accidents always do, transpired in an instant. It was over before any of them could lower their raised glasses. And yet it was experienced — at least by Elliot — frame by frame.

Rainblatt's screwy semicircular canals must have corrected his momentum in the wrong direction, for as he started to list, to tip, he seemed to push off from the chair, kicking it aside, as if it were part of some acrobatic party trick. He actually cleared the parapet cleanly, his feet flying high. He fell backward, his arms windmilling a desperate backstroke, twisting as he dropped. His head went first, facing the street so that his last sight would be the ROM Crystal he so despised, surely looking to Rainblatt like a baby barn rocketing to the heavens.

"—ioooooooooooooooot . . ."

❧ •• ☙

IT WAS, ELLIOT thought, peculiar to feel the need to see "news" of an event at which one had been present not ninety minutes earlier. Was nothing reality until it was on TV? And yet here he was, back at his condo, searching his television for coverage of Rainblatt's plunge.

During his perfunctory interrogation by the Toronto police, Elliot had noticed a sizable contingent of CBC newsies at the scene. Both the national and local teams were there, and a drunk from the radio service. But the story was not flagged in the billboard at the top of the national broadcast. Elliot clicked over to Pulse 24 in time to see a shot of someone hosing down the sidewalk outside the hotel but heard only, "For Pulse 24, I'm Peter Warne." He switched back to CBC and muted the volume; perhaps they would have an item together by the end of broadcast. He heard a cork pop in the kitchen. Hazel.

She'd poured herself a mug of the Isabelle d'Orange. "Poor bastard. To go like that. For a while there, when Victor caught wind of the plan to sell parts of the service to the Chinese, I worried that the Prime Minister's Office or CSIS might have his brakes fixed, but . . ."

"How's the wine?" Elliot asked, reaching for his best stemware.

"Oh, that's right, this is the bottle Victor gave you. If I hadn't seen it myself I would have assumed he'd been pushed."

Examining the bottle, Elliot saw that Hazel had poured a good quarter of its contents into her mug. He filled his glass to one-third its capacity. The wine had lost all colour at its edge; where the liquid met the glass was as clear as water. Then there came a wider region of amber or brickish orange. Only at the very centre of the sample, with a salmon aura, was there true red: glossy and sanguine like the heart of a small animal. Elliot sniffed it.

"I've never seen anyone die before," said Hazel, walking from the kitchen to the couch in the living room. "Wait, that's not true, I saw my father die. Never seen . . . a fatal accident, I guess."

"Are you okay?" asked Elliot.

He didn't hear Hazel's response; he was mesmerized by the aroma of the wine. That this was made from fruit was now difficult to detect: it was the scent of a world and a time. And it was transitory. There was something capric at the start, not at all pleasant, which was soon overwhelmed by truffle nail polish and sweetened coffee . . . Vietnamese iced coffee. These notes did not endure. Everything about it was fleeting. Was that curry? Not the genuine article, but the supermarket powder in his mother's spice rack? No, it was cinnamon . . . no, fresh gingerbread, and then . . . sun-baked earth, horses, roses wilting in the sun, a woman's neck.

"Did you say something, Hazel?"

"Helga! Who called Helga?"

"I got Troy to do it. He was great there tonight, poised. He kept it together, showed . . ." Elliot was distracted by the fumes from the glass. "I don't know, what? Grace under pressure? Never would have expected that."

"Helga. Poor woman."

"Yes, it's going to be . . . for her, difficult, I guess . . ."

Tentatively, Elliot took a sip. There were berries, or an extract, raspberries and blackberries squished between your fingers, there was unmistakably toffee and tamari, there was pan juice of roasted game, partridge or hare, and something from a hunting trip he'd taken with his father and his Uncle Bert, in the fall of the year, near Baie d'Espoir in Newfoundland, the decaying vegetation beneath the trees . . . and it was gone. The bottle was so old, its contents so delicate, that the oxygen in the air of the room was burning it up.

"How do you like the wine, Hazel?" Elliot thought he would try again.

"The wine?"

"Yes, the wine Rainblatt gave me."

Hazel sniffed at her cup and then gulped. "It doesn't have much of a taste, does it? It's . . . God! It reminds me of something . . . When I was a kid, we spent part of the summer in the family cottage in Muskoka and there was a smell of the woods . . . or no, that's not it." She inhaled again. "My grandmother, she was this wild woman. Is it her perfume, or the smell of her perfume fading on her clothes? When I was fourteen years old, she took me on a shopping trip to Paris. Or that's what she told my parents. We weren't there two days before we went on to Italy, to Siena. She had a rendezvous with a lover there. We stayed at his estate out in the country and in the morning, among the trees . . . I loved her, my Gran. She's the one who insisted I be called Hazel."

"After her?"

"No, everyone called her Mitzy. It was because I was born

at the height of a hurricane, Hurricane Hazel."

"Wine with notes of 'love affair in the country.' I got them too. It's high praise for a drink."

"More like 'fading, questionable memory of love affair in the country.'"

"Higher still. And it is a very old bottle."

"And here I thought one drank to forget."

"With a good wine, never."

Elliot looked back at the silent tube but the news was over. On instead was the premiere of *Benny Tries Again*. Benny was in a tussle with his first guest, was out from behind Elwood Glover's old desk and wrestling with Barry Hart. Scoring Barry was a coup Elliot had organized, asking a favour of their mutual agent Mike. Bennie was tugging at Barry's jacket. He ripped off a sleeve. Elliot reached for the remote.

"I have to sleep here," said Hazel.

"Of course," said Elliot, laying the remote back on the coffee table.

"I don't feel I can go home. I'll sleep on your couch."

"No, no, I'll take the couch."

"It's no trouble? You've slept on the couch before?"

"Not often."

"Okay, there's going to be all this awkward and needless back-and-forth now and . . . having seen poor Victor go over the edge like that . . . I don't have the patience for 'We'll sleep in the bed together, no hanky-panky' and then a comforting hug and next I'm feeling you all hot and hard against my back and we don't sleep until after we've had a fuck but by then it's four thirty in the morning. You know what I saying, Elliot."

"I hope so."

Hazel held out the mug. Perhaps stress, the sight of her boss falling off a building, had aggravated her arthritis, for her hand was knotted cordage.

"Give me another glass of that wine, will you?" she said. Elliot was retrieving the bottle from the kitchen when Hazel called from the living room, "Benny's show! He's got some woman on."

"That's his second guest," said Elliot. "I forget her name. She's the oldest gal on the LPGA tour. She's from Victoria."

"CanCon, anyway," said Hazel. "Is Barry Hart coming on later?"

"I believe he was the first guest," said Elliot, returning with the wine. "Cheers."

THREE

WESLEY JOHNSTON WAS being truthful when he informed the Customs official that his trip to the United States was for pleasure. He was beaming in anticipation when Walt picked him up at San Francisco Airport. He'd called Walt two days earlier to ask for the lift. No sense confusing matters at a car rental agency with a Wes Johnston Canadian passport and an Elliot Jonson California driver's licence. Jihadists had seen to it there was less habeas corpus than there once was in the Republic, and one wanted to act judiciously. Walt was happy to oblige, saying he and Elliot had at least three hours of vineyard and cellar issues to discuss.

The fifth floor of the parkade, where Walt had left his truck, was open to the elements, and the blast of air that met Elliot there was cooler and moister than that he'd last breathed in Toronto.

Walt took the 280 to the 101 just south of San Jose. It got warmer and drier as they went. At Gilroy you could tell you were heading south. At Salinas you could finally feel the heat they used for California's Chia Pet agribiz, the land a dead, porous medium into which seeds and their feed could be injected. He was watching dust devils dancing on the broiling flats when his cellphone rang. It was Hazel.

"Where are you?"

"I'm driving through a place called Gonzales."

"You went to California?"

"Yeah."

"You should have woken me when you left," she said. "Your cleaning lady arrived just as I was leaving."

"I envy that kind of sleep. I'd never mess with it."

"I haven't been that out of it in years. I was like a teenager, I didn't open an eye until ten o'clock."

"It's a reaction to the stress, to the shock."

"Thinking about it this morning I was almost sick. I assumed, Elliot, that you would have changed your travel plans."

"Anything in the papers?"

"Morbid fascination with how he died is overshadowing his accomplishments."

"Anybody call you about it?"

"Nobody yet. It's a local story about a guy falling off a building. The entire executive of the CBC could drown in Lake Ontario and nobody would notice. Is it beautiful where you are?"

"It's featureless. I can see a McDonald's."

"If there are questions, can I give out your cell number?"

"I would prefer if you could field stuff. You can call, but don't give them my number. I'm gonna be busy." Walter nodded at Elliot's assessment.

"People are going to be shocked you didn't cancel your trip, that you're not going to be here for the funeral."

"I can't choose when the grapes ripen."

"Your immediate superior fell to his death in a freak accident, the national public broadcaster is without a president, and you are taking a vacation at your hobby farm?"

"It's not a hobby, it's a business concern into which I have sunk considerable resources. Take the opportunity to mention the new season when you're speaking to the press."

"You are kidding me."

"Nothing crass, just slip it in. Let's not forget he was at the event to celebrate the new schedule. Mentioning that isn't a lie."

"Wow."

"Promoting the new season is the best way to honour Victor's life."

The cellphone reception seemed to break up; Elliot could hear nothing.

"Hello?"

"Eat a grape for me."

"I will."

Walter took Elliot's closing up the phone as his cue to start talking business. Various plots of the different varieties were becoming ripe at different times. There was much to calculate. He confessed to having been deeply pessimistic at the beginning of the year. The plants had flowered adequately but it never seemed to get warm enough, and he'd feared that some of the grapes would never ripen. He'd abandoned all hope for the heat-craving Mourvèdre.

"But it was dry," he continued, "dry enough to worry, except that this year it seemed the fog always made it just as far as our vines at night. Because of the dry farming — and I give you credit for it, Elliot — that's all it took to keep them going. Maybe this year was the first time some of the vines you planted had roots deep enough to cope with water stress, I dunno. And with the wind, you got away without spraying."

Heat had arrived only in August: temperatures constant and fierce. When the ripening commenced, the vines were still yielding little fruit, owing to the drought — but they were fully mature, with complex flavours from the skins to the pips.

"Miguel started a team picking the first Syrah this morning, you know in that amphitheatre we call 'the dip'?"

Elliot did know it, a shallow southwest-facing bowl in the side of a hillock, a location, Elliot thought in retrospect, better suited to Mourvèdre.

"I'd say we can finish all the Syrah within the week, just in time for the Grenache," Walt continued. "Counoise is well ahead so it won't be long after. There might be a week or even two to wait for the Mourvèdre. It's all had enough hang time — you can tell by the feel and look of the berries. There is more acid than most people would be happy with, but considering what I think you are going for . . . As long as it doesn't rain."

"I caught part of a news conference where the mayor of Los Angeles and the governor were praying for rain. I mean literally, with their heads bowed as some ding-dong spoke to God on California's behalf. Jesus."

"Rain is the only thing that can hurt us, Elliot. I have rough ideas about the sort of tonnage we can expect. The Syrah will be less than three tons an acre, so it's probably not too early to begin thinking about the blend. Every variety is looking terrific, even the old Cinsault that was part of the field blend is killer, it's a luxury I've never had before, so you . . ."

Walt's speech was almost frantic by this point; he leapt from harvesting to fermentation, ahead to the blend and back again. Elliot wanted to listen. More than anything he wished to dream possible dreams with long-suffering Walt. But ahead was a large billboard with the message "It's Happening in Soledad." "It," for his son Mark, was another four years in prison in a town called Loneliness.

He could not even think about attempting a visit, travelling as a former version of himself. It was as if, up there in Canada, he was reverting to an earlier draft, one abandoned for a page-one rewrite. And after all the trouble of reimagining the character, changing the setting and the storyline, the producer was deciding to go back to the original script, using some rationalizing hooey like "your first instincts are usually right." But Elliot liked his own rewrite.

". . . and despite what I've said, I agree with you." Walt was still going. "If the wine is built like that, you probably aren't going to know how it turns out until it's been ten years in the bottle. We won't live long enough to know how we should start, you know? Sometimes it's a best guess."

"You know what they say, 'Nobody knows anything.'"

"Who said that, Randall Grahm?" Grahm was a fellow California winemaker.

"No, it was William Goldman. He was talking about the pictures."

"Could apply to just about anything," said Walt.

Elliot could now see the walls of the low-slung prison

from the highway. Walls and walls and walls, punctuated with guard towers.

"It does, I'm sure."

"What's happening with Jasper Crabb?" Walt asked.

"Huh?"

"The dude from the Department of Agriculture, the suitcase clones?"

"That's sorted."

"You're kidding me."

"I told you, no one wants to open that can of worms, too many brand names in Napa would be implicated. I told him they were legit and he was fine." This was untrue.

They were passing the town of Paso Robles, taking exit ramp 230 off the 101, when they were overtaken by a short yellow school bus. Walt was forced to the shoulder by the speeding vehicle.

"What the fuck?" said Elliot.

"Goddamn Bread Heads."

"That was Farinists?"

"They drive around in those short buses. They've been coming in from the Bay area and L.A., they're having some kind of festival, some kind of unholy bake-off."

"They seem pretty harmless. I mean, bread shoes . . ."

"That's no cake shop up by the old mission, Elliot, it's a fortress. And I see them in Paso: they're crazy. It's in their eyes."

The tidy rows belonging to Haldeman Laboratories were an even green, in stark contrast to the leaves of Elliot's vineyard beyond, with their yellow skirts and rusty veins. A giant circular sign, cut and painted to look like a medal, stood next to the Haldeman gate. "97 Points, *Wine Advocate*," it said.

"I was talking to the General the other day," said Walter.

"About?"

"He wants your Zin. It's deadly this year. His . . . not so much."

"Let's sell it to him."

"I'll mention it. He also wanted to talk to Miguel about pickers."

"Haldeman is getting none of our team."

"We'll be done two weeks before he starts."

"Then by all means . . . Two weeks? Really?"

"Yep."

"You really think we can go for it?"

"The grapes are mature, Elliot. Most of the stems are ligni-fied. The phenolics there . . . and it puts armour on the juice. Maybe the wine will only come in at twelve percent alcohol, maybe people won't know what to make of it, but . . ."

Walt turned the truck through the gates of 303 Locura Canyon Road. Elliot could see Miguel's team coming up the hills toward the winery for lunch. Harvest was done for the day. The afternoon would see the grapes picked over, the busted, rotten, and raisined berries discarded along with the leaves and twigs and dirt. A select portion of the prize grapes that remained would be destemmed before they were placed into vats to commence their transition to wine. Already wild yeasts were beginning to consume the sugar in the berries. The end of the season was the beginning.

The midday meal was served under a long canopy, jerry-rigged from various flies and tarps. Every harvest, Bonnie put down her pen and cooked for the crews. Elliot needed her at her desk, but the seasonal KP detail was one of the few joys Bonnie found at Locura Canyon. And she was a terrific cook. She worked from a bounty of fresh veg from her organic farm. Today there were plates best described as heaps of sliced tomatoes and fresh goat cheese over which was poured herbed olive oil, and there were salads in infinite permutations of the green things she grew. There were at least three pork roasts, their heat lifting aromas of cumin and chile and garlic into the autumn air. There were pots of beans and rice.

Freed from the tractor beam of the computer screen, Bonnie was, every year, a new and better woman. Seeing Elliot, she hugged him.

"Prodigal boss."

"Don't think the fatted calf was killed on my account, but I'll take it."

"How long you here for?"

"Going to try to stay until the Mourvèdre is in."

"Business in L.A.?"

"Nope. Staying here the whole time. Gonna pull out the camp cot."

"I need to talk to you. Can we have a walk, or do you want to eat?"

"No, let's walk."

They headed out to the vines. At a judicious distance Bonnie produced a joint and lit it.

"I'm giving you notice."

"No."

"Not going anywhere soon. I knew you would need time to find someone else . . . so three months."

"Please, Bonnie . . ."

"You aren't going to be able to do this from up in Canada. You are going to have to stay, live the dream — or at least attend to it."

"What's that supposed to mean?"

"Nothing. This is shaping up to be your first decent vintage, so it's not going to be so hard getting another manager."

"That's bullshit, Bonnie, you run the operation."

"And that's not what I signed on for. Frankly I'm exhausted from fighting off the bank and the creditors."

"I'm devastated, Bonnie. Naturally, there's nothing I can do to make you stay . . . I'm just . . ."

"Elliot . . . have you ever thought that it doesn't matter what's in the bottle?"

"I don't understand."

"Something is always the new thing, right? Like Californian wines were the thing for a while and the French were in the shitter."

"Yeah."

"But those were fashions," said Bonnie.

"No, they were tastes."

"See . . ." She couldn't find the words. "For the first few people, the ones who were looking for something new, or at least claiming they'd found something new, it might have been about taste. But for everybody else . . . they were just following."

"I really don't see what point you're trying to make."

"I understand your desire to make something special, but I don't think you realize that most people don't care."

"You're wrong," said Elliot.

"Someone comes home from a long day at the office, fires

up the barbecue, kicks off their shoes, puts up their feet, looks out over the backyard at all the other backyards, and enjoys a nice, freezing cold glass of blush Zin from the fridge."

"Yeah?'

"Is that experience any less pleasurable than you'd have drinking a glass of . . . what was it . . . Dettori?"

"No. Yes. Dettori is a bad example."

"Why?"

"Its simplicity is too complex."

"I remember the look of pain on your face as you drank it."

"Yeah?"

"You said it was beautiful."

"Yeah?"

"Don't be a snob, Elliot. Maybe simple pleasures are the best of all."

"Even if I agreed with you, which I don't, what difference would it make?"

"You could irrigate, throw in a few oak chips, and make a nice Zin. With some of the other grapes it might even be a little different. And as the Grenache and Counoise get older, you could sell that fruit to some idealistic new guy in the 'hood."

Elliot couldn't think what to say. Bonnie needed to fill the silence.

"You're chasing this thing that's really of interest to very few people. Not that that's not a noble thing, but unless you are doing it at its best . . . Rather than failing at doing something great, why not just do something good for a bunch of people? What is wrong with making a few dollars making people happy?"

"Put a Zebra on the label, call it 'Zebra Zin'?"

"That's actually pretty cool, Elliot."

"It was Walt's idea."

"And you could always keep trying to make that wine you imagine on the side."

"Like a hobby?"

"Exactly."

"Bonnie, you've been so good to me over the years, so patient."

"Thanks. Don't put off looking for someone for too long. You were always a Canadian, Elliot, no matter how many years you spent down here."

"What's that supposed to mean?"

"It's not an insult, Elliot. You cling to things, good things that aren't working out, hoping they'll get better. Americans are quicker to change to the winning team, they forget any allegiance they had to the old squad. I mean, don't you still have a king?"

"A queen."

"'Nuff said."

THE TRICK WAS to get the grapes from the vineyard to the winery quickly and with as little handling as possible. Not only were the Mexicans faster at picking the grapes than Elliot, their fleet hands did less damage. Each time Elliot looked up, the distance between him and the hired pickers had increased.

By the end of the first morning, Elliot's soft hands were bloody and sore; his secateur-wielding right was now, in the midst of the first pass at the Grenache, numb and swollen. His lower back was rusted rebar. He dropped to his knees and leaned backward to stretch. The early-morning sun was low and honey coloured and special delivery to Locura Canyon. There was camphor on the wind and orange rind and sage in the dust. God had a tumultuous relationship with this land, shaking it, baking it, burning it, and then, because it was so damn sexy, so irresistible, kissing it.

The pickers started singing "La Adelita."

> *En lo alto de la abrupta serranía*
> *acampado se encontraba un regimiento*

They'd seen Bonnie coming, bringing them water and coffee and sweet, sticky buns. They were having a bit of fun, as if Bonnie were Adelita, the revolutionary heroine of the song.

> *y una joven que valiente los seguía*
> *locamente enamorada del sargento.*

To bottle all this, thought Elliot.

❦

ELLIOT HAD FALLEN asleep in his clothes. His cellphone was in his shirt pocket, which was bunched near his chin. The ringtone entered his dream: an alarm of some sort at the Broadcast Centre, and he couldn't get Hazel to leave her desk because they would have to escape by means of a plunge into the atrium. The vibration, felt in his lips, he took for electrocution, which woke him with a start. He smelled burning toast. Jesus, was he having a stroke?

"Hello?"

"Elliot, it's Walter."

"Yes, Walter?"

"You watching TV?"

"I try not to."

"Cops are trying to get into the Faranista compound, shots have been fired. There's a tank coming now, with one of them dozer blades attached to the front. What do they call those things?"

"Trouble?"

"Guess so."

"This is . . . Why is this . . ."

"No, I'm calling to remind you to check the temperature of the Cunny. It was getting hot."

"Right."

"I've found if you open the bay doors on the west of the building and the garage door we use for the tractor, air races right through the place, and tonight, where it's so windy . . ."

Elliot heard a distant *umph.*

". . . it shouldn't take long. If it stays up over eighty-eight . . . Shit! There's been some sort of explosion at their compound. It was just on television."

"I sort of felt it here. At what temperature should I start to get alarmed?"

"Ninety. It's like a horse, you've got to hold on. It's alive, remember; it's not a machine. I swear when the Grenache fermentation got stuck there two years ago it was because the yeasts committed suicide. You can take all the measurements you want, you've got to look in there and size it up. That's why I prefer just opening and closing doors to any cooling process, it doesn't . . . Uh-oh. Shots."

"I hear something. Is that what that is? That's gunfire?"

"That's gunfire."

"So, ninety degrees. I'm on it."

"Call me back if there's anything weird. I'll be up watching this shit go down on TV."

Elliot went to the garage. The tractor was an antique that Miguel somehow managed to keep going. It was parked alongside the vineyard's one truck, a 1989 two-ton Ford that urgently needed to be replaced. If this was a hobby, it was sure an expensive one. How many people with whom he worked at the CBC had ever signed the front of a payroll cheque instead of the back? None, he guessed. There was no one to catch you if you fell here stateside. Maybe Bonnie was right — maybe Elliot's wine dreams were a delusion. He could have sold the land high in the boom years — he'd bought it for nothing — but he'd hung on. This vintage was finally going to produce a terrific wine — but was it too late? Without Bonnie to run interference, would he be forced to throw himself at the mercy of the bank, let them have it all? He would sooner do that than sell to the General.

He opened the garage doors. It was blowing hard. The brittle leaves were rattling on the vines.

That was the American way: you strove. Despite the mythology, few made it. It was a tougher society than Canada's; it was Darwinian. Was it any better in the end? Had it created any more? Maybe not. Canada was probably a "better" place, more humane. There was less excitement north of the 49th but there came a time when one had had enough excitement. He set out for the other side of the building.

At first the vats of fermenting Counoise had filled the building with bready aromas; tonight other perfumes were coming on, a mix of fresh and stewed raspberry and, indeed, violets.

The bay doors had been installed to facilitate shipping and deliveries, but they were rather larger than necessary. When they swung open, they developed a good momentum. The air was cooler here than inside the winery, but it was still a hot night. Elliot climbed onto the bottom rail of the big door and let it carry him for the last course of its arc.

So brightly illuminated was the Faranist compound it was visible to Elliot for the first time. It was like a Tuscan fortalice. It was closer than he'd thought, just two hilltops away. How far? A mile? He'd definitely thought it was farther.

Tackatackatackatacka. The terse spittle of gunfire. Nothing like the movies. Automatic weapon, repeating firing, a machine gun. How far would a bullet from one of those things travel? Was he in danger of being hit by a stray? The bullets of the rifles they used for hunting moose back in Newfoundland could travel more than two miles.

He was startled by a pair of deer bounding out of the vineyard, doubtless driven by the noise at the Faranist redoubt. They disappeared into the darkness. Peering into the gloom, Elliot thought he saw more of them out in the vines. Something was moving around out there, but he couldn't be sure. Coyotes?

He went back inside to check on the fermentation.

There was a steady burble inside the concrete vat. Bubbles were fighting through the floating cap of grape skins, but with less fervour than the day before. The stuff was giving off a powerful fresh-fruit smell; it was lip-smacking. The wine this year would be irresistible; sips of it would compel you to fill your cheeks to indulge completely in the taste. He loved this Counoise, even if it was from illegal root stock. The contents of the tank were at eighty-nine degrees. Wasn't that, in effect, ninety? He heard another thud from the direction of the Faranist compound as he dialled Walt.

"I love this Counoise," Elliot said.

"Holy fuck, Elliot, can you see what's going on from there?"

"What's going on?"

"The Bread Heads must have had a fuel storage tank or something buried outside because there was this . . . Shit, man, there's another one. I think they're blowing themselves up."

"The Old Testament has that effect on people . . . Now the Counoise, I checked and it's —"

"Elliot."

"Yes, Walter."

"They've started a pretty big fire down there."

"It's their apocalypse, they want to do it up right. You can't have a modest, low-key apocalypse. It's driven deer up here."

"Go have a look and call me back."

"Yes, Mom."

Elliot took the stairs down to the winery's main floor. The still distant prospect of what the blend might be was starting to excite Elliot the way it had Walter. In every vintage to date, the blend had been forced on them as a way of minimizing damage. Now, if the Mourvèdre came in as well as all the other varieties, they would be working with impeccable ingredients. There was temptation to fashion a tête du cuvée, a premium wine composed of the best lots. But this went against Elliot's belief that it was somehow a cheat, or mere marketing or pretence, to produce anything other than a bottle labelled "red table wine."

He walked outside.

There was an intermittent wall of flame stretching from the Farinists' hilltop all the way to the next promontory to the north. Even from this distance Elliot could see how the wind was feeding it.

His cellphone rang.

"Holy Mother, Walt . . ."

"Are we insured against this?" said a voice other than Walter's.

"'We'?"

"The investors in the vineyard. Last time I checked I still had a piece."

"Who is this?"

"You wouldn't fuck my wife. That didn't look good."

"Mr. Silverman?"

Something flickered in the vines. In his peripheral vision Elliot caught a spark and heard the pop of an old glass flashbulb on a Brownie camera.

"Present."

"'Are we insured against this' . . . What's 'this'?" Elliot's confusion was cascading.

"There's been a fire down here. Started during the siege of the Faranist compound. Is this not on the Canadian news?"

"The Canadian news . . . I'm not following you," said Elliot. Oh — right. Silverman thought he was still in Toronto!

Elliot could smell the chaparral burning, smell creosote and the vapours of hot sap.

"Don't you get the news up there in the wilderness? Never mind. The Faranists are planning to kill people in Los Angeles, something from the Bible about separating the wheat from the chaff."

Now Elliot saw the bursts plainly: one, three, and then another two simultaneously. They were like flash pots. The popping sound was delicate but of a pitch that cut through the growing roar of the distant fire and a rising choir of sirens. Sinister forces seemed to be making some sort of mischievous movie out in his vines. Now flames were licking the vines at the site of the flashes. It was a tinderbox. Silverman was still talking.

"They've quite obviously gone insane."

"Very much so, obviously insane. What's this about a fire?"

"Started during the police assault. Conditions have been terribly dry down here and it started some wildfires . . . I don't like being the one to break the news, but we've lost the vineyard."

"Are you sure? I . . ." Elliot said. Fire had a solid hold in a grove of trees between the old field-blend grapes and the first Grenache vines he had planted years ago. Embers were passing overhead, shooting stars on a drunkard's course. A comet killed the dinosaurs, thought Elliot.

"Hey, don't sweat it, Elliot," said Silverman. It was as if he were merely giving Elliot notes on the new ending the studio wanted for a picture. "The land alone is probably worth more now with the grapes gone. Who's Walt?"

"My vineyard manager and winemaker."

"He down here in California?"

"Yes."

"Lives at your winery, I suppose?"

"Nobody lives there." A gust raced under the fire and lifted it up like a blanket from a bed, flames flapped in the air, the great sheet billowing and then landing gently at a distance and catching all there ablaze. Silverman was still talking but Elliot had lost him for a moment. "I'm too young to have worked with Walt Disney," Lucky was saying. "I will always regret that. He was a great man."

"I guess."

"You know why he wrote down Kurt Russell's name just before he died?"

"Walt Disney?"

"Yes."

"I didn't know he had."

"There's another reason I'm calling."

"About Kurt Russell?"

"No, your son, Mark."

"Yes?"

"He was that cute kid in *Family Planning*, right?"

"Yes, he played Little Ricky."

"I loved that show."

"Really?"

"'Really?' Like, for real, did I genuinely enjoy watching the show? No, I fucking hated it, Jonson. It's just something you fucking say! It was a fucking courtesy."

"Of course, sorry."

"So, Little Ricky is, I understand, doing hard time in Sole-dad Prison."

"Yes."

"A lot of child stars from our industry run into trouble later in life."

"Indeed."

"Animals used to be a bitch to work with too, but these days the training is . . . This town has been good to me, Mr. Jonson. I've become wealthy. I would like to give something back. I took the liberty of talking to the governor about Mark's case."

Elliot could hear shouts from the direction of Haldeman Estates and the sound of their irrigation system starting up.

"You what?"

"And it seems nobody sees any problem with him being transferred to a Canadian prison, to serve out the remainder of his sentence closer to you."

"This is . . . I . . . I will have to speak to his mother . . ."

"Lucy's in complete agreement that this is the right thing to do."

"You've spoken with Lucy?"

"Lucy Szilard, yes. I'm producing her picture."

"The documentary?"

"No, it's an action picture, vehicle for Barry Hart. Lucy wants what's best for Mark."

"I . . . I'm sorry about that thing with your wife."

"With Robin? It's okay, next time. Listen, even if she wants me to, I won't fuck Lucy and we'll call it even."

"I gotta tell you, Lucky —"

"Call me Mr. Silverman, please."

". . . Yeah, well, my position in Toronto, here . . . it's not long-term. I can't remember what was said on that conference call. If I was compelled to testify, I wouldn't be able to tell them anything."

"I was never on that call, Jonson, got that?"

"Right, sorry, I —"

"God bless Canada, Jonson. There's no place like home."

"They don't say God bless Canada up here." A gust fed the fire and Elliot could almost see something, something animated, beyond the vines. It did not so much emerge from the wall of trees as chalk itself out of the shadows with its white lines. Not lines — stripes. The animal advanced toward him in frightful bucks and kicks, with hard-muscled "horsehorsehorse" locomotion. There was too much spirit in the creature for it to keep straight, and it shied and danced laterally, side passing and half passing, on its way. When it stopped, as if considering where to next run, its show of teeth was more human than equine, the smile of someone deranged. It tossed its head, neck, and shoulders, pushed off with its hind legs, and was gone.

The phone was still at his ear but the line was dead. Elliot ran to the truck. Sprinklers, used to cover the vines in ice when there was a risk of frost, were whirling over at Haldeman. They had water galore there.

He was at the gates. In the side mirrors of the truck Elliot saw his winery as a hole in a towering curtain of incensed scarlet and orange. The smell was of something stronger than smoke: it was sour, a breath-stealing burnt black. It was elemental. Iron and sulphur and tar.

FOUR

HAZEL SAW TO IT that clippings of good press were placed on his desk every morning he was away. Critics were universally positive about the new season. Liberal cultural commentators heralded the return of the national public broadcaster to its founding principles. Victor Rainblatt, everyone agreed, had been a great Canadian.

But this night, two months after their debut, Elliot sat at his desk and confronted the numbers. *Reason* was perhaps their most critically acclaimed show in a decade. It had started poorly and declined steeply.

Les Les had benefited early from a measure of controversy, but now more people from Alberta were complaining about the show, by phone and email, than were watching it in the entire country. The show's producers, who'd fought every compromise in its development, smelled doom and sent Elliot a panicked note about introducing "paranormal" elements to the show.

501 Pennsylvania was being called the "smartest comedy of the season," an obituary in television. They had lost the gang at Elliot's weather office. They were big with the crowd that never watched television.

There was one exception. One show was that rarest of beasts, beloved by scribblers and rabble alike. *Benny Tries Again*, the program for which Elliot bore sole responsibility, was a smash. From his premiere, when Benny tossed Barry Hart, his first guest, off the set for being, as Benny put it, "a fake fuck," people had been tuning in and staying. Soon after the opening-night debacle, the category of self-promoting celebrities willing to risk the show when they passed through Toronto dropped from the B's to the C's and D's. But this did nothing to diminish Benny's charm. His self-deprecation was so truthful — "After my last show I didn't end up doing infomercials, I ended up living with a family of raccoons" — that it gave his cracks cred. And debased as he was, he was genuinely sympathetic to people's woes. Guests were utterly disarmed and opened up completely. Of course, if you were a fake, like Barry Hart, an appearance was perilous. Starved of celebrities, Bennie interviewed his rather ordinary Canadian guests as though they were huge stars.

The numbers for news should have been cause for dismissal, but they were no worse than the competition's. Television news was a dying animal. The one thing Elliot could crow about was the tremendous savings he'd made by purchasing International News Makers, a company in Mumbai, to gather and produce the broadcasts. They were fed the raw footage for the stories by satellite; the cameras in the studio in Toronto were robots controlled by a reliable cadre of cheap faraway Maharashtrians. There was a lot of grumbling about the change among the journalists, but watching as those of their peers who dared to complain were dispatched to the Yukon and Newfoundland, most kept their peace.

❧ ❧ ❧

"WHY DO I HAVE to tell them they're being cancelled?" Hazel was standing before his desk in an orange and cream gown, a girl's princess costume all grown up and regal. By the way it gathered at the waist to show off her shape, Elliot could tell it had been custom-made for her.

"Where were you, dressed like that?"

"A gala, a fundraising gala for the opera."

"That's one of those Toronto elite things, isn't it?"

Hazel ignored his remark. "You should tell them," she said. "You're the one cancelling them."

"Hazel, yours was the privilege of delivering the good news when they were scheduled in the first place," he said. "There's nothing I can do, it's the numbers."

"Fuck you, Elliot. You agreed it wasn't about the numbers."

"I said it wasn't entirely about the numbers. Whether the shows are worthy or not, I can't piss away the public purse."

"You are completely abrogating your responsibility."

"My responsibility to what?"

"To . . ." Hazel thought about it. "To nation-build."

"Maybe Canadians don't want any more nation-building. Maybe they want to remortgage and blow the cash at some shitty resort in the Dominican."

"Because Benny Malka is working out, now you think you're some kind of programming genius?"

"Who accompanied you to the gala?"

"None of your business. What are you going to replace them with?"

"Shows Alice likes."

"Who is Alice?"

"I told you about my weather office —"

"Not with the weather office again, Elliot."

"Yes. And there's a receptionist, Alice, a big woman, somewhat withdrawn, very private."

"So guarded that she won't even open up to the person who imagined her? Elliot, get help."

"What do you think she likes to watch?" Elliot asked.

"I have to get back to my event, this is ridiculous."

"She's watching television right now, while you're going to a gala. While I'm here at work. She's watching television. She doesn't surf the Web; husband Fred, with whom she hasn't had sex in thirteen years, lives on the Web. He's online now, in his room in the finished basement. Alice gets all curled up and cozy, maybe with a blanket and some snacks. Snacks are her weakness. Alice gets perfectly comfortable on the couch, and to forget it all, to forget the passive abuse she suffers at the office, the emptiness of her life at home, to forget that she is overweight and unloved, she watches television. So what does she watch?"

Hazel was avoiding his eye, as if contact would provoke a rage.

"She likes comedy," Elliot said, "broad stuff, hates that cerebral junk. Nothing with a showbiz setting, no smartypants inside jokes, absofuckinglutely nudding 'meta.' She likes game shows for their hosts, they've got to be good people. She likes curling, especially women's . . . She's one of that number we've never been able to understand. In a drama she wants a protagonist she can root for, not damaged with a spinning moral compass, but a good guy. She wants a redemptive ending. She likes 'uplifting.' Television is her bestest friend."

"Television has such a large circle of friends. How can anyone really be its bestest friend?"

"Because, at its bestest, television is a crowd-pleaser."

"You know Alice well."

"I do, finally, I do."

"What does she drink?"

"I'm sorry?"

"You, ex of the beverage industry, should know. What does Alice drink, Elliot?"

"Pepsi."

"I would have thought Diet."

"I give her more credit."

ELLIOT REPLACED *Reason* with a reality show called *Canada's Stupidest*. It was good-natured fun, feeding off viewer-submitted stories of funny, dumb things friends and relations did. The producers of the *Canada's Worst* series of shows called Elliot in a snit, claiming proprietorship and threatening a lawsuit. Elliot dared them.

Taking the *Les Les* spot and an extra half-hour, Elliot green-lit *Murph Village*, described by its producers as a "fun action-adventure-comedy-mystery-drama." It was about the derring-do of the eponymous Des Murphy, a dashing yet sexually non-threatening boy-man and private dick in Vancouver. The scripts Elliot read made no sense but featured peeling tops and tires. (There was something charming about the CBC's prudishness in the media age of the amiable anus. The national public broadcaster took the sight of a bra strap on a bare back for titillation, as well, thought Elliot, it should.) The pilot made Vancouver a character too, sunny as Malibu, colours digitally jacked so that it seemed built of Jolly Ranchers. *Murph Village* didn't aspire to originality; rather, it covered, almost credibly, hits of the genre. It was junk, but it was "our junk." Elliot's only intercession was to ixnay a tendency to David Caruso–style sunglasses acting. There were limits. Weren't there?

The cast of *501 Pennsylvania* were said to test high, so Elliot kept the show but had the producers sack and replace the creative team with some fat guys and gals from *Benny Tries Again*. He eliminated the Friday-evening news and replaced it with *Your Product Here*, which recycled the best television commercials shown around the planet that week.

And to put truth to the fibs that got him the job in the first place, Elliot was in business with Lucky Silverman — one of Lucky's outfits, anyway — as one of many international partners producing the miniseries *House of Saxe-Coburg*. The Canadian end was post-production at the CBC facilities in Mumbai and a young actor named Brad Hodder, who was to play a young Prince Philip. In an interesting turn, Barry Hart was taking the role of Wallis Simpson.

◦ ❦ ◦

IT HAD BEEN weeks since Elliot had heard directly from Hazel.

From: hazel.osler@cbc.ca
To: el.jonson@cbc.ca
Subject: chat
I want to speak to you in person. I understand you
will be in Niagara for a few days. I will drive down
there tomorrow. I have something for you.

She was standing six metres from the front entrance, by
the curb, smoking furiously.

"You're not coming in?" asked Elliot.

"To a management seminar? At the Niagara Institute?
You're kidding, right?" Hazel squinted at a glassed-in display
next to the front doors. "Which one are you? 'Challenging
Your Diagnostic Style'?"

"'Managing Stakeholder Expectations,' Node A17, actually."

"Dear God."

"My team are going to take away a lot from this experience."

She gestured with her smoke to the glass in Elliot's hand.
"How's the vino?"

"Oh . . . I don't know . . ." Elliot noticed that he was, indeed,
holding a glass containing a transparent yellowish liquid. "I
haven't given it much thought."

"I've just come from Dr. Palme."

"Doctor who?"

"Jurgen Palme, the host of *Reason*. He was inconsolable."

"You showed him the ratings, surely a rational man —"

"Everybody has feelings . . . yourself excepted, I suppose."

"I gave the shows a shot, Hazel. But we're the national public broadcaster. Without a public —"

"I also am obliged to convey a message from Kurt and Heather."

"I don't know any —"

"They're the creators of *Les Les*."

"Kurt?"

"They want to make it a drama. They want to make Claudette, the Québécoise, straight. She leaves Betty, the Newfoundland character, for a man, a nice one, South Asian Ontarian. Betty's tested poorly and —"

"It's too late."

Hazel knew this was true.

"They are going to ask you to be president," she said.

"I already got the call."

"I didn't think you had the French."

"I don't really, but theirs wasn't good enough to tell the difference."

"Is that why you raced off to California when Victor died?"

"What?" Elliot was genuinely perplexed.

"To look like you didn't want the job, to let the other aspirants cut one another down in your absence? It's being called one of the great Machiavellian moves."

"I was booked to go before Victor's accident. As for Machiavelli? The CBC's hardly worth the candle."

Hazel took a studied drag of her cigarette and exhaled the smoke over Elliot's shoulder, shooting a hot cloud past his ear.

"I also heard you are going to wind up the Newfoundland service," she said.

"I'm going to consolidate Atlantic Canada in the Halifax office. When they called me about the president's job, they wanted to know how I could meet some of the 'Three Priorities.' I couldn't think of much so I made shit up. It's all in the new strategic plan, TVC 2.0: I'm putting advertisements on radio — the mornings are a gold mine; there'll be more children's programming for adults; there are some cuts called "consolidation." It seemed the sort of thing they would want to hear. There's a vacancy for the regional director position in Newfoundland; it seemed as good a time as any to kill it and Winnipeg."

"Give me the job."

"Head of CBC Newfoundland? Are you nuts? Canada is already a backwater, there's no need to go to *its* backwater."

"I'm quitting this place. You owe me."

"I don't owe you."

"No, but something," Hazel said and Elliot understood.

"Sure, Newfoundland, have it. What do I care? Been there in March? The climate is like geology in a mood."

"I like the people."

"What you mistake for friendliness? They're just nosy."

"How could you be shutting down the shop in St. John's and green-lighting a show that's from there?"

"Jesus, but people are gossips. And they get it wrong. The green-lit show has a Newfoundland theme, that's all. It's going to be shot in Halifax — they've kissed my ass raw looking for something to keep the plant open. I'll make them produce it in St. John's if you want. I'm the president. I'll shut down the Halifax studio instead — they've got the navy, they can't complain."

"What's the show?"

"*Tiny Newfies.*"

"'*Tiny Newfies*'?"

"It's fun. We tested the pilot. Canadians love tiny Newfies."

"What about Newfoundlanders?"

"As long as it's about them, they're fine with it. You'll find they're needy that way. "

Hazel nodded. Elliot knew she was weighing whether she should object to the show now or wait until she was safely ensconced in St. John's with the Halifax studio already sold to developers.

"Remember," Elliot said, "the new governing principle is to make the assets attractive."

"Attractive? To the audience?"

"To the marketplace. If a part of the service isn't readily salable, it is going to be wound up. This comes from on high. I got a call from Russ Yelburton at the PMO, three o'clock in the morning. I could hear the Prime Minister swearing in the background. The job offer was conditional on my making the CBC a liquid asset. Don't repeat that; not even the Minister of Heritage knows."

"In terms of replacing me . . ." she began to ask.

"Troy's being groomed," Elliot said, looking back toward the building. "He loves these management seminars. Thinking of abandoning that ridiculous plan to become a milliner and going for his MBA. Put him in a made suit and he looks like he deserves the executive bonus."

"You casting or hiring?"

"I'm managing."

"You'll have to post the Newfoundland position, I suppose . . ."

"I'll have Troy do it all. It'll look legit. No one is going to question your qualifications . . . only your judgement."

"I appreciate it." Hazel searched the ground and air for something else to say. "Any luck with the transfer of . . . ?"

"Mark? It's done. He's in Beaver Creek, in Gravenhurst. It's a minimum-security facility, a break from that nightmare at Soledad. He's settling in nicely . . . if anyone settles in that sort of situation."

"I'm happy for you. It must be a relief."

"It is. Maybe I'll get a place in the Muskokas."

"It's a fit with the new job."

"Mark has started talking to me."

"That's wonderful." Hazel was clearly warmed by the news. "A breakthrough."

"He's satisfied that I'm out of showbiz for good."

Hazel was puzzled. "How's that, Elliot?"

"I'm in government now, Hazel. I'm a bureaucrat."

"Goodbye, Elliot," she said, and turned to walk away. She tried discarding her cigarette butt with a sharp flick of the finger but fumbled it, the stub falling to the ground at her feet amidst a shower of embers and ash. She stopped and came back around. "I forgot. This is why I came out here. The ratings." She fished through the purse hanging from her shoulder. She handed him a single piece of paper, folded three ways.

Hazel climbed into her car, a smart little Merc, and drove off. Watching her go, Elliot noticed that, across the highway, rows of grapevines were being unearthed. A plough was being pulled behind a powerful tractor. They were driving and dragging deep into the earth, hauling up roots many yards in length, so the plants must be old.

You used the best information you could get to put in vines suited to the location. That, and wishful thinking, governed what you planted where. The vines could be fifteen years of age before they produced grapes that could make a decent wine, and that wine might take another ten in the bottle before you knew what you had. It took a generation to realize you'd made a mistake and planted the wrong variety, even the wrong clone. It took many generations to get it right. You couldn't fight that. It was completely at odds with modernity's impatience. Was there a banker to whom you could pitch the century-long amortization of a field of berries? The world changed. You got to watch, which wasn't so bad.

What were they ripping out? Elliot wondered. Gamay? Pinot? This place felt to him like one to try growing Pineau d'Aunis, even Oberlin. Those grapes made interesting wines, but not of the sort that many people liked. He supposed, for a second, it could be Matou de Gethsemane; hadn't Patrick Cahill said the Clementines had grown grapes down this way? He could walk over and check — but then, why? It was too late, he'd sold his acreage to Haldeman Estates. The General was probably down in Enredo now doing the same thing, uprooting Elliot's burnt-over Grenache and Mourvèdre and Counoise to make room for more Zinfandel. Even if Elliot could finally hold a tangled root of Matou in his hands, he no longer owned earth in which to plant it.

He opened the paper that Hazel had given him and looked at the numbers for the first week of the new schedule. They were a hit.

ACKNOWLEDGEMENTS

Jim Diorio related having seen a Los Angeleno in bread shoes. Too many CBC employees to enumerate sang. The criminal case involving the Anthony Pellicano wiretaps was an inspiration, but I did not pay enough attention to the facts for it to be anything more. My research regarding the mysterious advocates for the Sixth Amendment to the Constitution of the United States was similarly fuzzy. Ken Harvey introduced me to Mr. Pat Hobby in 1979. Indosamnesia was a port of call for *The Great Eastern*.

The Newfoundland patriot Bob Gardner flew me over San Simeon and its zebras. Rob Mills was wheelman for part of that trip up Highway 1. Dr. Craig Ferguson did the job on the run between Uzès and Courthézon. Dr. Donnelly had the security detail in California. Steve Palmer, out of Enredo, was my *hombre español*. Gerald Lunz victualled a forward operating base.

Suzanne DePoe was an early champion.

I wish to thank Fabrice Langlois, then of Château Beaucastel, Amy Lillard and Matt Kling of La Gramière, and Robert Haas of Tablas Creek for inviting me in and sharing their great knowledge and best bottles. Randall Grahm was patient with my questions, witty and wise with his answers. The many simplifications and fudging of things viticultural were for the purposes of storytelling. The mistakes are mine alone.

The Canada Council is elsewhere acknowledged but I must reiterate that without their support this book could not have been completed. The Newfoundland and Labrador Arts Council has been a help over the years.

At House of Anansi Sarah MacLachlan was right on time and smart to put Melanie Little on my hard case.

ABOUT THE AUTHOR

Edward Riche, an award-winning writer for page, stage, and screen, was born in Botwood, on the Bay of Exploits, on the northeast coast of Newfoundland. His first novel, *Rare Birds*, was adapted into a major motion picture starring William Hurt and Molly Parker. *The Nine Planets*, his second novel, was a *Globe and Mail* Best Book of 2004 and won the Thomas Head Raddall Best Novel Award. Edward Riche lives in St. John's.